A SHOT TO THE HEART

"We need to put a rush on Hal's autopsy results," I said to Mort after we'd moved through the French doors.

"Already did," Mort told me, "so the funeral wouldn't have to be delayed. Just routine anyway." His brow furrowed. "It is routine, isn't it, Jessica? Or is that why you asked me to come outside?"

"I don't have to tell you there are several ways to murder someone and make it look like a heart attack."

"I can name a few of them myself that I didn't even know existed before I read your books."

"If Hal was actually murdered, hopefully his killer didn't get his method from reading me, too."

"I'll make sure his autopsy is screened as a potential murder," Mort said. "If it makes you happy, Jessica."

I thought of Alyssa, the little girl all grown up who might not have the funds to finish college. I thought of my friend Babs, forced to sell the house she loved so she could escape the debt her late husband had inexplicably left her.

"Thank you, Mort," I said, wondering how long it would be before we learned the truth about Hal Wirth's death.

A Date
with Murder

A *Murder, She Wrote* Mystery

A Novel by Jessica Fletcher,

Donald Bain & Jon Land

Based on the Universal television series created by

Peter S. Fischer, Richard Levinson & William Link

BERKLEY PRIME CRIME
New York

BERKLEY PRIME CRIME
Published by Berkley
An imprint of Penguin Random House LLC
375 Hudson Street, New York, New York 10014

Copyright © 2018 by Universal Studios

ISBN: 9780451489296

Berkley Prime Crime hardcover edition / May 2018
Berkley Prime Crime mass-market edition / October 2018

Printed in the United States of America
1   3   5   7   9   10   8   6   4   2

Cover photograph of skyline by f11 photo / Shutterstock Images
Cover design by Katie Anderson

For Don Bain
A great writer and an even better man

And a special acknowledgment to
Zach Bain Shippee,
Don's grandson,
for his invaluable contribution to this book

The true mystery of the world is the visible,
not the invisible.

—OSCAR WILDE

A Date
with Murder

A *Murder, She Wrote* Mystery

Chapter One

"Come on, Jess—everything's riding on you."

Those words of encouragement came from Barbara Wirth, known to everyone in the town of Cabot Cove as "Babs." Babs and her husband, Hal, hosted what had become an annual event on Labor Day, a barbecue complete with friendly games, tasty grilled fare, finger food passed by well-dressed servers, and sumptuous desserts. A high-spirited memorial to the summer that had passed and the fall season now upon us. The couple's tennis court had been busy all afternoon, and the free-form pool ensured that the youngsters would be tuckered out (with puckered skin) and ready for bed when the festivities ended.

The horseshoe pit had been active all afternoon as well. The sound of the metal horseshoes hitting the iron spikes driven into the ground was a constant reminder that horseshoes was a popular game for young and old alike. I'd once read that it was a spin-off from the game of quoits, dating back two thousand years to just after horseshoes themselves had been invented. All I knew was that they seemed to get heavier with each toss, making me wonder how the poor horses managed with them nailed to their hooves.

The party had started to wind down. But the families gathering their belongings and saying their good-byes to Hal and Babs seemed equally matched by newcomers arriving unfashionably late. It was the day before the traditional start of school, explaining why this party, inevitably, lingered into the early-evening hours under the floodlights the Wirths had set up with just that expectation in mind. The sun was poised to dip behind the mountains in the distance, and those who'd elected to spend their day on the beach, a short walk from the Wirths' expansive property, brushed sand off their feet and bathing suits as they arrived.

I'd intended to join those who were leaving until Babs convinced me to team up with her for a final game of horseshoes. Our opponents were the town historian, Tim Purdy, and Brad Crandall, an old-timer known as the best horseshoe thrower in town. Standing nearby, camera in hand, was Eve Simpson, Cabot Cove's premier Realtor and gossip, two avocations that apparently went hand in hand. Eve was holding the camera but didn't seem to be taking any pictures. Servers from Cabot Cove Catering, meanwhile, filtered through the crowd, dispensing their wares with napkins to spare. A healthy assortment of the company's most delectable treats, now that we'd entered the dessert phase of the festivities, had replaced the trays of finger foods. My mouth watered at the sight of the bite-sized brownies, but I watched the last one snatched from the tray just before the server reached me.

I guess it wasn't my day.

We were down to the final tosses. Tim and Brad had twenty points, one shy of the winning number. Babs and I had surprised everyone (including ourselves) by accumulating eighteen points, three shy of the winning number of twenty-one. It was my turn to throw my two horseshoes at the iron stake, which stood forty feet from where I was poised to take what would be the final turn. I'd need a "ringer," worth three points, in which the horseshoe encircles the stake, for us to win. I didn't suffer any illusions that I was capable of such a toss, especially now that the horseshoe I was hefting felt heavier than the bicycle I often had to lift over the curb to chain in place.

"You can do it, Jess!" Babs assured me, upbeat as ever.

Her rosy voice made for a fitting match with her appearance. She had a headful of red curls that framed flawless, smooth skin that looked as though it belonged in a skilled artist's portrait. And her trim, athletic figure hadn't changed an ounce in the nine years I'd known her, as she looked more like someone who rode horses than tossed their shoes.

I eyed the stake, which seemed to be farther away than forty feet. The horseshoe, which weighed all of two and a half pounds, made me list to the side on which I was holding it. I drew a deep breath and glanced at Tim and Brad, whose bemused expressions reflected confidence in their victory. Then I closed my eyes, opened them, focused on the stake, and pitched the horseshoe, which caught the final rays of sun as it sailed through the air.

To my delight, the harsh sound of the horseshoe clanging against the iron stake rang in my ears.

"It's a ringer, Jess!" Babs yelled. "You tossed a ringer! We won!"

I guess it was my day, after all.

Tim gave me a hug. Brad, a sour expression on his weathered face, mumbled congratulations and walked away.

"Wait till I tell Hal," Babs bubbled. "Where is he?"

I fell in behind Babs in search of her husband. As we approached the sprawling New England–style house, we passed my dear friend Dr. Seth Hazlitt, who'd driven me to the gathering. People in town wonder why I've never learned to drive a car and trust my bicycle to get around, and look askance at me for having taken flying lessons and earning my private pilot's license. I'm not sure that I can adequately explain why I have a license to fly but not one that allows me to drive, and I've given up trying to figure it out myself. I guess one of the great things about Cabot Cove is you don't need a car to get around, much less a plane. I also hadn't needed either when I spent much of my time at the Manhattan apartment I seldom visited these days.

"Anything you'd like to say to Babs and Hal?" Eve Simpson said, approaching with her Canon still in her grasp. "I'm making a video for their anniversary."

I'd forgotten it was coming up. "Making a video with what?"

She held up her camera. "This."

"I thought you said video."

"I did," Eve said, shooting me the kind of stare adults aim at ten-year-olds. "This records video, too—on a memory card," she added, popping it from its slot. "See?"

I watched Eve slide the tiny thing back in. "What should I say?"

She positioned herself before me. "Whatever comes to mind. You and Seth are the last ones I need to get."

I remembered Eve spending the party circulating through the crowd with the camera dangling from her neck, mining for gossip, I thought, but now I realized her intentions had been considerably more hospitable.

"Ready whenever you are," I said.

"Just start whenever you're ready."

I smiled and plunged right in. "Congratulations, Hal and Babs. I feel like I've known you forever and I guess I have, at least since you moved to Cabot Cove. I watched your beautiful daughter, Alyssa, grow up and can only hope you've dissuaded her from becoming a writer. On the chance you haven't, my offer to serve as mentor still stands, so long as I don't have to teach her how to drive!" I stopped and moved my gaze from the camera to Eve. "How was that?"

"Perfect!"

"Ready to leave, Jessica?" Seth asked, coming up from behind me.

"Sure, but you need to record a video for Eve first, congratulating Babs and Hal on their anniversary."

"Ayuh. Sure thing. But where's the camera?"

Eve had begun to launch into her explanation anew when her eyes widened at the sight of someone passing between us and the entrance to the kitchen.

"My God, do you know who that is?"

I followed her gaze to a youngish man striding toward the outdoor bar with an empty drink glass.

"Can't say that I do."

"It's Deacon Westhausen, for God's sake."

The name rang a bell, but it took me a moment to realize the source of Eve's excitement.

"Of course, the tech giant," I said, watching as Westhausen was intercepted by a trio of party guests en route to the bar.

"Tech giant? That's putting it mildly. The man's Steve Jobs, Elon Musk, and Richard Branson all rolled into one."

"I've read the stories, Eve," I said, not bothering to hide my lack of enthusiasm for Cabot Cove's latest local celebrity, who was building a massive home in a previously protected area of wetlands right on the bluffs forming the cove that gave our town its name. This in return for the sizable investment he'd made in the long-awaited expansion of our cherished marina. "And I've also read the stories questioning the source of his income."

"I think you're just jealous over not being the most famous person in town anymore. And look at all the jobs the amphitheater he's building at the marina has brought to town."

"Then we should dismiss the rumors about his cutting corners and using substandard building materials?"

"Yes, because that's all they are—rumors. Spread by those who are jealous of his success and all the good he's doing for this town."

"I don't count that monstrosity he's building off the docks as anything good, Eve."

She scampered across the lawn, weaving a zigzagging path toward Deacon Westhausen and leaving me to follow Babs through a door leading directly into the kitchen to say my good-byes.

"Hal?" Babs called out before I could say anything.

The kitchen was empty, or it seemed to be. But then I saw half of a man's shoe protruding from behind a large island used for prepping food. I approached it to have a better look. The shoe was attached to a leg— Hal Wirth's leg.

"*Hal!*" Babs shrieked.

I rushed out the door to get Seth, the primary care doctor for pretty much the entire town. But I didn't have to go far, since he was already running toward me, having heard Babs's anguished cry.

"What's wrong?" he asked as we shouldered through the door, trailed by Eve Simpson, camera in hand.

"It's Hal Wirth," I managed, barely. "I think he's dead."

Chapter Two

The sun had dipped behind the mountains when Seth and I set out behind the ambulance transporting Hal to Cabot Cove Hospital. I sat shocked in the passenger seat while Seth drove. He was uncharacteristically quiet, stunned by the tragic conclusion to what had been a joyous Labor Day. Hal's health had seemed to be fine throughout the party; he'd spent the day mixing and mingling with guests or tossing a football with a few teenagers.

There was a period of time toward the end of the day, though, when he and Seth ensconced themselves in a secluded corner of the property and sat together on a green wrought iron bench. From my vantage point, and from Hal's body language, I judged the subject of their impromptu conversation to be serious and not for other ears. They conferred for twenty minutes before Hal stood and walked away, leaving Seth alone on the bench to ponder what had transpired.

I hadn't seen him again until he lay supine in the kitchen. Had he suffered a heart attack? Although it's unusual for people in their late forties to succumb to a coronary, I'd immediately assumed that had to be the cause of his sudden collapse. Or . . .

As a mystery writer, I have to discipline myself not to imagine crimes unfolding on every corner and not to see something nefarious in every sudden and inexplicable passing. Still, in Hal's case, the fact that he'd been so buoyant just minutes before aroused my suspicions, whether warranted or not.

"I saw you and Hal huddled off by yourselves for a time, Seth," I worked myself up to say. "I have to ask what it was about."

"No, you don't, Jessica. Just like you know I can't share what we discussed. Doctor-patient privilege."

"Then you were discussing Hal's health."

"I didn't say that."

"You implied it. Just give me a notion."

"All I can tell you is that we didn't discuss his *physical* health."

It sounded strange the way Seth said that, but I didn't pester him further. People in Cabot Cove confided everything to Seth. He was the classic small-town doctor in an age where insurance companies were making such practices almost impossible to keep up. Seth was the exception to the rule, and I respected him too much to press him on the issue.

Meanwhile, thank heavens a medical professional

had been there. Seth had recognized a pulse in Hal's jugular vein and shouted for the crowd that had gathered to call 911. He'd also instructed people to direct the paramedics to where Hal lay, while continuing to tend to him.

"Every second counts in situations like this," Cabot Cove's beloved physician said, kneeling over Hal to continue his CPR efforts.

Although the ambulance and its crew of two EMS paramedics arrived within minutes, it seemed an eternity to me. Cabot Cove's emergency personnel don't typically have much to keep them busy, although that was changing with an influx of new residents packing the town to its very gills, especially in the summer season, which was now drawing to a close. But the speed with which they showed up impressed me. Hal was fitted with an oxygen mask and rushed into the back of the ambulance. Babs, who'd been standing at the rear of the crowd, her fist pressed tightly against her lips to stifle the cry of anguish building inside, climbed into the vehicle with her husband. The sun was setting and, with it, summer itself. I could only hope the darkening sky didn't prove a portent for Hal's prognosis.

When Babs and Hal Wirth had arrived in Cabot Cove almost ten years ago, they injected a burst of youthful energy to a town that had begun to grow insular and perhaps too set in its ways. Their daughter, Alyssa, was in grade school when they chose our village as their new home, and Babs immediately threw herself into town activities, particularly as an active participant in the PTA and the historical society. She was also a skilled painter. My friend Mara was delighted to hang an exhibit of Babs's work in her luncheonette, and one of Babs's best-loved pieces, a seascape of the view beyond the bluffs, hung permanently on the luncheonette's wall. I'd also bought one of her paintings, now displayed proudly in my own home.

Babs had become one of my most treasured friends, a bond that became tighter as the years passed. A woman I've trusted with my innermost sentiments and secrets, she'd always been there whenever I felt the need to reminisce about my late husband, Frank, and had done her best to put a smile on my face, a consideration I was ready to return in kind. Now that such a time had come, it would fall on me to help support her through this ordeal, facing the possibility that she was about to lose her beloved husband, just as I had lost mine. Call us kindred spirits, but not for the reasons you'd ordinarily choose.

And maybe my fears were premature. Hal would be receiving excellent medical care, after all. People survived heart attacks all the time, especially when that care came quickly, as it had in this case. Still, there was something . . .

My mind snapped back to reality when the ambulance turned so abruptly that Seth hit the brakes and swerved to stay on its tail, drawing so close he had to jam down on the pedal yet again.

"Sorry about that," he said, hands squeezing the wheel tight enough to drain the blood from his fingers.

The ambulance's flashing lights dimmed a bit as we fell back to a more comfortable distance.

"Are you okay to drive?"

"Why wouldn't I be?"

"You did have a beer or two."

"Hours ago. And that was all," he said, clearly wanting no part of this conversation. "I'm perfectly fine, Jessica. Besides, I'd better be sober enough to drive; it's not as if you can take the wheel."

I started to say something, but he rolled right over my words.

"Backseat drivers are bad enough, but when they don't even have a driver's license, like you, Jessica Fletcher, it's best to keep your advice to yourself."

I made myself laugh, and Seth appeared to relax a bit. Although his tone could, at times, be brash and even insulting, I knew he didn't mean it, at least not with me. He was one of my dearest friends. I rolled down my window halfway, trying to rid the car of its stale, stuffy feeling and hoping the fresh air might snap Seth back to full alertness.

I changed the subject to the reason we were following the ambulance containing Hal Wirth and his distraught wife, Babs. "You said Hal hadn't discussed anything about his physical health with you."

"Ayuh."

"What about mental?" I pestered, unable to help myself and thinking of the rumors that Hal and Babs had been having some . . . difficulties.

Seth remained silent.

"He's my friend, too, Seth."

"But you're not his doctor. Not last time I checked anyway."

He stopped there, but I could tell whatever they'd

discussed must have unsettled him. Dr. Seth Hazlitt was seldom off-kilter, but something had clearly disturbed him today, even before Hal's heart attack.

The ambulance entered a traffic circle leading to the main entrance of the hospital. We followed it until it veered off to the emergency entrance. Seth pulled into his usual designated spot in the parking lot, reserved for staff. We could see the emergency entrance from our vantage point and spotted two nurses and a physician rush outside to meet the paramedics. One held an oxygen mask to Hal's face while the other guided the gurney from the ambulance into the hospital.

I was poised to get out of Seth's car, but I noticed that he hadn't moved, his hands on the wheel, the motor still running. He stared thoughtfully out the window.

"Is there anything I can do to help?" I asked him. "Did that conversation you had with Hal have anything to do with Babs?"

Seth turned off the engine and faced me. "It had *everything* to do with Babs."

I expected him to continue, but I had to let my mind fill in the blanks when he didn't. Their conversation must've involved those rumored marital problems the Wirths were having. What else could it be? I'd read over the years that it was a commonplace enough occurrence with couples when their child left for college. Having never enjoyed that experience myself, I couldn't relate, though I could relate to the fact that every marriage endures difficulties. I imagined that Hal and Babs were going through a rough patch and that Hal had chosen to confide in Seth about the particulars.

"Anything you'd care to share?" I asked him, unable to help myself.

Seth scolded me with a stare. "Doctor-patient privilege, Jessica. Don't make me keep repeating that."

I eased open my door. "Let's go see how your patient is doing."

The corridor leading to Hal's room was painted a pasty pink color that made me uneasy. Everything about hospitals, in fact, made me uncomfortable: the colors, the lifeless artwork, the equally stale expressions on the staff's faces. They serve the function of mollifying patients, I suppose, yet this had always produced the opposite effect on me.

But hospital decorations aside, what mattered was the medical attention that Hal would receive. Despite being in a relatively small town in Maine, our hospital and its staff provided excellent care, certainly on a par with many big-city medical institutions.

Babs Wirth sat outside her husband's room. The door opened and closed as doctors and technicians came and went, their sense of urgency obvious in their body language and the pace with which they moved. She spotted Seth and me and moved toward us, her motions stiff and robotic.

"Oh, Jessica, it's so good of you to come," Babs said, giving me a hug. "And you, too, Seth. I don't know what I would have done, what would've happened, if you weren't around when . . ."

"Whatever you need," I said, "we're here. Hal seemed so healthy this afternoon, so full of life and upbeat. I can't explain what happened. I wish I could, but I can't."

"I don't understand!" Babs said, her voice cracking as it rose. "Alyssa would always scold him about his diet, but I never thought it actually made that much of a difference. He's so young."

"It's not unthinkable," Seth said, "that someone Hal's age had a heart attack." He pulled up a chair and patted Babs's knee.

"But at *forty-seven*?"

"*Even* at forty-seven," Seth said. "That age makes the odds of surviving with only minimal damage much better. Trust me," he added, trying to push some lightness into his voice. "I'm a doctor."

Babs tried to smile, but failed, turning her gaze back toward the room in which Hal was being treated. "What's going on in there, Seth? Tell me so I can picture it, so I can feel better."

Before Seth could answer, the door opened and Jacob Waverly, one of Cabot Cove's top cardiologists, emerged and walked toward us at the head of the corridor. He greeted Seth and me before he turned his gaze on Babs.

"Let's take a walk," Waverly said to her, a dour expression stretched over his face.

I grasped Seth's hand as we watched the doctor lead Babs down the hall so they could speak in private. When they were far enough away, the doctor held Babs's shoulders and spoke to her, his own frame

stiffening. I watched her knees buckle, the shoulders
Waverly had been grasping sag.

"He's *dead*?" she rasped, barely getting the words
out before the sobs consumed her.

Seth and I looked at each other, then fell into step
together toward Babs.

Waverly watched us take up positions on either
side of her, clearly grateful for our presence.

"It was a massive coronary," Waverly said, to all of
us. "I have no doubt of that much."

"At forty-seven?" Babs managed, using a sleeve to
blot her eyes. "He's only *forty-seven*!"

I could see she was shaking, her glazed expression
indicative of the shock I had grown all too familiar
with over the years.

"Unusual for sure, but not unprecedented," Waverly tried, in a tone somewhere between reassuring
and matter-of-fact. "Given his health history, it could
be genetic, something in his family."

Babs tried to take a deep breath, but gave up halfway through and just nodded. "Hal's father died of a
heart attack when he was only fifty-five."

"I wish I had more information to share with you,"
said Waverly, no longer trying to sound comforting.
"Something more definitive. For now, you need to know
there's nothing you, nor anyone else, could have done.
Getting him here so fast was the only thing that gave
him a chance, however slight." He swallowed hard; the
kind of news he'd just delivered was something you
never get used to. "If there's anything I can do for you
in the meantime, Mrs. Wirth, just let me know."

With that, Waverly squeezed Seth's shoulder, as if

to turn the reins over to him, and walked away, back toward Hal's room.

"I want to see him," Babs said, her voice pleading, on the verge of breaking down again.

"That might not be a good idea at the moment," Seth said.

"But I feel—I feel so lost. I thought maybe . . ."

Her voice trailed off. Her lips trembled. Her eyes flitted, tearing up again.

"That's natural," I said, remembering how I felt the day that Frank died.

I also know that while the intensity of the pain of losing a loved one lessens as time passes, it never completely goes away. Kind of like the way amputees describe still feeling their lost limbs.

"I'll stay with you," I told Babs.

"You don't have to."

"I *want* to."

"No," Babs said, with a firmness that surprised me. "I—I need to be alone. There's so much to do, so much that has to be handled."

"Let me help you."

Babs wasn't looking at me anymore; she wasn't looking at anything. "I have to call Alyssa. She needs to come home. I need to get her home."

"I can help with whatever you need. We're having dinner tonight, you and me. I'll pick something up for us."

"You don't have to make sure I eat, Jessica. I could stand to lose a few pounds anyway," she said, trying for a smile that didn't come. "And there's all that leftover food from the party."

Which she'd asked Cabot Cove Catering to donate to the nearest food pantry, I recalled, but didn't remind her.

"You shouldn't be alone," I said instead, "and I'm not taking no for an answer."

"Count me in, too," said Seth. "And I'm happy to pick up the food. I'm a wizard with takeout."

"Sounds like an offer we can't refuse," I said to Babs, forcing a smile as weak as hers.

She gave me a long, tight hug, then did the same with Seth. Her cell phone chimed from her handbag, and I thought of all the people who'd been at the gathering calling to inquire about Hal's status. Just a sample of what Babs's life was going to be like for the immediate future, much of which was sure to be lost in the fog of grief. That's the somewhat cruel thing about well-meaning folks offering you their prayers and condolences; their hearts are in the right place, but they don't realize their efforts will pass like water through a sieve. And every time Babs answered the phone, at least for a while, she'd be forced to relive the moment she was living now, starting with the call to her daughter, Alyssa.

Seth and I reluctantly left her alone in the hospital and returned to his car.

"She's a strong lady," Seth offered as he climbed behind the wheel and started the engine.

"I was, too—at first," I said, fastening my seat belt. "Seth?" I resumed.

"What?"

I wanted to say something didn't feel right about this, something I couldn't quite put my finger on. Dr.

Waverly was right about men Hal's age not being immune to heart attacks, especially with his family history. Still, something was gnawing at me. A feeling, a sense of something somehow out of place, like an itch I couldn't quite reach . . .

"What, Jessica?" Seth repeated.

"Nothing," I said, clearing my throat. "I just hope you're right."

But I couldn't chase that feeling, or my worries about whatever Hal had discussed with Seth just a few hours earlier, from my mind.

Chapter Three

There were no lights on in Babs's house, or at least none visible through the front windows, as Seth turned into the driveway a few hours later. Babs had called me to say she was leaving the hospital and again tried to shun our request to bring over some food. I told her we'd already picked it up—a lie, yes, but a well-intentioned one.

"I wonder if she fell straight asleep when she got home," I said, a bit worried. "I know she takes those pills occasionally."

"After all she's been through, I wouldn't be surprised," Seth said, his expression squeezed into something between a frown and a scowl. "Let's bring the food in anyway and see if she's awake. We promised her dinner and company, and the two of us standing on her doorstep might be just what the doctor ordered—literally."

"When Frank died, it was the friends persistently trying to cheer me up that made the biggest difference in my life."

"Present company included, I trust," Seth said, managing a smile.

I put my hand on his arm. "I want to be that kind of friend to Babs now."

We took the food—lentil soup, cold cuts, bread, and a Greek salad, all from Mara's Luncheonette—and knocked on the front door.

No answer.

I knocked again.

Nothing.

I stepped onto the moist summer grass and over to a dark window. I put my hand to the glass to diminish the glare and peered inside into the Wirths' living room. It was still a mess from their Labor Day party, with paper plates and utensils strewn about the tables. Some must have been blown to the floor by the breeze passing through the windows she'd neglected to close before joining her now-late husband in the ambulance. I was surprised Cabot Cove Catering hadn't cleaned the place up, but thought perhaps they wouldn't be sure if they should, given that Hal had suffered the heart attack on the premises. The way things are today, so litigious, people are always afraid of lawsuits, and it might have been just that very thing that had kept the company from completing its duties.

The events that had transpired seemed like they'd occurred days ago, not hours. It felt like I was returning to the scene of a crime, something I'd grown all too accustomed to over the years, although that clearly wasn't the case here. Unless . . .

I fought back the thought, resisting that odd sense that had struck me in the hospital.

"If Babs wants to be alone, we should let her," Seth said. "We should let her grieve however she needs to. We can bring her breakfast in the morning instead."

"I don't think she'd leave all the lights off even if she went to sleep, Seth."

"Let me give her a call on her cell phone, then. Maybe she's in one of the back rooms."

The Wirths' house was expansive, Hal's success in the world of high technology having garnered considerable perks. I recalled now him once speaking of his admiration for Deacon Westhausen when Westhausen expressed interest in relocating to Cabot Cove. Since they had plenty in common, I could understand that. I'd yet to meet Westhausen myself, and it had nothing to do with being supplanted as Cabot Cove's most famous resident either. No one was ever more right than F. Scott Fitzgerald when he wrote that the rich were different from you and me, as evidenced by the monstrosity of an estate Deacon Westhausen was building on a previously pristine patch of land now only he would be able to enjoy.

No, I wasn't jealous of him at all, I mused as I walked to another window to see if I could spot any indications of Babs's presence.

"The front door's open!" Seth called. "I'll leave the food inside the foyer, or maybe stow it in the fridge, and we can let her be alone."

"I guess that's a good idea," I said. "I don't see—"

I stopped speaking abruptly when the reflection of halogen lights off the windowpane momentarily blinded me. I turned to see a car, a taxi, pull into the driveway behind Seth's.

To my relief, Babs climbed out of the backseat.

She swiped at her eyes and ran over to give me a hug, forcing a smile when we finally broke the embrace.

"I'm so sorry you arrived before me," she continued. "I had to make some calls, and I found it easier to do it from the hospital, where there were people around. Dr. Waverly was a great comfort, too. He arranged for a taxi to bring me home," she added as the car reversed out of the driveway and was gone. "I don't know what I would have done if . . ."

The breath poured out of her like air from a balloon, and she looked suddenly ready to collapse, her eyes welling with fresh tears.

"Let's go inside," I suggested. "Seth and I brought dinner. As promised. Greek salad, your favorite."

She tried to smile again. "It was Hal's favorite, too."

The house was dark and chilly, as September nights tend to be in Cabot Cove, when summer winds down.

"My, it's cold. I must have left the back door wide open before I left. Hang on—let me check."

She walked toward the other end of the house to shut the door.

"Go into the kitchen and I'll meet you there!" I heard her call out to us.

We obliged, and eventually I found the switch to turn on the kitchen lights. Seth lifted the food onto the counter and began opening the various containers.

"Don't rush to help, Jessica. I've got it under control," he chuckled.

I barely recorded his sarcasm. This was where I'd found Hal collapsed on the floor earlier in the day. Now that it was quiet, the weight of the day's tragedy began to sink in. How much Hal and Babs meant to this community and to the people who'd come to their party. How many laughs we'd shared over the years. They always seemed so happy, so perfect for each other. It was impossible to conceive of them having marital problems. And that brought me back to spotting Hal speaking with Seth alone earlier in the day in what was clearly a serious, pointed exchange.

I noticed a folded piece of paper at the base of the counter beneath the sink, right where Hal had fallen. I picked it up, intending to place it on the counter, but couldn't resist lifting back the edges to open it up. I tried to tell myself I was doing it for Babs's own good; maybe it was a simple bill or something she didn't otherwise need to see at the moment.

It turned out to be a brief, hand-scrawled note, signed by someone named Eugene Labine.

Hal, I'm writing to extend an undeserved courtesy by informing you that I'll be taking legal action against you and—

"What have you got there, Jessica?" Babs said, suddenly by my side.

"Oh, it's nothing," I said, embarrassed, as if I'd been caught snooping.

I set the note on the counter, trying to appear casual. I wanted to ask Babs who Eugene Labine was and what the basis of his legal action against Hal might be, but I managed to hold my tongue, just as Seth finished laying out the food.

Babs forced a smile. "Then let's sit down. How about some coffee?"

"I'd love a cup of tea if you have it," I said, my gaze lingering on the letter now resting upon the granite countertop.

"Sure thing, let me get the water on the stove."

"And a coffee for me," Seth added.

I so wanted to read the rest of that handwritten letter, but wouldn't, *couldn't*, press the issue now; it would have to wait. My friend had been through enough for one day, and whatever the letter pertained to, it was none of my concern. Hal had done business all over New England since he and Barbara moved to Cabot Cove from Chicago with their daughter, Alyssa. He was a computer guru, and he'd founded a software company called Wirth Ventures Inc. in Granite Heights, a rapidly growing industrial area a little more than an hour's drive from downtown Cabot Cove, at the virtual halfway point to Boston. The company became very lucrative, turning the Wirth family into minor celebrities as Cabot Cove's local dot-com success story. And Hal and Babs had used that status to further causes important to them and had become true pillars of the community.

In the years of Hal's business dealings, of course, it was hardly unthinkable that he hadn't made an enemy or two. A rival, a disgruntled employee, an associate bearing a grudge . . . any of those could have been behind the hand-scrawled note I'd found on the floor. Nonetheless, the tone, and the fact that it had been handwritten, which was unusual in its own right, lingered in my mind.

A sprightly whistle sounded outside, and then a retort. I looked out the window to see if the song's source was just beyond the windowpane.

"It's an eastern whip-poor-will," Babs said, noticing my interest. "I've heard them less and less over the years, but this one's been serenading us all summer. I wonder . . ."

"What?" I prodded.

"Nothing. Just that maybe the birds have some sense that . . ."

"You must have trouble sleeping at night," I said when her voice trailed off again. "I would need earplugs."

"Those birds comforted me when Hal was in Granite Heights, sometimes for days. His software company had been demanding a lot of his time, but the work excited him so much. I don't think he'd ever been happier, although I wish the business hadn't forced him to be away so often." The expression seemed to slide off her face, her shoulders sagging with it. "Funny, I hadn't even thought about the business yet. So much to handle, so much to do."

She lapsed into silence, as if waiting for the bird to resume its singing, but the kitchen remained bathed in quiet.

"Well, be sure to tell Tim Purdy about your whip-poor-wills!" Seth said, trying to break the tension that had settled in the room. "He'd love to document their return to Cabot Cove. You said you haven't heard them in a long time, until recently?"

"Yes, they migrate south during the winters and return north for the summer to reproduce. The Maine populations have been dwindling, so their making a comeback is welcome news indeed."

The three of us stood in the kitchen, gazing out the window into the darkness beyond.

The kettle whistled on the stove and Babs lifted it from the burner, flapping away the steam that dampened her face.

"Let me help you," I offered.

"It's all right, Jessica," she said, laying out the mugs and tea bags for us.

She made Seth a "pour-over" coffee, which entailed placing a portable filter filled with coffee grinds over the cup and pouring hot water directly into it. It was a form of brewing gaining prevalence with the rising popularity of café culture and organic coffees spreading among the millennial generation. It seemed to me a bit too much bother for a single cup and made me glad I was a low-maintenance tea drinker. But the look on Seth's face, after he took a sip, told me it must've been worth it.

"Any milk or sugar?" Babs asked him.

"Typically, yes, but this is perfect as is."

Babs handed me my tea, and took a cup of her own, blowing the steam off the surface to cool it down.

"Babs," I said to her, "I'm sure there will be a lot to do at the house now, and I'd be happy to help with any preparations, paperwork, housework, etc. This will be easier if you don't have a million logistical nightmares hanging over your head."

I had an ulterior motive, of course, for offering my assistance, my curiosity having been piqued by a combination of that odd feeling that had struck me at the hospital, now coupled with that strange handwritten letter from someone named Eugene Labine threatening legal action. I'd based some books, and become embroiled in some very real-life investigations, on less than that.

Babs's voice was shaky when she answered. "I'd like that—I'd like that very much. For the company alone. Alyssa will be home tomorrow, but I don't want to depend on her or burden her. I don't even want to think about her voice when I called her from the hospital."

Babs looked like she had more to say, but just sighed and shook her head.

Seth was left shaking his head, too. "I've had to facilitate too many of those conversations in my time."

"So Hal's computer business was going like gangbusters," I said, trying not to sound like I was prying.

Babs smiled reflectively. "He always hated when people called his business that."

"What?"

"Computer. His work was actually centered on technology itself, particularly software, writing it to satisfy the needs of individual companies. Getting their platforms set up, that sort of thing."

"That's way beyond me."

"Me, too," she conceded. "But the company was

doing so well from its base in Granite Heights, bringing in so much revenue, that Hal had brought on a whole bunch of new hires. Kids straight out of college, if you can believe that. But they needed supervision, and that's what took him away for so many days at a time."

I noticed Seth bristle when Babs mentioned how well Wirth Ventures was doing, and kept an eye peeled for his further reaction as I responded.

"I thought all those kids were going out to Palo Alto for that kind of work."

"You'd be surprised. Granite Heights has really grown since we relocated Wirth Ventures from Chicago. It's become an attractive place for young people to settle down for tech work, especially those who don't want to join the rat race out west."

"I guess that influx helps explain the rising popularity of Cabot Cove, especially in summer."

"Not a great trend," Seth groused, "given the effects rising real estate prices have already started to have. I always liked our town better when it was quaint, instead of fashionable, ayuh."

"Well," I said, "I guess we have to learn to live with the fact that now it's both."

"Yes," Babs mused, clearly glad for the distraction. "I always liked how resistant Cabot Cove was to change, but it seems that the world finally caught up to our little New England town. I remember when we first moved here, Alyssa was so enamored with the ocean. She'd never seen it before, and you'd walk on the beach with her, Jessica, when Hal and I were at work. You helped guide her through those first couple years in so many ways, even sharing some of your writing with her. She wants to be a mystery writer herself now."

That took me by surprise. "What happened to studying criminal justice and becoming a lawyer?"

"She's still studying criminal justice. But she's having trouble with the notion of three more years of school after college."

"Maybe it's just a phase," I said, catching Seth fidget again.

"Like it was for you?"

"I was still an English teacher when I got started. Well, at least by studying criminal justice, she'll be starting off writing what she knows."

"Just like you've put what you know to practical use plenty of times outside of your books."

I shrugged her comment off, even as I checked Seth for a reaction again. "Right place, right time. That's all. Fate more than skill."

"You're selling yourself short, Jessica. Wasn't it Sherlock Holmes who said, 'The world is full of obvious things which nobody by any chance ever observes'?"

My eyes widened. "Indeed, he did. In *The Hound of the Baskervilles*. I didn't know you were such a dedicated mystery reader."

"You mean besides your books?" she quipped. "You bet I am. Nothing better than a good mystery to take your mind off everything else."

"I couldn't agree more," I told her.

Chapter Four

"Don't ask," Seth said once he'd reversed out of Babs's driveway and commenced the short drive to my home.

"Don't ask what?"

"What Hal Wirth and I were discussing at the party. I know you were about to again."

"Well . . ."

"I don't want you barking up trees where there's no cat."

"What's that mean? And how do we know there's no cat?"

Seth offered no further comment and I stopped pressing him. He dropped me home and I immediately made myself another cup of tea and sat down on the couch in my living room, where I did much of my best thinking. I was glad to have something to focus on other than the memories of my own grief in the wake of Frank's passing; anything was preferable to that, including whatever Seth was hiding about Hal Wirth. Rumors had been floating around town about his long absences from home for some time now, and romantic flings he was purported to have engaged in during those periods. I had dismissed them, because I was so close with Babs and trusted her judgment over gossip.

My eyelids drooped, and it was to thoughts of Babs's vulnerability and Hal's indiscretions that I began to drift. . . .

I awoke on the couch at 10:37 p.m., to the sound of the phone ringing. My tea was still warm, and I took a sip as I pressed TALK on my cordless phone.

"Hello?"

"Mrs. Fletcher?"

"Yes?" I answered back, even though I already knew who was calling.

"It's Evelyn Phillips of the *Cabot Cove Gazette*."

"Yes, hi, Evelyn. I thought I recognized your voice."

"I'm so glad to have caught you awake! I know it's late, but as long as you're not asleep, I hope I'm not disturbing you."

"Well, as a matter of fact . . ."

"I've just heard the news that Hal Wirth suddenly passed away of a massive coronary."

I remained silent, letting Evelyn continue.

"And I also heard you were there," she added, sounding almost gleeful, as if she smelled a scoop in this somewhere. "Can you tell me the circumstances surrounding his death? I heard it happened during the Wirths' annual Labor Day party."

Evelyn was the last person in the world I wanted to talk to right now. Hal, for one, had frequently mentioned that he did not particularly care for her, nor the *Cabot Cove Gazette*, which he considered to be a rag of a local paper, just a notch above a tabloid.

"Circumstances? He suffered a heart attack."

"That's all?"

"Isn't it enough?"

"I understand you were at the party," she persisted. "Is it true that Hal was acting strangely? Not as if he was sick—more like he was worried about something?"

I immediately recognized Evelyn's usual trick to make me assume she knew something she didn't, like about Hal's terse conversation with Seth Hazlitt.

"I don't know what you're talking about, Evelyn," I said, to halt her in her tracks. "I stopped by the party with Seth for an hour to say hello and—"

"Seth Hazlitt was there?"

"Well . . ."

I continued to stammer, regretting my misstep. Lingering fatigue and the stress of such a difficult day had conspired to make me fall right into Evelyn's trap. Now she would contact Seth, who knew more about Hal than most people in Cabot Cove.

"I have nothing more to say, Evelyn. I have to go now, and frankly, you snooping into a deceased man's life hours after his passing is disrespectful at best. Excuse me for saying this, but you should be ashamed of yourself."

I could feel Evelyn bristle, even over the line. "I have readers, Jessica. My responsibility is to them and I can't help that they want the truth. You should know that as a fellow writer."

"Our styles have nothing in common, besides the fact we both, apparently, write fiction."

"That doesn't change the fact that Hal was an important man in this town. My readers want to know the real story of the man they so revered."

"Real story, Evelyn?"

"My sources tell me he was known to have engaged in affairs with several women."

"Affairs? And how would your 'sources' know this exactly?"

"I didn't ask them. I was hoping you might shed some light on the details. For instance, how many women, how many of these affairs, were there?"

"As far as I know, one, and her name was Barbara, his wife. Beyond that, I'm afraid I can't help you."

"Jessica, I understand you want to protect Hal's reputation. I just don't want to run a story that might damage his standing in this community before first getting all my facts straight, and that's where you come in. You know the Wirths as well as anybody, but if you have nothing to clarify, I'll have to make do with what I've got."

"Which is what?" I asked, suspecting this entire line of conversation to be yet another of Evelyn's journalistic wiles.

"Oh, come on, Jessica. You know Hal Wirth was less than scrupulous in his business dealings."

"I know no such thing, and neither do you."

"Don't be so sure about that. Tomorrow morning you can read all about it in the *Gazette*. I'm thinking front page, unless you have something to dissuade me."

"You know, Evelyn, the Wirths' daughter, Alyssa, is due home from college tomorrow to attend her father's funeral, and many of your readers will be stopping by to express their sympathies. You're right, Hal Wirth was a well-liked man in this town, and I sincerely doubt these readers of yours will take kindly to you disparaging his name with unsubstantiated rumors. I suspect there may be a rush by those same readers to cancel their subscriptions."

"It's not like they have other options to get their news in Cabot Cove."

"No news is better than poorly reported news. You go ahead and print this gossip piece on such a beloved man's life while his family grieves, and I just might see to it the *Gazette* has some competition at long last."

It was an empty threat, spoken in haste, but Evelyn didn't know that and mustered no reply, allowing me to compose myself over the dead air.

"You might be right, Mrs. Fletcher," she said, dispensing with the familiarity of using my first name. "I admit the timing is . . . regrettable and suppose the story, the truth, can wait. But there will be a time, and you and I both know there's a story here you can't quash with your threats."

I couldn't help myself. "What do you think you know about Hal Wirth's business dealings?"

"Will you comment on the record?"

"No."

"Then you'll have to wait for the story to run to find out. And it will run, I promise you that."

"Maybe you'll win a Pulitzer," I said to the younger woman. "A regular Woodward and Bernstein rolled into one."

"Who?" Evelyn asked.

I hung up the phone, glad that, if nothing else, I'd at least delayed her running the story for a while.

I rose from the couch and wandered into the kitchen, wondering if I was any better than Evelyn for seeing dark doings in Hal's dealings and untimely death, reading too much into that letter I hadn't even finished and whatever mysterious conversation Hal had engaged in with Seth Hazlitt. Everybody confided in Seth because he never betrayed a confidence. I should've known better than to have even asked him. When your life requires you to live inside your imagination, sometimes you just can't help seeing something that isn't really there.

I knew I'd never be able to fall back to sleep now and decided to ride my bike to Mara's Luncheonette, which stayed open until midnight, to grab one of Mara's famous muffins to have for breakfast.

It was a beautiful night, and I heard the faint songs of whip-poor-wills as I pedaled. Their music was a sound I had always taken for granted. I was oddly comforted by the consistency of the call, a dependable trill that satiated the organizational portion of my mind as I counted the cries and retorts, wondering what they might be communicating. Babs had said that they returned to Maine during summers to mate, which made me remember she'd lost her mate forever.

Mara's was winding down for the night, but I heard voices from the newly built terrace behind the restaurant when I chained my bike. There I found my friends Tim Purdy, head of the Cabot Cove Historical Society; Mort Metzger, the local sheriff; and Mort's wife, Maureen. They were huddled around a table with a round of beers.

A man I didn't recognize sat alone a few tables away, nursing a cocktail with his head down. He wore a beige jacket and a black felt hat, and was scribbling words in a notebook as my friends rose to welcome me.

"I was just on the phone with Seth," said Mort. "He told me about Hal. How awful! I hope Babs is okay. How's she doing?"

"Hanging in there," I said. "Devastated, of course, but she has plenty of friends to help keep her spirits up, and her daughter Alyssa's coming home tomorrow."

"That's good," Tim Purdy said. "Babs and I have been getting closer this past year and Hal's death struck a real chord with me."

"Babs told me that you two have been cataloguing the local birdlife. She pointed out that the whip-poor-will population is coming back. I heard them singing on my bike ride over."

"That's right." Tim laughed. "Between you and me, I had no idea what the heck a whip-poor-will was until Babs and I embarked on this project. Now I know why I can't sleep at night."

"I hope we don't all catch a case of insomnia." I smiled, so glad in that moment I'd decided to ride over there.

"If I don't sleep tonight, it'll be because of Evelyn Phillips," Maureen said.

"You spoke with her?"

"She was here maybe ninety minutes ago, snooping around and probing us for information on Hal's indiscretions, marital and otherwise."

Evelyn must have called me as soon as she left, I calculated.

"Impersonating a journalist, no doubt," I couldn't help but say, not bothering to add she'd pestered me as well.

"Want a drink, Jessica?" Mort asked. "Last call's come and gone, but I have some clout in these parts."

"No, Mort, but thank you. I just came to clear my head and grab a muffin for the morning."

I sauntered up to the counter, pretending not to notice the man at the corner table rising to follow me. In a close-knit community like Cabot Cove, all strangers stood out, but something about this one made him stand out even more.

The waitress, meanwhile, was nowhere to be found, and the cook had just poured water over the grill to cool it down, releasing a curtain of thin steam that drifted toward me.

"Excuse me—are you Mrs. Jessica Fletcher?"

I turned to find the stranger standing right alongside me at the counter. "That would depend on who's asking."

He settled onto the stool next to where I was standing, his face caught by the wafting steam, which dimmed his features and made his skin look shiny. I was still able to discern a pair of eyes that looked too small for his face, set deep in his head over a pug nose and a mouth that similarly looked too small. His teeth, too, looked tiny when he smiled at me, and they carried the brown stains of a cigarette smoker. He had thinning hair pasted to his skull in patches and some beard stubble marking his face.

"It's an honor to meet you," he said, through the steam that had settled between us, nothing threatening or ominous in his voice. "I've heard about you over the years. I was hoping I'd get the chance someday to meet Cabot Cove's most famous resident."

I could smell bourbon on his breath, accompanied by the stench of cigarettes lifting off his clothes. "I hope you don't mind being disappointed."

"I'd ask you to sign a book for me had I brought one."

"And who would I inscribe it to if you had?"

"I'm Lawrence Pyke, Hal Wirth's attorney," the man said. "I've driven up from Boston to speak with Barbara about some issues regarding Hal's estate, which— as you might have guessed, being such a dear friend, according to Hal—Barbara is inheriting in full."

I hadn't known that, but nodded anyway.

"And this whole business with Hal's ex-business partner," the man continued. "Such a nasty state of affairs I thought he'd put behind him."

"Oh, yes." I nodded, still pretending, in this case that I hadn't glimpsed that handwritten letter from one Eugene Labine. "Truly unfortunate. Regrettable," I added, leaving it there.

"What do you know about that?"

"About what?"

"Hal Wirth's business partner."

"What makes you think I'd know anything about him?"

"The fact that you're such good friends with Barbara."

"Hardly something that would make me privy to her husband's business affairs."

Lawrence Pyke leaned forward—a little, which seemed like too much. "Barbara always spoke of you as a pragmatic woman. She needs an astute ear, such as your own, to guide her in these difficult times. She is an effervescent spirit, but naive, I think. And now, with the responsibility of taking over Hal's corporation falling on her—well, let's just say things might get hairy."

"Babs is a brilliant and headstrong woman. I don't think you have anything to be concerned about."

"I do hope so. I have only affection for Barbara. Hal's old partner is . . ."

"Is what, Mr. Pyke?"

I could see the man claiming to be Hal Wirth's lawyer fishing for words. "There's no easy way to say this. He was scorned after Hal screwed him out of the business they cofounded, and recently stopped making good on the financial settlement they agreed upon."

"I'm not aware of any such thing."

"A structured settlement whereby Hal would make regular payments to his former partner, Eugene Labine, which he did for several years until they stopped abruptly a little over a month ago."

"Strange that you'd be sharing information I'm sure is privileged with a stranger."

"You're not a stranger, Mrs. Fletcher. I thought we'd already established that, and I'm only looking out for Babs's best interests."

"Well, Mr. Pyke, I am indeed a stranger to the interests of Hal's estate, and my concern for Babs doesn't include being made privy to her husband's private affairs."

"Then Mrs. Wirth has said nothing about those affairs to you?"

"I believe I just made that clear." I should have let things go there but, again, couldn't help myself. "Tell me, Mr. Pyke, are you Hal's lawyer or the estate's lawyer?"

"Both, I suppose."

"Don't suppose, please. Because it occurs to me that those pursuits may represent a conflict of interest. Perhaps I should inform Mrs. Wirth of that fact."

Pyke stiffened, the steam riding him like an aura. "I'm sure she has other things on her mind tonight."

"There's always tomorrow, Mr. Pyke."

"As her friend—"

"Tell me again how you even know we're friends."

Pyke tried for a smile that didn't quite come. "It's in Barbara's best interests that you share with me anything you may have learned about her husband's business dealings prior to today, anything potentially awry, for instance."

"I never took an interest in Hal's business dealings. And, excuse me for saying this, but you don't sound like a lawyer looking after the interests of a departed client's wife."

Pyke slid off the stool and stood close enough for

me to almost be able to name the brand of the whiskey on his breath.

"Be a friend to Barbara, but steer clear of issues pertaining to her husband. It's for your own good and hers."

"Is that a threat?"

"Just a bit of advice from someone who knows the territory and who has your best interests at heart."

"You don't even know me."

Pyke smiled, showcasing twin rows of tiny teeth. "I know your books, and now I know you. Be a friend to Barbara," he finished. "Be a friend, and nothing more."

Lawrence Pyke took his leave, eyeing me all the way to the door. I waited for it to shut behind him before I returned without my muffin to the table, where Mort Metzger was looking at me with his cop's eyes.

"Who was that?" he asked.

"I'm not sure" was all I could say, still staring at the closed door.

Chapter Five

"And this one?" I asked Babs as we took stock of Hal's possessions the following day, at her insistence.

The memories of my brief and disconcerting conversation with Lawrence Pyke had faded somewhat, and I had avoided any mention of our encounter at Mara's Luncheonette the night before, figuring Babs had enough on her mind. Surely, he'd been in contact with her by now to begin the process of getting Hal's affairs in order. I purposely steered clear of the issue to prevent causing Babs any further strain, especially since keeping herself active was proving to be the best therapy.

We were standing in Hal and Babs's bedroom, staring at an abstract portrait of a woman formed of thick oily smudges, which reminded me of a crude Van Gogh. As best I could discern through the hodgepodge, the female subject of the painting was not Babs.

"That's Hal's work, believe it or not. He tried his hand at painting seven or eight years ago. It didn't stick." She laughed. "But I agreed to hang this to indulge his ego."

I couldn't help myself. "Has Hal's lawyer made contact with you about settling the estate?"

"Several times. I'm expecting him shortly as a matter of fact." Her face crinkled in concern. "There's so much to get in order. Hal had so many dealings across the state, and across New England—Boston, Providence, Worcester—and it's all much more complicated than I could have ever realized. I tried to make sense of what I could dig up last night, when I couldn't sleep, but didn't get very far."

"When's Alyssa due home?"

"She got here late last night, after you left. She's running a few errands right now. I wanted her out of the house for a while—thought it best. We had a long conversation about her father last night, and what needs to be done over the next couple months. She's insisting on taking the rest of the semester off, tells me Boston University has agreed not to charge her and she'll be readmitted without question next spring."

"She'll have time to read my latest book, then," I said. "The first draft is finished and she can be my first critical read."

That drew a smile from Babs. "I remember her reading your books when she was, what, ten or eleven?"

"Twelve, I think."

"I'm sure she'll be thrilled. I was planning to put her to work around the house, but reading your latest manuscript sure beats that."

"When's the lawyer due?" I asked Babs, hoping I wasn't snooping too much.

She looked toward a clock radio with a bright red LED display set on a night table. "Any minute now. Hal named me executrix of his will and I'm inheriting his entire estate. Pyke wants to do an accounting and inventory of Hal's paperwork. It's all down in the basement, where he kept his office here, but I haven't been able to bring myself to go down there yet."

"Perfectly understandable, under the circumstances."

Babs swallowed hard. "Would you come down there with me, Jessica? Would you come down there with me now, before Pyke arrives?"

"Of course. Say no more."

She led me down a flight of narrow hardwood stairs to a basement I had never seen in the ten years I'd visited the Wirths' beautiful home. The decor upstairs was sleek and modern, minimalist: stainless steel appliances, sharply angular furniture, and walls graced with pieces of modern art. But descending into the basement was like regressing a century and a half. The floor was uneven and unfinished. I was grateful to be wearing hard shoes, because splinters jutted from the cracks between the floorboards, which were lodged with lint, crumpled pieces of trash, crumbs, and other refuse.

One of the walls of the walkout basement was brick and indented in the middle by the imprint of an old fireplace that had since been filled with cement. There was a sliding glass door that did not quite mesh on the opposite wall. It clearly hadn't been washed for years, and it led out to a small overgrown terrace. The terrace was enclosed by a wooden fence, and I did not see a gate, so no one could access it from the yard during, say, one of the Wirths' annual Labor Day parties. The only sign that the terrace was even used, what with the victory of weeds over the entirety of its terrain, was an ashtray situated on a glass outdoor table beneath an umbrella, brimming with half-smoked cigarettes, telling me something else I didn't know about Hal: that he'd been a smoker.

"It's me," Babs chimed in as I formed that thought.

"What?"

"I'm the smoker. Hal knew, but not Alyssa. I'm swearing you to secrecy here."

"Done."

"Scout's honor?"

"I was never a Scout."

Against the third wall, there was a desk and two large filing cabinets on either side, with a unit of shelving above, which held office supplies, a printer, paper, the works. The paint in the room was white, but water stains riddled the surface, which was turning a sickly yellow. Clearly, this had been the original basement of the old house leveled to make room for the Wirths' mansion.

"Hal always threatened to renovate things and clean the basement up, but never got around to it." Babs's tone was again apologetic, as she bent down to pick up stray papers scattered on the floor. "I guess he preferred keeping it as his man cave."

"I can see that," I said.

"The way things worked out, this became more a

place for personal projects and to just escape—from me, among other things, I suppose."

"I can hardly believe that," I said, taking pains to make sure my expression showed nothing of my knowledge of the rumors that Babs and Hal were having some marital difficulties, and that Hal might have been engaged in an affair.

"Everyone needs their privacy, Jessica. You of all people should understand that, given the insular nature of your work. This was Hal's way of replicating that, I guess."

Her tone had grown glum again and I felt a need to keep the conversation going. "What's in the filing cabinets?" I asked.

"Somewhere in here are his financial records, mingled among a myriad of documents and personal material. I was hoping you'd be able to look through the folders and begin categorizing everything."

She pulled a set of keys from her pocket and opened the first cabinet before I had an opportunity to answer.

"Of course, Babs. Whatever I can do to help."

She handed me the keys. "This small one opens all the drawers."

She sidestepped back toward the stairs, a clear indication she much preferred that I handle this chore on my own, both to spare her the pain and so she could get on with other things.

"I just remembered I have some more calls to make," Babs said as if reading my thoughts. "If you don't mind, of course."

"I don't mind at all," I said, quite comfortable down there, where I might find some inkling of the enigmatic doings that had characterized Hal Wirth's final months and days.

"I can't thank you enough, Jessica. And I mean that sincerely."

"Go make those calls, Babs," I told her. "I'll be fine down here."

She smiled and clambered up the old stairs, leaving me alone in Hal's dingy basement with a silver key in my hand and eight drawers full of who-knew-what to sift through and categorize. I took a folder from the drawer Babs had already opened, labeled "Tax Returns—2002," and a cursory glance at the remaining folders revealed, predictably, the annual tax records for every year since Hal founded his company.

Not exactly a financial whiz or maven myself, I expected to glean nothing from them and returned the tax files to their rightful drawer and used the key Babs gave me to open the one below it. I did this for all the drawers, to assay what I was up against.

The cabinets were all filled to the brim, except the last drawer, which contained only a pile of neatly stacked papers, the top sheet of which read in bold lettering: "HAL WIRTH: AN INTREPID LIFE."

A subtitle followed: "The Memoir of an Idealistic Entrepreneur's Rise to Software Giant."

I had no idea Hal had even entertained the notion of writing a book. If Babs had ever mentioned anything about it, it must have slipped my mind. Being no stranger to the perils of publishing, I always smiled at how those from other walks of life believed transitioning into that industry would be a seamless escapade, having no clue of the challenges involved in both successfully writing and selling their work. It appeared Hal was no exception and I found it odd he hadn't at least tried to pick my brain.

I took a seat in the desk chair in which Hal must've spent countless hours, ignoring the thin layer of dust that had collected on the leather, and opened the manuscript to the first page, when I heard a voice call my name.

"Mrs. Fletcher!"

I practically jumped out of Hal Wirth's desk chair, my heart pounding in my chest when I spotted a figure silhouetted in the murky light. My overactive writer's imagination conjured an image of Lawrence Pyke from the night before, so clear I could almost smell the whiskey on his breath. But it wasn't Lawrence Pyke at all.

It was Alyssa, Babs's daughter!

"Mrs. Fletcher!" she repeated, as if afraid I hadn't heard her call the first time.

I sprang out of my chair and met her halfway across the floor, where she swallowed me with her outstretched arms in a firm hug. Was this the same Alyssa who'd been a little girl the last time I blinked?

"Alyssa, you've grown so much!" I said, a bit lamely, since my heart was just starting to slow.

She was taller than me by at least two inches. Though we'd corresponded off and on about her interest in writing, I was always left picturing her in pigtails with skinned knees and bony elbows. Now she was all grown up, a beauty just like her mother, only with stronger features that included sharply defined cheekbones and hair that tumbled gracefully past her shoulders.

"It's so good to see you, Mrs. Fletcher."

"You're not little Ally anymore, that's for sure! And call me Jessica, for God's sake."

She stepped farther into the dim lighting, and I noted deep bags under her eyes, evidence she probably hadn't slept since getting the news from her mother.

"I'm sorry about your father, Alyssa."

I gave her another hug.

"Thanks for being there for my mom," she said, her eyes moistening.

"What are friends for?" We both aimed a glance toward her father's desk. "I'm looking through your dad's old papers, organizing them and setting aside important documents pertinent to his business, so your mom will have everything handy."

"That's a mighty task. Dad was a secretive man and never let anyone else deal with that part of his life. The business part, I mean. Can I help with anything?"

"No need. This is just secretarial work. I'll be done in no time. I was just going through your dad's drawers," I said, making no mention of Hal Wirth's memoir and positioning myself to block the pages atop the desk from Alyssa's view. "I need to ask you a stupid question."

"How am I doing?"

"That's the one."

"I'm okay, better now that I'm home. My boyfriend is coming to stay with us tomorrow, so that will be good for me, too."

"Your mom didn't mention that."

"Because I didn't tell her. His name is Chad. I'm sure you'll like him."

"You met him at college?" I asked.

"He lives in the same dorm building as I did last year. We hit it off right away. He's, like, a computer genius. An absolute whiz with a keyboard."

"Meaning . . ."

"Are you always this suspicious?"

I shrugged. "I'm a mystery writer. It's my nature."

"Then let's just say Chad plays computers with the skill of a concert maestro."

"I get the idea," I said, figuring Chad must be a hacker or something.

"I've told him all about you, Jessica. I think he's even read a couple of your books and said he was going to take another with him for the bus ride up here."

"I can't read on buses, or cars. Planes and trains, yes, but not your ordinary moving vehicles."

"Me either."

"I guess Chad's lucky, then. Me, too, for the royalties he's making me. Why don't I sign a copy of my latest for you to give him?"

"Would you?" Alyssa beamed.

"Of course. My pleasure."

"We're having dinner when he gets in tomorrow. You could join us and Mom. You could give it to him then."

"Wonderful! It's a plan!" I held her eyes briefly, accustomed to addressing Alyssa the adult now. "Now, tell me how your writing is going."

She frowned. "My classes keep me really busy, but I try to make time to write."

"So long as your boyfriend knows to leave you alone when you're in the creative mode," I said, smiling inwardly at the memory of how Frank always kept his distance when he heard the keys clacking, reluctant to disturb me. "When the time comes, I'd love to introduce you to my editor."

"Really?" Alyssa said, squeezing my arm tenderly.

"Absolutely. I still remember those stories of yours I read when you were a little girl. You've got real talent, and talent only gets better with age. You're also the closest thing I have to a daughter. You're family to me, Alyssa, and I truly mean that."

She hugged me again, dabbing at her eyes as we separated.

"Anyway," Alyssa said, pawing at the floor with her boot, "Mom sent me down here to get you. My dad's lawyer, Lawrence Pyke, just arrived and she wants you to meet him."

I already had met him, of course, and could only hope our second encounter was more pleasant than the first. At the very least, I expected him to be sober.

"Then let's get ourselves upstairs," I said, and followed Alyssa up the steps.

We walked to the living room together like old friends, all that time since we'd last seen each other bridged by a combination of her father's death and my offer to mentor her career. Something told me Alyssa was a talented writer, although I couldn't put my finger on what. But I wasn't sure she'd settle into the mysteries. Something else told me this was a young woman with more literary aspirations than genre fiction may have provided. I've had that discussion, or argument, countless times with those for whom mindless entertainment is too trivial to bother with, since to me creating such mindless entertainment is the greatest gift a writer can give.

I noticed Babs standing atop the living room's Persian carpet, speaking to a gentleman whose back was to Alyssa and me. I wasn't looking forward to another encounter with Lawrence Pyke after the first one had gone so strangely, but resolved myself to play the good friend to Babs and not pick up where I'd left off with Pyke in the diner.

"Ah, Jessica," she said, spotting us coming, "you're here. I'd like you to meet Hal's lawyer, Lawrence Pyke."

The man turned, revealing a shock of thick salt-and-pepper hair and a perfectly coiffed thin mustache riding his upper lip. Smiling as he extended his hand.

It wasn't Lawrence Pyke.

Chapter Six

At least not the man who'd introduced himself in Mara's Luncheonette the night before as Lawrence Pyke.

"Jessica," I heard Babs say, "are you okay? You look like you've seen a ghost."

I wanted to tell her I had—well, not exactly a ghost, but close enough. "It's just that—," I stammered, the words stopping as quickly as they started.

"A pleasure to meet you, Mrs. Fletcher," the real Lawrence Pyke said, sparing me from having to complete my thought. "I'm a big fan."

I almost said *Of whom?* but managed a smile as I took his hand and replied typically, "Oh, so you're the one."

"I suspect you have a few more than that."

"Not as many as I used to, with fewer bookstores and the like. These days you need to send a search party out to find one of my old paperbacks."

Pyke nodded, as if he understood. I had no idea why I was making small talk with him. I suppose I was trying to give myself time to let the shock subside and plan out what I was going to say next. Then Babs saved me the trouble.

"Lawrence was just going to review some things he needed to discuss with me. Maybe you'd like to sit in."

I could tell from the soft plaintiveness in her voice that Babs's offer was more than just a gesture; she wanted me there because she needed the support, even if it was only moral.

"Of course, Babs," I said, smiling. "I'd be happy to."

I noticed Pyke fidget a bit, his tall frame scrunching slightly. He looked past me, and I realized Alyssa had been standing there, a bit behind me, through the entire exchange.

"I've got some things to do," she said, taking Pyke's expression as a proper cue and heading for the stairs, and her bedroom, in all likelihood.

"Let's adjourn to the kitchen," Babs suggested. "I'll make some coffee."

She used the pour-over method again. I was fine with just regular coffee, so this whole thing about designer coffee drinks, flavored and otherwise, escaped me. But Babs managed the effort in rapid fashion. She hadn't asked me which of her many flavors I wanted, because she knew I'd pick the most ordinary. Something close to Maxwell House or Folgers for someone who normally preferred tea.

The whole time the coffee dribbled down into the mug, I studied Lawrence Pyke's expression, which wavered between anxious and concerned. He kept tapping his fingers together and shifting about in his chair, as if trapped in some form of unease I couldn't otherwise identify.

"How much did Hal share with you about the state of his finances?" Pyke asked, through the light mist of steam that had risen from the cup set before him.

Babs squeezed a handful of hair and threaded it through her fingers. "We didn't talk much about finances, other than the usual husband and wife stuff. You know, expenses, repairs—that sort of thing. I've been giving some thought to opening a business and did ask for his input on that."

"And how did he respond?"

Lawrence Pyke sounded very formal, clearly getting at something.

"He didn't, not really. He changed the subject," Babs said. "But that's not unusual. I don't think Hal had a lot of respect for my skills in business, the idea of renting space on Main Street in the Cove to . . ."

Babs's voice trailed off as she seemed to notice Pyke's taut expression for the first time.

He nodded and then continued. "Your husband didn't mention any issues with the business he'd opened down in Granite Heights?"

"I thought we were here to discuss his estate," Babs said, concern edging into her voice.

"We are."

Babs picked up her steaming mug of coffee and set it back down just as quickly. "Then, no. Hal never said anything about any issues with the business."

"You had no fiduciary involvement?"

"None. Our accountants believed it was better for tax and legal reasons." Babs glanced at me, then leaned closer to her late husband's lawyer. "You're scaring me, Lawrence. Should I be scared?"

The expression on Pyke's face told both of us she should be. He leaned in closer to Babs, trying to appear as comforting as he could.

"I don't know a gentle way to say this, so I'm just going to say it. Your husband's business was insolvent."

I reached over and grasped Babs's forearm. I could feel the gooseflesh rising as the color washed from her face, my gesture, aimed at reassurance, feeling mostly lame.

"That's . . . impossible," she managed, her voice barely audible.

"I only wish that were the case. I truly do. Since I have power of attorney for Hal's business dealings, I accessed all of his financial records in preparation for this meeting. I didn't expect to find anything amiss or awry. Hal was always meticulous with his record keeping and conservative in his borrowing, never extending or overleveraging himself. And he never made a major move or investment without consulting me. I've been there with him every step of the way. He was never shy about asking for counsel, even if there were no real legal ramifications involved. I once joked that he wouldn't lick a postage stamp without consulting me."

Babs pulled her arm from my light grasp, as if forgetting I was even in the room. "But that must not have been true, was it? I mean, based on what you're suggesting."

I thought back to what had clearly been a tense conversation between Hal and Seth Hazlitt the day before. Could this have been the subject of their conversation? Had Hal sought Seth out to confide this to him, perhaps in the form of some kind of confession?

Lawrence Pyke looked as if he didn't want to go on, needing to pull the words up his throat and push them out of his mouth. "In the past month, he'd opened six separate lines of credit, totaling over ten million dollars. I haven't been able to track down all the paperwork, but apparently, he used the assets of his business as collateral. I'm assuming he must have done so fraudulently to some extent, and must have had his reasons, because the sources of these credit lines, which were drained almost immediately, were less than reputable."

"What's that mean?" Babs asked him.

"The kind of shady sites you go to when you don't want, or can't go to, traditional lenders like banks." Pyke hesitated and tried to hold Babs's stare. "He never approached you about refinancing the mortgage on this house?"

"No, of course— Wait, did he do that on his own?"

"No, he would've needed your signature. You would've had to attend the closing. I can only assume he wanted to keep whatever he'd gotten himself involved in, how he'd ended up so overextended, secret from you." Pyke glanced about, as if looking through the walls into the entire sprawl of one of Cabot Cove's most impressive homes. "Refinancing this house would have covered at least some of the money he found himself in need of."

"It might have, if we weren't carrying such a significant note on it—Hal said it was good for tax reasons." Babs glanced at me, as if remembering I was there. "Why didn't he say something to me?" Her eyes darted back to Pyke. "What's going on? What did he use the money for? Have you been able to figure that out?"

"Is there a paper trail?" I blurted out.

"I'm afraid there's nothing."

"*Nothing?*" Babs repeated, just as I was ready to utter the word.

"It's gone, all of it."

I couldn't help myself. "Ten million dollars doesn't just disappear, Mr. Pyke."

He flirted with the thinnest of smiles. "From reading your books, Mrs. Fletcher, I can tell you obviously know that's not the case."

"I write fiction."

"And money vanishes in fact as well, I'm afraid. A deal gone bad, a debt called in, a bad investment from the past returning to the fold, or one in the present gone bust. Our sins always catch up with us. And, in my experience, those sins almost invariably involve money."

Babs was shaking her head, her eyes narrowed, as if trying to focus on something that remained a blur. "This makes no sense. This isn't Hal."

Lawrence Pyke said nothing, his silence speaking for him.

"There's got to be some explanation, something we're not seeing. You're telling me Hal was broke.

You're telling me *I'm* broke." I could see the tears welling in Babs's eyes. "The mortgage, Alyssa's college bills, the expenses—what am I supposed to do?"

"I've ordered a full forensic audit of your husband's assets," Pyke offered.

"What will that accomplish?"

"Hopefully provide clues as to what Hal did with the money, what he'd gotten himself involved in, or whom he'd gotten involved with."

"We shared *everything*, even when . . ."

"Go on," Pyke urged.

Again, Babs glanced toward me, her pained expression taking on a tint of embarrassment. "We were having . . . problems."

Pyke didn't urge her on this time.

"But we worked them out. At least, I thought we had." She was shifting her gaze between Pyke and me with her words, as if looking for the one thing neither of us could give her under the circumstances—reassurance. "That's what the Labor Day party was all about this year: a celebration of us putting all that behind us, with our anniversary coming to boot. We were married on Labor Day twenty-four years ago now, almost to the day. Did you know that?"

"I, er . . ."

Babs started to choke up and Pyke stopped his words there. We all slipped into silence. I twirled my coffee mug about, wishing I'd opted for tea instead, something more soothing. A heaviness filled the stagnant air. The humidity had ticked up, typical of the season here on the Maine coast, and I realized Babs hadn't turned on the central air. I missed the dank cool of Hal's basement office, my thoughts drifting to his memoir and whether somewhere in the pages he'd penned, there might be some clue as to what had become of the ten million dollars Lawrence Pyke insisted had vanished into thin air.

That brought me back to Mara's Luncheonette the night before and the man who'd introduced himself as Lawrence Pyke, how his vaguely threatening nature had left me unsettled. His presence in town now made no sense, no more than why a man like Hal Wirth would squander the entire fortune he'd built up in Wirth Ventures.

"There's something I need to tell you," I started.

They both just stared at me when I finished my story.

"Rather cryptic," the real Lawrence Pyke said finally.

"I'll say."

"And you have no idea why this man claiming to be me sought you out?"

"Information, like I said. Because he knew Babs and I were friends, or seemed to."

"How could he know such a thing?"

"Cabot Cove is a small town."

"Only for those who live here," Babs noted, even more discomfited now, so much so that I regretted telling the story.

I reached over and grasped Babs's arm anew, firmer this time so she wouldn't be able to escape my clutch as easily. "You remember that handwritten note I was reading last night?"

It was clear she didn't. "What note? I don't remember any note."

"Seth and I were getting dinner ready when you returned from the hospital. You caught me reading it when you came into the kitchen. I pretended it was nothing."

"Was it something important?"

"It might be. We need to tell Mr. Pyke about it, because the letter clearly implied a threat. It was from someone named Eugene Labine." I swallowed hard, feeling uncomfortable with even this small measure of deceit. "I left it on the counter."

"Oh, that." Babs rose, moved to one of the kitchen drawers. "I thought it was something Hal just dropped when he . . ."

Her voice trailed off and I could see Babs fighting back tears.

Pyke's expression had tightened, a look more befitting the courtroom than the kitchen, his purpose in coming here evolving. "Who was this Eugene Labine?"

"Hal's business partner," Babs said, swallowing hard.

"No such name appears in any of your husband's financial records."

"Because Labine was his *original* business partner. Years ago, when Hal was just getting started. They had a falling-out."

Pyke turned his gaze briefly on me, as if I'd invented that detail in the plot of one of my books. "And when would this have been?"

"Years ago. Before we moved up here and before

Hal found success. I haven't even heard or thought of Labine for years."

"Where's this letter now?" Lawrence Pyke asked her.

Babs opened the drawer where she must have tucked the letter after I'd seen it. Something occurred to me and I trailed her across the floor, holding her arm just as she was about to lift the letter out.

"Perhaps we shouldn't be handling it," I advised. "Could be evidence now, after all."

"Of what?"

"I don't believe it was a coincidence that this letter came at the same time these revelations surrounding Hal's business interests have surfaced. I'm just wondering who this Labine was and what his part in all this might've been."

I spotted a pair of rubber dishwashing gloves on the counter and moved to get them, intending to lift the letter from the drawer only once they were donned, when my cell phone rang.

I missed the old flip one that had served me just fine for years. I'd upgraded to the smart variety because everyone told me I should, what with e-mail and texting, which I hardly ever used my phone to do. Should have just kept the crusty flip.

I recognized Sheriff Mort Metzger's number.

"Mort?"

"Where are you, Jessica?"

"With Babs. At her house."

"Can you get away? I'll send a car so you don't have to bike into town."

"What's in town?"

"Remember the man you met at Mara's last night?"

Given we'd just been talking about him, I couldn't believe Mort had chosen that moment to mention the man who had introduced himself as Lawrence Pyke. "Yes. Why?"

"He's been murdered."

Chapter Seven

The deputy Mort had sent dropped me right before the entrance to Hill House of Cabot Cove, our own quaint hotel. Hill House was a step above the local bed-and-breakfasts, blessed with a rustic demeanor and charm all its own. No two rooms were alike, and with Labor Day's passing and the summer season now gone, the rates were very reasonable.

Mort met me outside amid a sea of revolving lights. Four cruisers, as many as I could ever recall in Cabot Cove in one place at one time.

"Second floor, corner room," he told me. "Manager said the victim requested it. What's that make you think?"

"If he heard footsteps, he'd know they were coming his way."

Mort nodded. "That's what I think, too. Don't suppose you're rubbing off on me, do you?"

"More likely, the opposite."

The exchange was meant to be light but, under the circumstances, only added to the tension fueled by the patrol cars' spinning lights.

"You don't need to see the body. It's a bit . . . messy. It could well be you're the only person, besides the front desk clerk who checked him in yesterday, who spoke with the victim after he arrived in town. Anything stand out from your conversation?"

"He introduced himself as Lawrence Pyke, Hal Wirth's lawyer. I was speaking to the real Lawrence Pyke when you called."

Mort raised his eyebrows. "The victim could only know to do that if he was somehow acquainted with Hal."

"Just as he knew I must not have been acquainted with Lawrence Pyke, or he wouldn't have bothered with the ruse."

"What else do you remember from your discussion?"

Excuse me for saying this, but you don't sound like a lawyer looking out after the interests of a departed client's wife.

It was the first thing that sprang to mind, those words I'd spit at him that now rang oddly prophetic. I settled myself and reconstructed the scene as best I could. It took shape in my head the way a scene does when I'm writing, though conjured from memory instead of imagination. But it formed the same way, starting with the steam rising between us from the cooling stove, which had seemed to settle over the man who'd claimed to be Lawrence Pyke.

"He spoke of Hal's business partner," I recalled, reconstituting the conversation in my mind.

There's no easy way to say this. He was scorned after Hal screwed him out of the business they cofounded, and he has not been successful since.

"He said that?" Mort probed.

"Or something very close to it, yes."

"What else?"

It's in Barbara's best interests that you share with me anything you may have learned about her husband's business dealings prior to today, anything potentially awry, for instance.

"He wanted information about Hal's business dealings. He was vaguely threatening. And I remember the smell of whiskey on his breath."

Mort made a note on a small memo pad. "I'll check all the local watering holes, see if our victim may have stopped in to have a drink before heading over to Mara's."

"I thought he was there when I came in and joined you."

"My back must've been to his table."

"But it occurs to me . . ."

"What occurs to you, Jessica? I can see that suspicious mind of yours working."

"What if he followed me there? What if he'd been watching my house?"

Mort didn't look overly concerned. "Not easy to follow someone pedaling a bicycle, I daresay."

"Good point."

"What made you say he was threatening?"

"I said *vaguely* threatening. It was the last thing he

said to me, something like 'Be a friend to Babs and nothing more.'"

"And you found that threatening?"

"It was the way he said it."

"What else?"

"That I should steer clear of issues pertaining to her husband. But, Mort, there's something you need to know, something about Hal's estate. Hal was nearly bankrupt and was being threatened with legal action by a former business partner."

Mort made another note on his pad. "Got a name for me?"

"Eugene Labine."

His pen froze in the middle of a word. "Jessica, that's who was murdered upstairs."

I heard myself speak, but the words sounded as if they came from someone else. "I think I better have a look at the body, after all, Mort."

Entering the Hill House of Cabot Cove was like stepping back in time. The big wooden door opened into a spacious, airy Victorian lobby that featured ornate furniture spread atop elegant carpeting, along with a genuine Oriental rug. A uniformed officer stood vigil just inside the door, not far from the front desk, which was actually a counter currently staffed by an anxious-looking clerk whose name I couldn't recall.

I followed Mort through the comfortable sprawl, passing a sitting area and built-in bookshelves toward a lavish stairway, featuring a hand-carved railing that spiraled toward Hill House's upper levels. The guest rooms located there retained a measure of the original charm, along with some furnishings, from the hotel's origins as the family home of a wealthy sea captain who'd gone on to run an entire fleet of merchant ships.

"I've stopped counting the murders that have taken place here," Mort said. "Too many to keep track of. You know what some of the old-timers have taken to calling Hill House?"

"Hell House," I said, before he had a chance to, "though I suspect the owners aren't too happy about that, given that it may drive away guests. It's amazing Cabot Cove still has such a thriving tourist trade."

"Just like it's amazing anyone wants to live here anymore," he added. "The murder rate must be higher than in any big city."

"Maybe that's what attracts people, Mort. An obsession with the macabre, like being unable to turn away from a traffic accident."

He let out some breath in what I thought might've started as a chuckle or laugh. "We might suggest to the chamber of commerce that they start up a tour of the locales where all the bodies were found."

"Like a murder tour."

"To go with your murder sense, Jessica."

The second-floor corner room in which Eugene Labine had been murdered was currently being guarded by a pair of Mort's uniformed deputies. The pair of crime scene techs Mort employed on a part-time basis as needed must have fortunately both been available, no small feat in a village the size of Cabot Cove, and, I could see, were busy at work inside the room as we neared the open entry. Their forensics cases were open and they were busy checking the room for any clues and evidence not discernible by the naked eye. One was working the area between two love seats facing each other kitty-corner to the room's fireplace, and the other was currently moving a UV light over the drawn covers of a rumpled but still-made double bed.

They certainly weren't disturbing Eugene Labine, who was lying on the carpet with his arms splayed wide to either side and his head propped up against the base of one of the love seats. It looked from a distance in the ambient lighting as if the love seat were resting on his chest. A neat hole that had oozed blood, now dried, sat dead center in his forehead, surrounded by a symmetrical burn mark from the bullet that had killed him. He was wearing the same clothes I recalled from Mara's Luncheonette, and his blank expression was remarkable for nothing other than the illusion that the angle of his fall had left his gaping eyes drooped downward.

"Shot at close range," I heard myself say.

"You must be a mystery writer," Mort said, leaving the body to the crime scene techs for now, although I recalled glimpsing outside the local funeral home hearse that doubled in these parts as the coroner's wagon.

Of course, an autopsy wouldn't be required to tell how Hal Wirth's former business partner had died.

"I think it happened as soon as he opened the door," I resumed. "Based on the trajectory and placement of the wound, I'd say he recoiled backward and fell just short of the couch, accounting for how his head ended up against it."

"Agree on both counts," Mort said. "Anything else come to mind?"

I glanced toward a mahogany desk, situated just beneath a wall-mounted wide-screen television, the one compromise this room in the Hill House had made with modernity.

"His wallet and cash are still in evidence, so robbery wouldn't appear to be the motive."

"Appear?"

"We can't see what we can't see," I reminded Mort. "So we can't be sure something else wasn't taken. He wrote Hal a letter."

"Who did?"

"The victim. Eugene Labine," I said, glancing back down at the body.

Such scenes were nothing new for me in reality as well as in fiction. Somehow seeing the actual product of what was normally conjured by my imagination felt less real. Crime scenes were always more intense for me when I was creating them in my mind, my imagination left to connect the dots, fill in all the creases and crevices. Real crime scenes like this had a cold, antiseptic feeling to them, right down to the scent of alcohol that hung in the air from the various forensic materials. The exception was those cases where I found the body myself, having had no forewarning of what I'd been about to encounter. That left me feeling many things, but mostly a violation of the victim's most intimate privacy, as if I were somehow intruding. More than once, I'd wondered if his or her spirit might still be lurking about to watch over my actions and efforts, perhaps trying to steer me in the right direction like a real-life muse.

But I had no sense whatsoever of Eugene Labine in this Hill House room right now, nor did I feel as if anyone were watching me except Mort.

"Letter," Mort repeated. "You didn't mention that before."

"He was threatening Hal. That's what the part of his letter I glimpsed implied."

"You can't be any more specific?"

I shrugged. "Not beyond the fact that Hal and Labine parted ways as partners years ago, and Hal stopped making payments on the structured settlement agreement they had between them."

Mort nodded, weighing my words. "Makes you wonder about the timing of Hal's heart attack, doesn't it?"

"I was already wondering. Something . . . well, something just didn't sit right with me."

"That murder sense of yours, Jessica?"

"You never called it that before."

"You've heard the story of the cat in the nursing home that sits outside the doors of residents soon to join the dearly departed."

"Are you comparing me to that cat?"

"Only in the sense you have the uncanny ability to see things nobody else can. And if there's something about Hal's death that set off your radar, that's enough for me." His eyes drifted back to the corpse. "Especially in view of the untimely passing of Mr. Labine."

"It's all connected, Mort—it must be. Hal's sudden

and inexplicable insolvency, the letter he received from Labine, Labine's coming here on his trail."

Mort consulted his fabled memo pad. I wondered if it was the only one he'd ever owned, somehow blessed with an inexhaustible supply of pages for him to flip over the wire top. I had my sixth sense for crime and he had his magic memo pad; now I knew why we'd made such a great pair over the years.

"According to hotel records, he checked in the day of Hal's death," Mort informed me.

"Before or after?"

Another glance at the pad. "After, by all accounts. Early evening, according to the front desk." Mort left the memo pad open and looked up from it at me. "Do you think he might have stopped by the Wirths' party before coming to the hotel?"

"I don't remember seeing him there, but I suppose it's possible."

Mort made another note on his pad. "Won't hurt to flash his picture around, see if anybody recognizes him."

Something occurred to me, lingering at the edges of my consciousness. A disconnected memory trying to rise to the surface, something to do with the party that I'd dismissed from my mind because it bore no meaning, its progress halted when Mort resumed.

"And the letter, what do you remember about that?"

Hal, I'm writing to extend an undeserved courtesy by informing you that I'll be taking legal action against you and—

I recited the words I recalled reading before Babs appeared in the kitchen.

"Sounds serious. Threatening, too. And connected, obviously, to these financial troubles Hal was having. We have Labine's home address from the registration card he filled in. I'll contact the local police down near Boston to inform them."

"Hopefully securing their cooperation in obtaining a warrant to search his home."

Mort's expression crinkled as he stole a quick glance back at the body. "Except Mr. Labine's not party to any crime, besides his own murder."

"That we know of, you mean."

"That we know of," Mort acknowledged, with a nod. "And there's only one way I can see right now we're going to learn any more."

"We need to have a closer look at that letter," I finished for him.

Chapter Eight

Lawrence Pyke was still at Babs's house when I arrived with Mort minutes later. True to his lawyerly instincts, the handwritten letter from murder victim Eugene Labine remained undisturbed; even the drawer remained opened, just as it had been when I left. That said, a number of folders pulled from Pyke's still-open briefcase littered the kitchen table, and the look of concern and anxiety on Babs's face had only worsened since my departure upon being summoned to Hill House by Mort. Clearly whatever revelations they'd discussed had unsettled her even more than she'd been already, the shock of Hal's sudden death exacerbated by the insolvency that left Babs's entire future shrouded in a cloud of darkness. I wasn't privy to Hal's specific business dealings, or whatever tailored arrangements had been made between husband and wife in that respect. It stood to reason, though, that the mess Hal had left behind would end up dumped in Babs's lap, the debts he'd recently incurred about to become hers.

Alyssa had joined her mother at the table and hugged me tight as soon as I stepped through the door, her look more fitting a child clinging to an adult after a bad dream, hoping he or she could chase away the boogeyman. I imagine Alyssa was hoping I could do something similar here, only with a different sort of boogeyman in the form of the financial mess she and her mother were only just learning about. I didn't know when Alyssa had joined them at the table, or how much she knew, but from her expression, I imagined it was quite a bit.

Mort greeted Babs and introduced himself to Lawrence Pyke, while I kept my attention fixed on Alyssa, feeling an extraordinary obligation to help figure out whatever was going on with the family finances. I think, more than anything, that's what has inspired me over the years, fueled my obsession with getting to the bottom of things and helping to set them straight. Providing entertainment for my readers had always been my life's mission, but connected to it on a deeply intrinsic level was my desire to help those, like Babs and Alyssa, who had no one else to turn to.

And that's what I intended to do here, through whatever means I could.

As Mort fitted evidence gloves over his hands and moved to fetch the late Eugene Labine's letter from the still-open kitchen drawer, I looked toward Lawrence Pyke.

"These lines of credit Hal opened that so depleted

his worth—did you find any clues as to what he did with the money?"

"Not a one, not even an inkling. Of course, I've only been at it for twenty-four hours, so I've merely scratched the surface. But for anything mundane, like major purchases, debt relief, paying back investors, or putting the money back into the business, the paper trail would be easy to trace."

"But there's nothing."

Pyke shook his head. "Nothing I've been able to find so far. Absolutely nothing."

At that point, Mort laid Eugene Labine's letter on the table. Looking at it made me think of the fact I'd just viewed the corpse of the man who'd penned it, sending a chill up my spine. Hal's former business partner now had a face.

The letter's contents filled a single side with a tight signature etched at the bottom. Labine's penmanship seemed to get worse with each sentence, each word, making me recall the whiskey I'd smelled on his breath at Mara's. It wasn't hard to envision him penning this letter in a drunken state, accounting for the impulsiveness of handwriting his words in a barely legible scratchy scrawl. But I could read it well enough, beneath the heading FROM THE DESK OF EUGENE LABINE:

Hal, I'm writing to extend an undeserved courtesy by informing you that I'll be taking legal action against you and proceeding with it immediately. We've shared so much, you and me. We started out together and back then I thought we'd be business partners for life.

I'll shoulder my share of the blame for our parting ways. When I started drinking again, you had every right to force me out because I was hurting the company we started together.

How long ago was that? I don't even know. But I always appreciated the fact you never forgot where the money came from that got us started. I put every penny of my inheritance into our start-up and never begrudged the terms that allowed you to push me out without returning a single dollar of my share. I still owned fifty percent of the company and so long as you made good on compensating me with my share of the profits, I was able to live with that.

But I can't live with the ~~borderline~~ criminal behavior on your part when you borrowed against the assets of the company for reasons you refuse to explain or divulge. I'm not going to say I'm perfect, because I'm far from that. But that doesn't mean I deserve to be left with no visible means of support, having come to rely on my regular stipends to survive.

Since you refuse to make good or make me whole, you've forced me into this corner where I have no choice but to sue. So I'm writing this letter to give you one last chance to make good, to find a way to continue honoring the terms of our settlement agreement. If that means selling your Cabot Cove estate, so be it. And I'll be paying you a visit in person over Labor Day weekend.

But, be warned. If I leave Cabot Cove without satisfaction, the next correspondence you receive will be from my lawyer, and I won't stop until I learn the truth behind what you got yourself into without con-

sulting me as is spelled out in our dissolution agree-
ment. So I'm warning you, Hal, I'm warning you that
I won't rest until I find the truth, unless you make
good. Do the right thing here, Hal, do the right thing.
                                        Eugene Labine

My eyes kept coming back to the word "border-
line" having been crossed out in the letter. I could feel
Eugene Labine's anger through his hastily scrawled
words, which reeked of desperation as well.

"He must have learned of Hal's death when he
reached town," I said, rereading the section about
coming to Cabot Cove over the Labor Day weekend
that had ended so tragically.

I wished Alyssa weren't in the room. If only she
could've been spared hearing all this . . .

"But who in Cabot Cove could possibly have
wanted Labine dead?" Babs wondered out loud.

"My guess," advanced Mort, "is that someone followed him up here. That's the way it is with trouble—
it follows you. And my other guess is this Eugene
Labine made plenty of enemies over the years. Once I
run him through the system, I'm sure we'll be up to
our necks in potential suspects. Someone he owes
money to, maybe. Or just someone he spouted off to
about coming up here to collect on a debt, and they
followed him up here to relieve him of whatever he
was able to collect."

"You're talking about a robbery," Pyke suggested.

Mort shrugged. I knew he didn't believe that any
more than I did. First off, by all accounts, Labine was
shot as soon as he opened the door, so there couldn't

have been any argument that had ended in his death. His room at Hill House showed no signs of any disturbance, from either a struggle or a thorough rousting to find the money his killer would've come for.

No, the murder of Eugene Labine was about something else entirely, and some connection to Hal's yet unexplained desperate financial plight was unavoidable. I might not be a professional sleuth, but like Sherlock Holmes, I didn't believe in coincidence.

The quaint Hill House had no security cameras, so Mort would be afforded no clues as to the identify of Labine's murderer that way. Even now, his deputies were interviewing everyone they could find who'd been at the hotel in the hours leading up to and following the murder, inquiring if any of them had seen anything amiss. With Labor Day having come and gone, only a third of the rooms were occupied, the halls sparsely traveled enough for a single man, or woman, to stand out.

If circumstances weren't what they were, Hal would have been the prime suspect in Labine's murder. Of course, since Labine had been murdered after Hal's death . . .

My thoughts ground to a halt there, as I was struck again by the same odd, inexplicable feeling I'd first experienced in the hospital when the doctor had tried to explain away a heart attack being suffered by a man in excellent health. Such things did happen, after all.

People died.

People got murdered.

But when those two people are connected . . .

"Mort, could you come outside with me for a moment?" I said, interrupting something he was saying to Babs and Lawrence Pyke.

"We need to put a rush on Hal's autopsy results," I said to Mort after we'd moved through the French doors onto a patio made from imported granite. I remembered how proud Babs was of the job, one of her primary contributions to the rebuild of the old mansion she and Hal had spent a fortune renovating.

"Already did," Mort told me, "so the funeral wouldn't have to be delayed. Just routine anyway." His brow furrowed. "It is routine, isn't it, Jessica? Or is that why you asked me to come outside?"

"I don't have to tell you there are several ways to murder someone and make it look like a heart attack."

"I can name a few of them myself I didn't even know existed before I read your books."

"If Hal was actually murdered, hopefully his killer didn't get his method from reading me, too."

"Do you know how ridiculous that sounds?"

"No more ridiculous than Hal's former business partner being murdered at Hill House."

Mort scratched at his scalp and shook his head. "I swear, Jessica . . ."

"Swear what?"

"Do you know how many murders were committed in Cabot Cove before you moved here?"

"No, I don't."

"Neither do I. It's like they followed you here."

"Are you suggesting I leave town?"

He smiled tightly. "Not until we figure out who killed Eugene Labine."

"What about Hal Wirth?"

"I'll make sure his autopsy is screened as a potential murder," Mort relented. "If it makes you happy, Jessica."

I thought of Alyssa, the little girl all grown up who might not have the funds to finish college. I thought of my friend Babs, forced to sell the house she loved so she could escape the debt her late husband had inexplicably left her.

"Thank you, Mort," I said, wondering how long it would be before we learned the truth about Hal Wirth's death.

Chapter Nine

That night, I took the whole of Hal Wirth's manuscript, "Hal Wirth: An Intrepid Life—The Memoir of an Idealistic Entrepreneur's Rise to Software Giant," to bed with me. I had planned on reading only a few chapters, but the mysteries that had consumed the day left me thinking his words might hold some clues as to the circumstances of his insolvency and, perhaps, to the murder of Eugene Labine. I wasn't ready to openly theorize murder in the case of Hal's death, but wondered if something in his manuscript might yield something to that effect as well.

Losing my own husband, Frank, made Babs's pain resonate with me in a way few tragedies ever had. I guess it's the way of the world. I think of Frank every day, yet I hadn't really thought of his passing in years, until Hal's death brought it all back home to me. How much, and how long, it hurt. How empty the house had felt. We weren't blessed with children—the way of the world again. But we did raise my nephew, Grady, for a time, long enough to know the challenges that come with child-rearing. And that made me think of Alyssa, the challenges that lay ahead of her as well.

Starting with how she was going to pay for college in the wake of Hal's financial misfortune. I didn't recall Lawrence Pyke mentioning anything about Hal's likely sizable life insurance policy, but imagined the bulk of it would be needed to pay off these substantial debts he'd incurred for reasons that remained a mystery. I could have let it all go if not for the murder of Eugene Labine. Someone had obviously followed Labine to Cabot Cove and killed him for something he either knew or possessed. And if that *something* involved the financial plight of his former business partner, Hal Wirth, I feared that Babs and Alyssa might very well be in danger, too.

That redoubled my commitment to get to the bottom of all this, starting with what had led to Hal's financial impropriety. The fact that he had borrowed what Lawrence Pyke had intimated was more than ten million dollars without telling his wife or former business partner suggested something nefarious afoot. Blackmail of some kind? Gambling? A secret investment gone wrong? But Hal Wirth wasn't a gambler and had a well-deserved reputation for watching every penny. He'd grown up poor and had learned the value of a dollar. I remember him once deriding those who'd trusted their money with the likes of Bernie Madoff, believing above all else that when something seems too good to be true, it usually is. I don't ever recall Hal discussing the stock market beyond that, and wasn't sure he had a single investment staked in Wall Street other than a retirement plan that would likely end up similarly drained to pay off his debtors.

My train of thought was interrupted when my phone rang—the old-fashioned landline as opposed to the cell—and I snatched the cordless extension from my night table, fearing late-night calls, just as everyone else did.

"Hello?"

"Jessica, it's Seth. I got your message. Hope it's not too late, but you said it was important. I trust you're well."

"Of course. I just—," I stammered, having forgotten I'd even phoned Seth upon returning home. "I was hoping you could do something for me."

"I heard about that murder at the Hill House. Might this have something to do with that?"

"No," I told him, not going into further detail about the victim's identity and connection to Hal. "It's about Hal Wirth. I'd like you to review his blood work, the toxicology studies."

"You see a pathology degree hanging anywhere on my wall?"

"You know your way around a lab report as well as any pathologist I've ever known. I'd just like to know if anything in the results stands out, raises flags. You know, something awry."

"That the doctors at the hospital missed?"

"I'm talking about something they may not have had call to notice."

Seth hesitated. "I know that tone, Jessica. Ayuh."

"What tone is that?"

"You have reason to suspect foul play in Hal's heart attack?"

"That murder you heard about at Hill House . . ."

"Yes."

"The victim's name was Eugene Labine. He was Hal's former business partner, who Hal apparently still owed money to through some kind of structured settlement. Payments Hal could no longer pay because he was insolvent. But you already knew that, didn't you? From that conversation you had with Hal at the party."

I heard Seth sigh. "I guess there's no point in keeping the secret anymore."

"He shared the truth with you, didn't he?"

"Hal's been a patient ever since the Wirths moved to town. I could tell something was wrong with him— something was off. I pulled him aside and he told me pretty much what you just did."

"What about details, specifics?" I said, anxiously hoping to have at least that part of the mystery solved.

"He refused to offer anything beyond the fact he'd lost everything. But I definitely got the impression it wasn't his doing, at least not all of it."

"What's that mean?"

"I think he may have been the victim of a stock swindle, sham investment—something like that."

I shook my head on the other end of the line. "That doesn't sound like Hal at all."

"Well, all the same," Seth said, leaving things there.

"I'm thinking Hal's heart attack may have been induced."

"You tell Mort about this?"

"He's not a doctor."

"No, just the town sheriff."

"Who prefers to wait for the autopsy results."

"While you, Jessica . . ."

"Want to hear it from a more trusted source."

"I can access the hospital records online. Why don't we meet tomorrow for breakfast at Mara's? If it's still raining, I'll pick you up."

"Sounds like a plan," I said.

I was so focused on the events of the day, I hadn't even realized it had started raining since I biked home from Babs's. Even if Hal hadn't been murdered, Eugene Labine had been, and I wasn't going to let the same thing happen to Babs or Alyssa. I settled back in bed to read as much of Hal's memoir as I could before sleep claimed me, but then the storm intensified with blowing winds and rumbles of thunder, ruffling my already frayed nerves and stealing whatever thoughts I had about drifting off with Hal's life scattered on the sheets alongside me.

In the end, I read it all, every single page, skipping only the dedication. I knew Hal well enough to be sure he'd dedicated the book to his wife and daughter, and had glossed right over that page because it would rekindle the heartache I was feeling for their plight.

Maybe I should've read only that page instead, because Hal's memoir was god-awful. The writing was rambling and scattershot, in need not so much of an editor as a coauthor capable of lending order and substance to Hal's random thinking and stream-of-consciousness narrative. It was an endless muck of ramshackle thinking that had no business being strung into words, increasingly unreadable as my pile of read pages grew, as if whatever financial issues Hal was experiencing had begun to affect him.

Whatever they might have been, his memoir made no mention of them or even suggested something awry in his business life. Hal's personal life, though, was something else again. The memoir dissolved into a true mess when he switched from the world of business, in which he was comfortable, to the problems he and Babs had been experiencing that, at least for a time, had threatened their marriage. In my experience, all couples go through such struggles these days, and I suppose, if I looked back without donning my rose-colored glasses, I could find comparable struggles during my life with Frank. He'd been an air force captain and a war hero, and to this day I believe that some of the issues we had sprang from what is now called post-traumatic stress disorder. We didn't have a formal term for the PTSD-like symptoms Frank displayed from time to time, and the greatest regret I hold of our relationship was that I wish I had known then, so I could have helped him more.

Just like I intended to help Babs and Alyssa. The funeral had been scheduled for Friday, three days from now, and it promised to attract much of the town's populace, given the couple's popularity and the sudden, tragic nature of Hal's passing. I found myself pondering again if the cause of death had truly been a heart attack.

The storm conspired with my dark thoughts to steal any notion of a true night's sleep. I had taken to skimming Hal's memoir when I came to a portion that reclaimed my attention. The words seemed misdirected for the chapter in which they'd been placed, the way I sometimes include scenes in one spot yet know they will find a more appropriate home in my final draft.

In Hal's manuscript, mired within a chapter dominated by professional triumph, was a sudden allusion to the issues that had threatened to upend his marriage to Babs. He seemed to be lamenting his decision to stray when a combination of estrangement and time spent away from home in Granite Heights had led him to seek companionship elsewhere. He wrote in halting, embarrassed language about what he called the "juvenile" decision to sign up with an online dating service, the source perhaps of the rumors floating around town about marital infidelity on his part.

> I was a believer in the ultimate power of computers to succeed where humans had failed. My marriage was a mess at this point, a mess.
>
> A mess!
>
> So many random factors had come into play, the kind of things machines can avoid in their mechanical thinking process.
>
> A dating service?
>
> Why not?
>
> A good friend, a man whose judgment I trusted, recommended I give them a try, swearing by his own

experience. I won't mention his name because you probably wouldn't believe he'd ever need to use an Internet dating service. He told me he'd gotten such great results, he ended up buying the company and that I could trust it completely. And if it was good enough for a man like him, what did I have to lose? I was lonely, all right? And if that makes me sound like a jerk, then, okay, I'm a jerk.

It wasn't that I hadn't tried to work things out with Babs—I had. Boy, had I ever. And I'm not saying we didn't equally share blame for the problems we where having. People change, I guess, either together or apart. And at the time I registered on LOVEISYOURS .com, I thought we were finished. Saw no hope for finding a common ground or some form of reconciliation. We'd gone too far, strayed too far.

This part of Hal's memoir read like a confession, a man racked by guilt trying to explain away his sins, work things out through the writing process. I knew about that firsthand, but the stream-of-consciousness thinking, coupled with this section of the book seemingly dropped in out of context, made me think that Hal's opus was more therapy than memoir. A man trying to make sense of his life and finding only more complications along the way.

I read on:

I came home purposely several times unannounced, hoping to catch Babs with another man. I wanted an excuse to find something on LOVEISYOURS that maybe I'd been looking for all along. I wanted some-

one who defined me by how I chose to define myself.
That meant filling out a lengthy profile the site
claimed was the most exhaustive in the industry and,
thus, the most likely to find the right woman.

The problem, as it turned out, was I didn't know
what I was looking for. I turned down several ad-
vances, or "arrows," as the site called them, after Cu-
pid, until I finally answered one of them. The
woman's name was Naomi, but for some reason she
went by "Nan."

Nan . . .

At this stage of my life I wasn't looking for love,
because love hadn't worked beyond giving Babs and
me a beautiful and intelligent daughter.

Was that enough?

It should have been.

But it wasn't.

It went on like that, short paragraphs followed by
even shorter paragraphs. Snippets of Hal's longing and
angst, assembling the puzzle of what sounded like a
classic midlife crisis. He was searching for order amid
the chaos, as his writing grew increasingly chaotic. The
memoir didn't feel to me as if it had been written for
anyone else but him, although I'm certain that wasn't
the case when he started, at least not consciously.

I continued reading:

I was "matched" with Nan and proceeded with no
expectations or preconceptions. It was one date and I
hated every minute of it.

Hated!

I wish I could've taken a mulligan and made the whole thing go away, so deep was my embarrassment and discomfort. Yes, Babs and I were having problems. Yes, we had raised the "D" word. But being with another woman, even if it was just over dinner, even though Nan turned out to be even more lovely and attractive than her picture indicated, felt so wrong. What did she want with a man my age anyway? Twenty years or so my junior and as charming as she was beautiful.

What is it they call women who chase after successful older men for their money? Black widows or something, isn't it?

Was that what Nan was?

Had my lack of interest and clear discomfort waylaid her plans?

I doubt it.

It was the most difficult dinner of my life. I barely ate, can't even tell you what I ordered. I never missed Babs more than in that moment and genuinely believe the experience vanquished the doubts I'd been harboring of our future together.

What a fool I was! What a

The memoir, what Hal had managed to complete of it anyway, ended there in the middle of a sentence, as if it hurt too much to finish. I'm sure he intended to come back to it another day, but never got around to writing more. Maybe he'd realized, mercifully, that the process wasn't for him. Maybe in trying to tell his story, he recognized, as many do, that he didn't have much of a story to tell. Clearly, though, the single date

with whom he'd been matched, and that one miserable dinner, had proved a cathartic moment that
showed him the error of his ways and made him realize how much he still loved his wife.

I swabbed my eyes at that final realization he'd set to
type, his love for his wife restored and indiscretion acknowledged. I felt as if this was something Babs needed
to know, though perhaps I'd be opening the proverbial
can of worms by even broaching the subject and thus
forcing her to discuss a part of her relationship with
her late husband better left alone. I had no way of
knowing what Hal had told her, if anything, about the
LOVEISYOURS dating site, how much he might have
confessed about this Nan. And the last thing I wanted
to do at such a difficult time was risk casting any asper-
sions on a relationship that had indeed been salvaged,
especially given how they seemed to be getting along
just two days earlier at their Labor Day party. Sometimes it's best to leave things alone, even for a meddle-
some sort like myself. Just be a friend. That's what Babs
and Alyssa needed now and that's all I'd be.

The hard copy of the memoir I'd just read had no
time or date stamps, like the document on Hal's computer surely would, so I had no idea how long ago
Hal's date with Nan had actually occurred. I knew
only that the pages I'd just finished had made no mention of his financial impropriety or the circumstances
that had somehow led Hal to lose the fortune he'd
painstakingly built, including the business he loved,
virtually overnight.

Strange, to say the least, unless he'd typed that last
word before everything went to hell and—

My thinking froze there. I thought maybe it was a thunderclap that had shocked me alert, and it was in a way: a thunderclap of realization. Remember what I said about coincidence?

I needed to do some serious digging, but it would have to wait until tomorrow.

Chapter Ten

The day dawned sunny and bright and I biked across town to meet Dr. Seth Hazlitt for breakfast at Mara's Luncheonette. It's not that driving a car scares me, but rather that the older I've gotten, the more intimidated I've grown by the whole process. Even as a passenger, I prefer the backseat because things seem to move slower from that vantage point. I guess that's what has turned me off in general about driving: things moving so fast that I couldn't expect to control them.

When I arrived at Mara's, Seth had already staked claim to a table and was sipping from a steaming mug of coffee.

"Breaking news," he said, after I'd taken the chair across from his. "Hal Wirth died of a heart attack."

"You're sure?"

"I'm sure I checked all the blood work and toxicology reports that were done on him, and I'm sure they revealed not a single anomaly that would make even your suspicious mind think twice."

"Nothing, Seth?" I said, considering anew the revelation that had come to me the night before. "Nothing at all?"

Seth took another sip from his mug and the steam floated up from it, adding a sheen to his skin. "Nothing this old country doctor can find, anyway. But I don't have to tell you, Jessica, that there are several ways to bring on a heart attack that wouldn't necessarily show up in blood work or a toxicology report."

"And I've probably used every single one of them, at one time or another, in my books. Enough to know that the most likely ones, virtually all, must've occurred at the Wirths' Labor Day party. Since every guest was a Cabot Cove resident, that doesn't allow for a lot of prime suspects."

"I can see this insolvency thing of Hal's has got your ears perked up, ayuh."

"There's more," I said, seeing the final pages of Hal's memoir in my mind.

"Care to share it with this old country doctor? At my age, I'll probably forget whatever it is anyway."

"We're practically the same age."

"Then I suppose you'd best get back to your writing while you remember where to find the letters on the keyboard. Now, about this thing you were just about to share with me . . ."

Before we got any further, the waitress came and took our breakfast order.

"It's nothing, really," I said, struck by a craving for

the cup of tea I'd just ordered and not ready to share the thought I'd had last night, which maybe didn't hold up as well in the light of day.

"If it was nothing," Seth said, "you wouldn't have bothered bringing it up."

"Maybe I'm just getting old."

"We're practically the same age, remember?"

Seth smiled and sipped his coffee as my phone rang and I snatched it from my bag, again regretting the decision to replace my old flip variety.

"Jessica Fletcher," I greeted.

"I'm calling for Sheriff Metzger down at the station, Mrs. Fletcher," a female voice greeted. "He was wondering if you could come down straightaway."

"I'm just down the street at Mara's. Tell Mort I'll be right there. Oh, and did he say what this was about?"

Click.

Too late. She'd already hung up.

I wolfed down my English muffin and left Mara's without finishing my tea, or sharing the revelation that had struck me last night like a figurative lightning bolt not long after I'd completed Hal's manuscript. Outside, I climbed back on my bicycle in the warm, late summer air laced with humidity left over from last night's storm, and set off on my way.

The thing that never ceases to amaze me while pedaling about Cabot Cove is how I seem to see something new every time. A nook, a cranny, something tucked where it never seemed to be before, or a fresh coat of paint or siding splashed over a weather-beaten building facade. Our village was struggling with the challenges posed by encroaching modernity; the resident population (especially in the summer) had become the sort that lured all manner of chain stores capable of outlasting the more staid village staples that were disappearing one by one. Rents were skyrocketing and the real estate speculators who'd staked their claim to Main Street years ago were seeing their profits multiply dramatically. And the expansion of the Cabot Cove Marina, coupled with a spacious amphitheater, thanks to Deacon Westhausen, was certain to draw even more to a place that had previously been a secret well kept from the world.

Not anymore, though.

The SeaBasket, for example, was our new supermarket and part of a growing chain in Maine that had helped put the quaint old Cabot Cove Market out of business. Maybe the market's demise was inevitable, but the coming of the SeaBasket to town certainly quickened it. I felt guilty whenever I shopped there, as a result, and could never pedal past the place without feeling pangs of nostalgia for the Cabot Cove Market, which had put in a special display in the front of the store for my books.

I could hear the sea nearby, waves crashing against the rocks. Seagulls hovered in the wind, scoping prospective opportunities to pilfer unattended food. I rode past the hardware store and the pharmacy and the sheriff's station, just past the next intersection. I'd heard the low rumble of an engine for a couple of blocks, and thought nothing of it until it sounded right behind me. I turned and spotted a dark sedan

I'd never seen in town before that seemed to be following me.

At first I appreciated that the sedan didn't speed past me, as most cars do around bicyclists, but the close proximity became conspicuous. I slowed down and moved to the far right of the road to let the vehicle pass, but it slowed, too, and maintained the same distance. Up ahead a car was fast approaching, so I chalked the sedan's hesitation to cautious driving. My head told me that.

My heart told me otherwise, and it started to feel more like my heart was right when the engine sounds picked up and the sedan drew close enough for me to feel the heat sprouting from its hood.

I held my pace steady, fighting the urge to look back, and decided to make a right turn at the next intersection, figuring I'd take a detour to the sheriff's station, just to get the tailgater off my back. But its engine revved behind me, and it trailed my bike around the corner, drawing closer, so close I began to look for a yard or parking lot to dart into for cover. I couldn't try the sidewalk because the sedan could easily trail me onto that as well, and I wasn't about to endanger any bystander strolling innocently about.

Could I use my cell phone to call Mort and keep pedaling at the same time? I didn't dare stop, but I also didn't dare slow my pedaling enough to allow me to lift my cell phone from my bag. Maybe I should have bought the voice-activated model that allowed you to order the phone around with verbal commands.

Like, "Dial nine-one-one!"

I fought against panic, and thought about just grinding to a halt and confronting whoever it was there and then. But I felt the sedan at my bike's rear bumper, tapping up against it. I pedaled faster and it kept riding the back wheel, pushing me forward now. I realized I was approaching the next intersection much too fast to stop safely, knowing then I couldn't have stopped even if I'd wanted to.

Even as I heard a horn blaring.

A red pickup truck had just started on again through the four-way stop when my tires locked up from the handlebar brakes I was squeezing with all my strength. I remember hearing the screech of tires, their rubber bleeding smoke against pavement. The pickup clipped my bike's rear tire and sent me flying, tumbling to a soft patch of grass fronting a Massage Envy storefront that had just moved into an old Victorian building.

A Massage Envy in Cabot Cove? Really?

Much to my surprise, I bounced back up in time to see the dark sedan screeching away and the red pickup grinding to a halt just slightly down the road from where we'd collided. A woman I didn't recognize dropped down from the cab and rushed my way.

"Oh, my God, are you all right? Please tell me you're all right!"

I checked myself over, found I was just that. A little sore, of course, but nothing seemed broken. I could move just fine and seemed to be intact.

"I think so," I said, through the shock sinking in.

I knew that shock could mask injury for a time,

even pain, but I also knew my body well enough to realize I'd been remarkably fortunate.

"Maybe you should sit down," the woman said. "That was quite a tumble. You did a full flip through the air."

"I did?"

"Looked like something from the Olympics."

"Too bad nobody was around to film it," I tried to quip, casting my gaze down the street in the general direction the dark sedan had fled.

"We should call the police," the woman offered.

"I was actually on my way there."

The woman looked at me strangely, not sure how to take that. "What about an ambulance? You should be checked at the hospital, to be on the safe side."

"No need. I'll just call . . ."

My voice trailed off when I realized the contents of my bag had been scattered in all directions around my demolished bicycle.

"I have a doctor friend I just left at Mara's. Do you have a phone I can use to call him?"

The woman fished it from the pocket of her jeans, more people gathering around us now, the ones who knew or recognized me approaching.

"Are you all right? Are you okay?" I heard again and again.

"Just fine," I reassured, as I dialed Seth's number, glad I was able to pull it so easily from memory. "Did you happen to notice that dark sedan?" I asked the woman while waiting for Seth's phone to ring.

"Dark sedan? No."

Seth's phone was ringing now.

"Because I think it was following me. That's why I sped into the intersection. This wasn't your fault. We can go to the police together and tell them everything."

If only she'd gotten a better look at the dark sedan, good enough even to remember its license plate. Seth's phone went to voice mail, so I pressed the end button and redialed. I noticed the pickup's bumper and part of its fender were badly scuffed.

"I'm sorry about the damage to your truck," I said.

We looked toward my ruined bike, surrounded by the spilled contents of my handbag, and then back at each other.

"Looks like your bike suffered the worst of it." The woman shrugged.

"Hello? Hello?"

I could barely hear Seth's voice through the phone's speaker and realized I hadn't taken my helmet off yet. It had probably saved my life by cushioning the impact, and featured a trio of indents that looked like golf balls had struck it.

"Seth," I said finally, realizing my hand holding the phone was shaking.

"Jessica? Where are you? What's this number?"

"I've been in a minor accident. Nothing serious, but—"

"Stay there! Don't move! I'm on my way! I'll be right there— Wait, where are you?"

"Okay, Jessica. Follow the light."

A small flashlight, about the size of a pen, slid left

and right across my field of vision. Seth had driven me to his office, insisting he check me out after I again refused transport to the hospital. We'd waited until one of Mort's deputies arrived, so he could hear from both me and the kind woman in the red pickup truck who'd lent me her cell phone, after sending me flying from my bike through no fault of her own.

"And again," Seth said, holding the light about a foot from my face, now moving it up and down. I crossed my eyes and smiled, wobbling to and fro. "If you're not going to take this seriously, I can take you to a different doctor."

"Maybe I should see a *real* doctor, Seth, if this is as serious as you seem to think," I said with a smirk. "Just don't tell Mort that."

"Tell Mort what?" Cabot Cove's sheriff asked as he strolled into the examination room.

"I called him," Seth explained, pocketing his penlight. "Let him know you weren't going to make your meeting."

"That's why I came straight over," Mort said, an edge of concern in his voice. "Because my office never phoned you."

Chapter Eleven

"And then this dark sedan followed you," Mort said. We were still inside Seth's exam room, and the shock of Mort's telling me it hadn't been his receptionist who'd called me hadn't worn off.

"More than followed," I told him. "It rode my tail, forced me into the intersection."

"You could have been killed," Mort noted.

"Maybe that was the idea."

"I may be just an old country doctor, ayuh," Seth started, "but I want to see if I've got all this straight. Yesterday, a man closely associated with Hal Wirth gets murdered, and today Jessica, who believes foul play may have been involved in Hal's death, nearly gets run down."

Mort shot me a glare. "You involved Seth in this?"

"I asked him to check out his blood work and toxicology report in advance of the autopsy results, that's all."

"And?"

"Nothing," Seth and I said together.

"But there's something else." I picked up from there, finally getting to what had struck me the night before, after finishing Hal's memoir. "Hal Wirth was writing a book, a memoir."

"Surefire bestseller, certain to threaten your status as Cabot Cove's preeminent author?"

"We'll never get to find out, since it was left unfinished—literally in the middle of the line."

"Didn't I read somewhere you do that so you have a running start when you pick up the process the next day?"

"Something like that, but I don't think Hal learned it from me. This was something else."

"Like what?"

I was finally getting to the point, testing my realization to see if it bothered Mort, and Seth, as much as it did me. "Hal used a dating service for a while when he was away from home down in Granite Heights."

"Go on," Mort urged.

"He only went on a single date he expressed deep regret for, profound guilt, even though nothing occurred other than dinner with a woman named Nan. That's where his memoir ends: in the middle of a sentence without any mention whatsoever of whatever led to his financial ruin."

Mort and Seth looked at each other.

"Hal uses this online dating service, LOVEISYOURS, one time and one time only," I elaborated. "Then he forgets all about his memoir and finds himself in financial ruin what must've been a short time later."

"When would this have been?" Mort asked. "What's the time frame?"

"I'm not sure. I need to check the actual document on Hal's computer to find when he left off writing. That will tell us the general time frame of the date as well."

"What about the time frame of these financial issues that surfaced yesterday?"

"Well, the estate's lawyer, Lawrence Pyke, mentioned that the lines of credit that were almost immediately drained were opened between three and four weeks ago."

"And if that's the same time frame as this date Hal went on . . ."

"Then maybe the two things are somehow related," I said, completing the thought for him.

"You know how crazy that sounds, Jessica?" Seth asked, before Mort had a chance to speak.

"Be gentle with me. I had a fall, in case you've forgotten."

"Nope, haven't forgotten. But that doesn't mean you left your mind in your busted-up bicycle helmet."

"He's right, Jessica," Mort interjected. "This does sound pretty outlandish, even for you."

"I don't believe in coincidence."

"So you always say."

"And I'm betting his not going back to the memoir and the financial calamity that led Hal to open those credit lines happened at almost the same time."

"After this date with someone named Nan."

I nodded, affirming Mort's statement.

"Then what do you say we go have a look at Hal's computer?"

It turned out Hal did all his writing on the laptop I'd noticed on the desk in his basement office. I led Mort down there, putting on as brave a face as I could, because, truth be told, my head was starting to throb. I didn't want to say anything, lest Seth have me spirited away to the hospital, in Mort's handcuffs if necessary. I attributed the pounding headache more to the shock of the accident and my lack of sleep than anything else, especially since Seth had cleared me of any concussion. Still, I wasn't myself and didn't want anyone to notice.

We brought Hal's MacBook Pro upstairs. It wasn't password protected, and the file icons appeared across the screen, just a double click away from opening, as soon as I turned it on. Sitting at the kitchen table with Mort and Babs looming over my shoulder, I found an icon marked "Memoir." I didn't have the password to log on to Hal's e-mail, nor did I want to under the circumstances. So I opened his Safari browser and logged on to my own e-mail account. Then I clicked on COM-POSE and attached the Word icon marked "Memoir" to an e-mail I never intended to send.

"What are you doing?" Mort asked me.

"You'll see."

What all three of us saw, once the attachment loaded, was a box containing it on the right-hand side of the page that featured the file name, the size, when it was created, and when it was last opened.

Almost four weeks ago—twenty-six days, to be exact.

Which, according to Lawrence Pyke, jibed almost perfectly with Hal's opening of lines of credit amounting to over ten million dollars, his and Babs's entire net worth.

"There's your timeline," I said to Mort. "And if we look further into—"

I cut myself off there, just in time to avoid mention of Hal's use of the dating service LOVEISYOURS in front of Babs. She didn't need to hear about that for the first time in the midst of planning his funeral services. It could be that Hal had shared the news with her already, confessed it after they'd reconciled their differences, but I couldn't be sure. And I could tell from Mort's expression that he was drawing the same conclusion I was.

"Sorry to have disturbed you, Mrs. Wirth," he said, backing away from the table. "We'll get out of your hair now."

"You're not disturbing me at all, Sheriff. My daughter's out running some errands, so I'm grateful for the company. And, for God's sake, when are you going to start calling me Babs?"

"How about now . . . Babs?"

We sat in Mort's squad car for a time, leaving Babs's house for her driveway.

"You want to tell me what that mind of yours can conjure of a possible link between that date Hal went on and the financial crisis that followed?" Mort asked, looking at me across the front seat.

Not to mention Eugene Labine's murder and a dark sedan trying to run me over, I almost added. "I think we need to find out more about this woman Hal went on a date with."

"You said her name was Nan."

"It's what she called herself, but according to Hal's memoir, her real name was Naomi."

"How many Naomis could there be in the dating site's database?"

"I have absolutely no idea."

Mort pulled a phone that looked as big as a small television from his pocket. "Let me check something," he said, working the keyboard with surprising dexterity, which reminded me how much I missed my old flip phone. So much that I almost wished my so-called smartphone had been ruined in the accident, which would mean I'd get the chance to go back to my flip.

"It's based in Boston," Mort reported, turning the screen toward me so I could see the LOVEISYOURS logo displayed on their Web site. "Chestnut Hill, actually. There's a break."

"You're thinking we should take a drive down there and have a chat with them, find out more about this Naomi."

"I'm thinking that *I* should take a drive down. But if you're game, I could use the company."

"I'm game."

"Tomorrow morning, then."

"So long as you pick me up," I told Mort. "In its current condition, my bike doesn't have room for two."

Chapter Twelve

But first there was dinner with Babs, Alyssa, and her boyfriend, whose name, I seemed to recall, was either Chad or Zach. Maybe the fall off my bike had done more damage than I had initially thought. The pounding in my head got worse as the day wore on, no relief found from the aspirin, which was all I allowed myself to use. And I knew the feeling in my mind as well.

Overdrive.

It happened when I was in the all-consuming midst of penning the first draft of a book and also when I found myself embroiled in one of the investigations that kept finding me, rather than me finding them. But this was different, because the victim had been a friend—or at least an acquaintance, since I knew Babs far better than I knew Hal.

I kept circling back to the same thoughts.

Eugene Labine had been murdered.

And maybe Hal had been murdered, too, his thriving business rendered insolvent virtually overnight.

Then there was this online dating service, LOVEISYOURS, to which Mort and I would be paying a visit tomorrow.

When I do appearances and interviews, I get asked a lot whether I outline my books. The answer is yes and no. I have all the pieces, but am never exactly sure how they're going to fit together when I start. I like to surprise myself, like to imitate a real detective piling clue atop clue, in search of a suspect. But real life defies that kind of symmetry. Real life doesn't come with order; it brings chaos, and the unfortunate fact is that in real life criminals get away with it. Schemes work because real heroes aren't living in a writer's mind where whatever they need is always a paragraph away. So I had to face the fact that I might never find how everything surrounding Hal Wirth's death was connected, but I resolved to do all I could to fit together the pieces of the puzzle.

Because of Babs. Because she needed me. Because her future quality of life and her daughter's ability to finish college where she'd started it depended on what I might be able to uncover and string together.

I tried to take a nap before heading back over to Babs's house for dinner, but my mind wouldn't let me, wouldn't shut off. Every time I closed my eyes, financial balance sheets, manuscript pages, Hal lying on the kitchen floor, Eugene Labine shot dead in his Hill House hotel room, the bright airy logo of LOVEISYOURS displayed across Mort's giant phone screen, flitted through my mind. Exactly as things did when I was working out the connections in my books, where the clues led. It was so much easier when I was writing, because I could make them up.

I only wished I could do that here. Identify Labine's killer and how he might've been connected to whatever financial plight had befallen Hal. Because Labine was the key. He must have known something his killer couldn't risk being revealed. Something he'd uncovered in the course of preparing this lawsuit he was threatening to file, something he'd come to Cabot Cove to confront Hal with, but had arrived too late. Someone watching him, following him the whole way.

And now someone was after me, too.

What else could explain the dark sedan riding the rear of my bike, forcing me into traffic in the hope of causing exactly what had almost come to pass?

The connections were unavoidable. Labine was dead because of something he'd uncovered, and I was a threat because somebody must have thought I knew it, too. But who?

And *what* exactly?

My so-called smartphone was dinged up a bit but still fully functional. Not wanting to ride my older, spare bicycle to Babs's or bother anyone for a lift, I brought up the Uber app and requested a ride. Our tiny, tony hamlet had several residents who made extra cash as Uber drivers, especially in the summer, when business was brisk, although I had to think this would be the first time someone who was nearly killed while riding her bike had called them for a ride.

I remembered I'd be meeting Alyssa's boyfriend

and I resolved to be on my best behavior. I would not peer into any closets in search of skeletons or hit the young man with particularly probative questions, as was my instinct, more in this case out of my affection for Alyssa than anything arising from suspicion.

She greeted me at the door, doing her best to look happy, and hugged me tight.

"Jessica, I heard what happened. I was so worried. Are you all right? You look okay."

"I'm fine," I reassured, holding her by the elbows. "Just a touch of a headache. Nothing a good night's sleep won't cure."

"Are you sure? Were you checked for a concussion?"

"I'm a writer, Alyssa. My brain is always banging around in my head. Get used to it."

She smiled again, less forced this time, and turned toward the living room, where a young man rose from the couch through a cloud of tumbling hair. It was dark and carried past his shoulders, his features soft and flat, deep-set eyes shadowed by the locks of hair that dropped over his forehead to his brow.

"And this is Chad," Alyssa said, introducing us. "Chad, this is Jessica Fletcher, my—" She stopped and looked at me. "How do I describe you exactly?"

"How about *mentor*?"

"Or the aunt I never had. Aunt Jessica," Alyssa tried out. "Has a nice ring to it."

"How about old widow?"

"You're not an old widow."

"I'm not your aunt either."

"Are you two always like this?" Chad asked, grinning as he extended his hand. He was wearing those jeans I never understood how young people, men especially, could squeeze into, made of denim so rough it looked starched. He was thin and lanky, with his soft face nearly swallowed by all that hair. "Nice to meet you, Mrs. Fletcher. I've been reading your books. Didn't think I'd like them, but I do."

"I'll take that as a compliment."

Alyssa cleared her throat. "I told Chad I mentioned him to you."

"You mean the fact that he's a genius with computers," I said, leaving out any mention of Alyssa's noting Chad's expertise with coding and hacking. "Maybe you can teach me how to work my smartphone, which makes me feel exceedingly dumb."

"No problem, Mrs. Fletcher. I can also load any apps you might like."

"Is there one for an autodriving bicycle?"

Chad's eyes flashed brightly. "Not yet, but . . ."

"Chad's going to be staying for Dad's funeral."

"In one of the guest rooms," Babs pronounced, emerging from the kitchen with an apron tied round her waist. "Isn't that right, Chad?"

He grinned at her, not at all embarrassed. "I'm already unpacked, Babs."

"My houseguests call me Babs. My daughter's boyfriends call me Mrs. Wirth."

"Understood . . . Mrs. Wirth," he said, flashing that grin again.

It was nice to see a degree of normalcy, however strained, returning to the Wirth household. Hal's funeral was the day after tomorrow and I was sure it was going to be difficult. But I was immediately glad I'd fought back my headache and come over for dinner. Being around Alyssa had inevitably perked me up when she was a little girl, and that remained true now that she was in college. The kindness, unbridled optimism, and generally good natures displayed by the young could be both restorative and enriching, and I understood deeply how much it must have meant to Babs to have Alyssa there. It's easy to overlook the fullness the company of young people brings into our lives. And, besides my nephew, Grady, Alyssa was the closest thing I had to a child myself.

"Soup's on, as they say," Babs announced.

We ate at the smaller, more intimate table in the kitchen, forsaking the formality of the dining room. Babs had made a chicken dish I don't recall her ever trying her hand at before, her apprehension at how we'd respond to the dish almost palpable.

"It's delicious, Babs," I offered for the three of us.

"She's right, Mom," Alyssa chimed in.

Chad's mouth was full, so he nodded his affirmation.

Babs breathed a sigh of relief. "I got the recipe from Cabot Cove Catering at the affair they did at the library. Almost added it to the Labor Day menu, but I didn't want to risk a riot by replacing the hot dogs, hamburgers, or lobster rolls."

I cut another slice of the chicken, grateful to have my appetite back. "Take away the lobster rolls and I would've led that riot."

Chad angled his gaze toward me. "So, Mrs. Fletcher, Alyssa tells me you're the reason she wants to be a writer."

"She would do well to find a better role model— one whose books aren't sold between the deodorant and the hosiery. And call me Jessica, please."

"That seems to have worked pretty well for you . . . Jessica."

"I've been lucky. That's the nature of this business. Right place at the right time beats talent any day of the week."

"You've still sold an awful lot of books. Sixty million or something like."

"Some Internet site tell you that?"

"Several of them, actually."

"That's probably the number of copies I have in print. Sales, well, that's something else altogether."

Alyssa grinned, as she worked some broccoli onto her fork. "I'd take those numbers. For my first novel anyway. We'll do better on the second."

"When I was in junior high," I offered, "you know what the bestselling book of all time was?"

"Not the Bible?" Chad chimed in.

"No, it's too easy to steal them from hotel rooms. *Valley of the Dolls,*" I pronounced. "By Jacqueline Susann."

"Never heard of it," said Chad.

"Or her," Alyssa added.

I leaned closer to her. "That's the point. You can be better than me or Jacqueline Susann. You can write something that matters, but I'm honored I influenced your dreams."

Something chirped inside a pocket of the vest Chad was wearing, and he pulled out the same giant phone Mort had.

"I got it!" He beamed at Alyssa.

"Got what?" Babs asked.

"The new *Star Wars* movie," Alyssa answered before Chad had the chance.

Babs looked confused. "But that's not coming out for weeks."

"Not in theaters," Chad acknowledged. "But the studio sends advance copies out selectively. Everything's digital these days, even much of what you see played in the multiplexes. No more prints—just digital files sent through secure networks."

"Apparently," I noted, "not very secure at all."

"You give me the firewall and I'll find a door," Chad boasted, exuding confidence.

"But that's a crime," Babs said, her tone difficult to decipher. "By downloading that movie, you're a criminal."

"Well, we don't actually download it—nobody does. The people the film is sent to are provided with a code that enables them to watch it on what the studio thinks is a secure server."

"So he's not really stealing anything," Alyssa piped in, smirking. "He's too pretty to be a criminal."

"Hey, don't call me pretty."

"Then cut your hair and get a tattoo."

"Good idea. I was thinking 'Alyssa.'"

"I," Babs interjected, clearing her throat, "was thinking no."

I leaned closer to Chad, my interest in this hacking

thing piqued. "So you hacked the studio's secure server."

"I wrote code that allowed me to talk to it, machine to machine. So I didn't really steal the film—the server gave me permission to watch it."

"Isn't that still hacking?"

"Hacking," Chad told me, "is level one. What I do is level ten."

"Modest," Babs joked to Alyssa, "isn't he?"

"If you ever want to write about hacking in one of your books, Jessica, I'm available to consult."

"I don't think I'll be able to afford you much longer."

"I take care of my friends," Chad said, smiling across the table. "Just ask Alyssa."

"I'd rather not," said Babs.

Chapter Thirteen

"Thanks for seeing us on such short notice, Mr. Booker," Mort said to Sean Booker, president of LOVEISYOURS, after we were ushered into his office the following morning.

"When you mentioned the murder of one of our clients, Sheriff," Booker began, leaving it there.

He was a nondescript man who looked very much like the sort who might need the services his own company provided. An administrator as opposed to the older version of Chad I was expecting. He wore a tie and shirt, his suit jacket draped over the back of his chair. The kind of man you forget as soon as you leave his company, the kind who prefers anonymity, shuns the spotlight, but runs a tight ship. Mort and I were facing him from matching chairs set before his desk that were stiff and uncomfortable, making me think meetings didn't last very long at LOVEISYOURS.

The company's headquarters was situated in Chestnut Hill, Massachusetts—anywhere from a few minutes to an hour from downtown Boston, depending on traffic. It was housed in a stately white building that still carried the dark window awnings of the law office that had previously occupied it, and overlooked Route 9 beyond. The three-story building also turned out to be just down the street from Frank Pepe Pizzeria, which for my money was the best anywhere. I found myself craving a slice, or two, or more, while seated across from Sean Booker.

"Please tell me how I can help you, Sheriff Metzger and Mrs. . . ."

"Fletcher," I reminded him, glad Booker had never heard of me, "Jessica Fletcher."

"She consults with my department from time to time," Mort offered, by way of explanation for my presence.

"That would be up in Maine, Cabot Cove to be exact," Booker noted. "Not a place you'd expect to be synonymous with murder."

You don't know Cabot Cove, I almost said, before Mort responded.

"We like to think so," Mort told him. "This is a most unusual case and the actual murder victim wasn't your client."

"Oh, no?"

"But we believe the circumstances of your client's death may have a direct bearing on our case. Isn't that right, Jessica?" Mort said, passing the ball to me, as he often did.

"Mr. Booker, your client became embroiled in unusual, and potentially criminal, circumstances in the immediate aftermath of a date he arranged after registering on LOVEISYOURS. His name was Hal Wirth, and we've come here in the hope of learning the name of the woman he arranged the date with."

Booker's flat expression seemed to crack. "I'm afraid that information's privileged. Legally, I'd need a warrant to produce to it. Nothing personal, just policy. Our clients expect confidentiality from us at every turn."

"Let's not get ahead of ourselves," Mort suggested. "Right now, we're not even sure there's anything to seek a warrant about. We're just talking here, having a friendly conversation. Isn't that right, Mr. Booker?"

"If you say so, Sheriff, I guess."

"And I do say so. I most certainly say so. You don't need a warrant to bring up what you can on Hal Wirth, do you? His death should void the confidentiality agreement. That's right, isn't it?"

"Well," Booker said, clearly hedging.

"I'll get that warrant if you like, Mr. Booker. I'll tell the judge I need a broad overview of your company's workings. Who knows what I might find on top of what I'm looking for?"

Booker swallowed hard.

"So I'm going to ask you again. You don't need a warrant to bring up what you can on Hal Wirth, do you?"

"No, Sheriff, I don't," Booker relented.

Mort leaned back again. "Well, there you go. Now we've got a place to start."

Booker started working the keys of one of three computers dominating his desk. I realized not a single scrap of paper was in evidence anywhere, nor could I see any pens. "Please spell the man's last name."

"W-i-r-t-h. First name Hal, although it's possible he registered under Harold. And he may have listed his location as Granite Heights, not Cabot Cove."

"That information is optional and not necessarily recommended," Booker said, typing away and not looking up from his screen. "States or the nearest cities are normally all clients supply. Very seldom specific hometowns. Nobody wants to risk becoming a target."

"Does that happen?" I said, unable to help myself. "Do some of your clients find themselves targets?"

"The more vulnerable ones are susceptible to a wide range of scams including identity theft and catfishing, so we take every precaution, both in the registration process and our own internal security measures, to keep our clients' personal info secure. Generally, they reveal only what they wish to and never anything like Social Security numbers or passwords. Nothing like that. These are people who uniformly value their privacy above all else, because, after all, using our services very much falls under the auspices of their private lives. I can tell you that while we have our share of complaints we have to deal with and negative reporting on clients we have to address, our options are limited."

"Why's that?"

"Because if we kick someone off our site, that doesn't stop them from registering on another, where they are likely to repeat the same behavior. Others have been known to reregister on LOVEISYOURS with a new username and password, so we have no way of recognizing them." Booker's eyes narrowed on the screen. "Could you spell that name for me again?"

"W-i-r-t-h," Mort answered this time.

"Well, that's a bit odd," Booker followed.

Mort and I leaned forward together, me speaking before he had a chance. "What?"

"We have no one by that name in our database and never have."

Mort looked at me before responding. "But you just said clients didn't necessarily have to use their own names when registering."

"Not when setting up their pages, but their accounts are different. We need a credit card to process our monthly fees, and for that, we do require their actual documented identities. Birth date, Social Security number—all that sort of thing."

"Social Security number?" I said, exchanging another gaze with Mort.

"It's the best way to protect our clients, Mrs. Fletcher. I'm sure you've heard at least some of the horror stories associated with dating sites, including, unfortunately, ours."

"Actually, I haven't."

"I'll spare you the details. Suffice it to say these incidents are rare, exceedingly rare, but when they occur, the burden falls upon us to do everything in our power to make sure that they're documented and reported to the proper authorities. If you'd like me to be more specific . . ."

"That won't be necessary," Mort told him.

"Since Mr. Wirth's online profile may have included an alias, would you happen to know the name as it appears on his credit card?"

"You could try the name with the middle initial *F*."

I could see Booker enter the data four separate times, each to no avail, judging from his expression.

"Nothing, I'm afraid."

"Try 'Wirth Ventures,' his company's name," I suggested. "Or 'Wirth Ventures Inc.'"

Booker obliged, trying any number of combinations again before shaking his head and looking across his desk at us once more. "I'm afraid we have nothing on record under any of those names."

"Is it possible he deleted his profile and canceled his registration after his first date didn't go well?"

"Of course, and I probably shouldn't say this, but that's not at all uncommon. However, I would still have access to both, since the profile and customer information remains archived in our system. And, by all indications, no one named Hal, or Harold, Wirth has ever had an account with us."

Mort and I looked at each other again, equally mystified. This was something we'd had no reason to anticipate, and it made no sense.

"Is there any other means you have of checking?"

"Well, we've added software that allows clients to tell us not only what they're looking for in a match, but also what they're not. The qualities, physical and otherwise, they want to avoid. So we've developed a very sophisticated facial-recognition program that goes hand in hand with that. If you could have a picture of Mr. Wirth forwarded to me . . ."

"No need," I said, reaching into my handbag and

clawing past my so-called smartphone to pull out an envelope. "I brought one with me."

I'd asked Babs for a picture the night before, without explaining my intentions, in anticipation of just this eventuality. Mort looked flabbergasted that I'd thought of such a thing, as I slipped the picture of Hal from the envelope and handed it across the desk to Sean Booker.

He ran the picture through a scanner perched on a ledge behind his desk chair, and then I watched him work some keystrokes to likely input it into the LOVEISYOURS database in search of a match. I settled back to wait, having no idea how long such a process would take.

It didn't take long.

Wordlessly, he turned the computer on which he'd been working around so Mort and I could see the screen.

NO MATCH FOUND

"I don't know what to say," Booker offered apologetically. "Perhaps Mr. Wirth was using a different dating service instead of LOVEISYOURS."

"I suppose that's possible." I shrugged. "But all indications led us here."

"Have you checked his credit card and bank statements to confirm that?"

"Not yet," Mort told him, "but we will now."

"Could you check your database for the name 'Naomi'?" I interjected.

Booker got his fingers poised anew on the keyboard. "Any last name?"

"No, but she went by 'Nan' and would have been somewhere close in terms of zip codes."

It didn't take long for the results to come up on the monitor screen Booker had tilted back to face him. "We do have several Naomis, and even a few Nans, in our database, but none whose profile lists both names and none within several hundred miles of Granite Heights, Cabot Cove, or the city of Boston."

We'd been flummoxed again. Unless Hal had included something in his memoir either purposely or inadvertently false, none of this made any sense.

Booker rose a beat ahead of us. "I'm sorry I couldn't have been of more help. If you could tell me one thing . . ."

Mort nodded.

"Do you have any reason to believe Mr. Wirth's death was connected in any way to his use of our services?"

"It's an ongoing investigation."

"How am I supposed to take that?"

"As the only thing I'm at liberty to say at this time, Mr. Booker," Mort said sternly. "The Cabot Cove Sheriff's Department has their policies about such things, just as you do."

Booker handed us both a card. "Well, if there's anything else I can do, please don't hesitate to call."

Mort handed him his card. "And if you think of anything in the meantime . . ."

He took Mort's card and pocketed it absently. "Of course, Sheriff."

Mort started for the door, before turning to look

back toward Booker. "One more thing, Mr. Booker. Am I the first law enforcement official who's been in this office inquiring about a criminal matter?"

"No, Sheriff," Booker said without hesitation, "just the first when it comes to murder."

Chapter Fourteen

We walked into Pizzeria Napoletana, more affectionately known just as Frank Pepe's, shortly after the lunchtime rush had abated. It was located in a mall right next to Morano Gelato, and Mort and I managed to snare a table inside the restaurant proper instead of having to sit amid a tight cluster of establishments in the mall's food court.

"I'm sorry I wasted your time, Mort," I said, after we'd ordered a large, half-plain (for me) and half-spinach-and-mushroom (for Mort).

"How could you have known? Usually your hunches are spot-on. What do you make of what we learned in there, or didn't learn?"

"I have no idea what to make of any of it. It just makes no sense."

"Unless Hal Wirth used a different matching service. Maybe he lied about using LOVEISYOURS in his memoir."

"Why would he do that? The whole point of a memoir is to tell the truth. And if Hal wanted to lie, or omit, he could have just made up a name. No, Mort, it was LOVEISYOURS."

"Not according to Mr. Booker. You think he was holding something back, covering his ass?"

"No. He didn't find Hal in his system because Hal's not in the system. At least, he no longer is."

"Nor is this Naomi."

"You have that giant phone of yours handy?"

"You just saw me check my e-mails and text messages to see if the station was trying to contact me."

"Figure of speech."

Mort worked the phone free from his pocket. "What would you like me to do with it?"

"Bring up the LOVEISYOURS site on your browser."

He started to do just that. "There's a free app here for it, too."

"I want to see what's on the Web. I want to see exactly what Hal saw when he registered on the site."

Mort whistled at what he saw displayed on his screen, drawing the attention of the tables nearest us. "Thirty-nine ninety-five per month fee. Wow! And that's for the basic package. For that much, you better fall in love."

"Me?"

"Figure of speech."

"Ah," I said, taking the phone from him.

I fiddled with it briefly as I figured out how to work

the screen, but ultimately located "FAQ," for Frequently Asked Questions. Then I scrolled down until I found the question I was looking for.

"Mort, it says here that a client can delete his or her profile whenever they choose."

"But as far we know, Hal Wirth didn't delete his profile. According to Booker, he never created one in the first place. And even if he created an alias, a straw man, his credit card confirmation would still have to be his own."

"Which never existed in the system either." I nodded.

"So what's your point, Jessica?"

"What happened to it? A question, not a point. If we take Hal at his word in his memoir, he registered on the site, went on one date, and then realized he'd made a terrible mistake, at which time he then would've likely deleted his account."

"Which, according to Booker, never happened because he never had one," Mort elaborated, then thought for a moment, while I sipped my iced tea. "Since Booker also claimed there was no credit card for Hal on file either, on the chance he used an alias, maybe we should have a look at his credit card statements to see if there's a charge or not. One of us may have to ask Babs for help there."

"You want my guess?" I asked him.

"I've got a feeling I'm going to hear it anyway."

"We won't find anything on the credit card statement. I'm thinking it, too, would've been erased online, maybe at the same time someone wiped Hal Wirth from the LOVEISYOURS database, before a paper statement could be generated. Beyond that, there's another reason I wanted to check the LOVEISYOURS Web site. It says here the first month is free. So Hal would've needed to enter his billing information even though he wouldn't start paying until the second month."

"But he likely deleted his account, or it was deleted for him, before that first month was up."

"Meaning the charge won't show up on any credit card statement period."

"Damn," Mort said.

"Exactly."

"So where does that leave us, Jessica?"

Precisely what I'd been pondering. "The issue here isn't just Hal—it's this Naomi, or Nan, as she preferred to be called. It's one thing for Hal's profile to have never existed. It's quite another when the profile of the woman he was matched up with also never existed."

"And then he conveniently dies."

I hardened my stare involuntarily. "I don't think it was a convenience at all, Mort."

"You've got that look, Jessica. . . ."

And I continued to use it on him.

"Need I remind you that Seth Hazlitt's reading of Hal's blood work and toxicology results suggested nothing nefarious?" Mort followed.

"I wouldn't expect it to. If Hal was murdered, whoever did it knew exactly what they were doing."

"Whoa, hold on there. Getting a bit in front of yourself, aren't you?"

"I think, maybe, he was poisoned."

"When?"

"I don't know."

"How?"

"I don't know that either."

"By who?"

"*Whom*, Mort," I corrected.

"Don't hide behind a grammar lesson, Jessica."

"Then, no to that one, too."

He gazed about as if wondering where our pizza was. "So you're discounting your own theory?"

"It's not a theory, not yet anyway."

"So what is it?"

"A possibility, given what else we know."

"And what's that?" Mort asked me, seeming to enjoy his role as my inquisitor.

"That Hal Wirth used a dating site that has no record of his ever having registered, and arranged a date with a woman from that site who doesn't exist."

Mort crossed his arms and nodded. "He could just as easily have made the whole thing up to spice up his memoir a bit. Writers do that all the time, don't you?"

"Do what?"

"Embellish."

"Fiction writers, yes. Nonfiction writers, or biographers, not so much."

"But Hal wasn't really a writer, hadn't published anything before. So maybe he just tired of trying to make his life sound interesting and decided to make stuff up instead."

"Or embellish."

"I already said that, Jessica."

I leaned forward to narrow the distance across the table between us. "And it's possible. You know what else is possible? Drugs that can cause a heart attack almost immediately."

"Like potassium chloride. Only even an old country doctor like Seth would've noticed elevated levels of that in the blood work. And if he missed it, any decent pathologist certainly won't, because potassium chloride stops the heart; it doesn't cause an actual heart attack, which is what killed Hal." Mort checked his watch. "We should have the autopsy results any minute."

"Assume there's another drug, or drug cocktail, that can cause a heart attack."

"For argument's sake?"

"For argument's sake," I agreed. "And, also for argument's sake, we're going about this the wrong way."

Mort feigned disinterest, turning his gaze to the floor again. "Where's that pizza . . . ?"

"Forget how the heart attack was induced, *if* it was induced, for now. Let's focus instead on the timing."

"The Wirths' Labor Day party?"

I nodded. "Somebody would've needed to get close enough to him to slip something in his drink, even give him some kind of injection."

"That's pretty close." Mort hesitated. "You were there. How many guests are we talking about? Just a ballpark figure."

"Two hundred. Given all the comings and goings, maybe as many as three hundred. There must've been an invite list Babs can provide."

Mort shook his head. "So my department can interview all three hundred. . . ."

"Maybe closer to two hundred. Interview them to

find out if anyone saw something, or someone, they didn't recognize and didn't seem to belong," I suggested. "Seth and I were there for several hours and didn't see a single person who didn't at least look familiar. It was all Cabot Cove residents, with a few of Hal's business associates sprinkled in."

"But not his former business partner, who, at least, had motive."

"That's the point."

"It is?" Mort asked, as the waitress set our pizza down between us.

"Hal's ex–business partner was murdered because he knew something. I was almost killed because the murderer must've thought I was getting close to the same thing. We were both seen as threats. And that makes no sense, unless Hal was murdered, too."

"Can we eat now?"

I spun the pizza around so the spinach-and-mushroom side was closer to him. "And all this is somehow connected to that dating service, LOVEISYOURS. It must be."

Mort laid his first slice down on the plate set before him. "Good luck proving that without a place to start."

"Who said I didn't have a place to start?" I asked, easing the first slice onto my plate.

Chapter Fifteen

Five hours later, I was seated at Babs's kitchen table next to Chad, with Alyssa on his other side. Chad had his laptop open and fired it up.

"Is this for a book?" he asked me.

"Assume that it is," I told him. "Do you have a consultant's fee?"

Chad flashed his boyish grin. "Just put me on the acknowledgments page. And tell me what you need."

Seconds later he had the LOVEISYOURS Web site up on his screen, awaiting further instructions.

"So, what now, Jessica?" He smirked, clearly comfortable in his element.

"I want you to create a fake profile and then make it disappear."

"You mean, like, delete it?"

"No, I mean make it like it never existed in the first

place, no record whatsoever. And that would include billing data."

"Why not just use an existing customer? That's what you want to get at, isn't it?"

I nodded, not yet considering the ramifications of actually wiping a member of LOVEISYOURS off their listings altogether. "If we can find someone, say, who hasn't visited their page in a while."

"You mean a dead man walking."

"What's that?"

"A man who opens a page on social media, then neglects it entirely. How about we use three years as a filter?" Chad suggested, fingers already clacking away atop the keyboard.

"Sounds good to me."

His fingers danced and flew some more, and the start of a long listing with picture click-throughs appeared on-screen. "There you go. All the clients on LOVEISYOURS whose accounts have been inactive for three or more years, but who've continued to pay their monthly fee, probably because they never bother checking the contents of their credit card statements." His expression wrinkled the way it might if he'd tasted something sour. "Who uses a site like this anyway?"

"Desperate people," Alyssa suggested.

"You mean like us, if we hadn't found each other?"

That earned Chad a kiss from Alyssa, making me glad Babs was currently in her upstairs office working on the final preparations for Hal's funeral tomorrow.

"Want to pick one?" he asked me.

"No, you do it."

He clicked on the profile of a man whose first name was Mark and began working the keys in a blinding blur, pausing on occasion to check on the progress of whatever he was doing, before resuming. It seemed like a long time had passed, when it was probably only about five minutes.

"Okay," he pronounced after a final keystroke, "we're in."

"You found his password?"

"Not exactly. It's easier in these cases for hackers like me to just give him a new one. I'll spare you the details."

"I wouldn't understand them anyway," I told him. "What's next?"

"Let me show you what happens when I just delete the profile."

Chad's fingers flew across the keyboard again until he pressed Enter in majestic fashion. "Gone!" he pronounced, adding, "Voilà!"

I peered at the screen. The man named Mark's profile was indeed gone.

"Now," Chad resumed, "I want to show you something."

He worked the keys some more, before he angled his laptop toward me and entered the name "Mark" in the search bar, then hit Enter again.

"This is a list of everyone named Mark currently registered on the site next to their profile picture. Notice anything?" he asked me, scrolling down the screen slowly.

"Stop!" I said, almost yelling. "There's our Mark, the one we deleted."

"Exactly. And look what happens when I click on his picture."

File not found appeared on-screen.

More keystrokes, followed by clicking on a Restore icon, and Mark's profile was displayed on-screen again.

"Okay, Mark's back."

"Not for long. What I just did was delete his profile. Now I'm going to wipe it."

"There's a difference?"

"A huge one. Deleting the profile means it's still there, but the software can no longer find it. Wiping the profile makes it vanish altogether from the server. Like magic. Watch."

His fingers danced across the keys longer this time, with only a few pauses. It looked as if he was on the clock, never letting more than a second or so elapse between clicks. Then he repeated the search process and this time Mark's profile picture didn't appear as it had before.

"That's amazing," I said, meaning it.

"The bad news is that I can't restore Mark's profile again, because it's gone, like it was never there in the first place."

Which had been exactly my reason for requesting this demonstration. "What about Mark's payment information, his credit card or something? Would that be gone, too?"

"Because it's part of his profile, absolutely."

"And the site would have no record he'd ever paid

them, even if he'd been archived?" I wondered, recalling what I'd learned from Sean Booker.

Chad nodded, a bit noncommittally. "Well, they'd still have whatever money he paid them—that doesn't go away. But there'd be nothing to archive—no trail, paper or otherwise, of where it actually came from, as there would still be if his account was just deleted."

I looked back at his computer screen, amazed by what I'd just witnessed. "You made that look easy."

"Because it is. Sites like this, LOVEISYOURS, operate on a binary system to be user-friendly. But the more user-friendly a site is, the more susceptible it is to intrusion from people like me."

"Hackers."

"I prefer the term cyber ghosts."

"Whatever you say. But you're really telling me it's that easy to make someone, like this Mark, *disappear*?"

Chad nodded and whipped the hair from his face with a snap of his head. I watched Alyssa reach over and fan it back into place, Chad first pretending to fight off her hand before taking it in his.

"The answer is yes," he said, without missing a beat. "And it's only from a single site. Virtually all of them are based off the same platform, and learning the ins and outs of how that platform operates allows someone like me to use their operating systems against them. It's a question of finding the vulnerabilities. They're always there, Jessica. You just have to know where to look for them."

I decided to grasp at a straw. "Any chance of reconstructing a file that somebody else has made disappear?"

Chad shook his head, suddenly looking glum over having disappointed me. "No. Sorry, Jessica . . ."

I glanced toward Alyssa, careful of my words. "Even if you had a name or additional personal information?"

He shrugged. "Once it's gone, it's gone."

I stepped outside to call Mort and update him on what I'd learned from Chad. I'd uncovered the means by which both Hal's and this Nan's profiles had vanished from LOVEISYOURS, along with Hal's billing information. In spite of all we'd learned at the dating site's corporate headquarters, we'd come to a proverbial dead end.

I felt guilty as I explained it to Mort, guilty that I'd let myself be consumed by this mystery instead of helping Babs finalize the arrangements for Hal's funeral tomorrow. Any clues leading to the truth behind his death, at least the sudden insolvency he'd suffered, would have to come from another source.

Eugene Labine's murder perhaps. Or the dark sedan that had forced me into the intersection yesterday and nearly killed me.

The problem was Cabot Cove had no traffic cameras—any more than Hill House had security cameras. I had to figure that solving all manner of crimes in big cities was infinitely easier than this.

"Has the autopsy report on Hal come in yet?" I asked Mort, remembering it had been due today.

"I didn't want to spoil your night, Jessica. He died

of a heart attack with no signs or indications of anything pointing to foul play whatsoever."

I thanked Mort and said good night, discouraged but far from ready to give up. Despite lacking evidence to that effect, I still believed Hal Wirth was murdered at his Labor Day party. I could see no way to prove it, though, my efforts stymied on all fronts.

After hanging up with Mort, I remained outside to ponder what I had left to pursue. There was the guest list from the Labor Day party to consider. A lot of guests for Mort and his deputies to interview, yes, but if one of them had seen something, *anything*, even remotely out of place in the hours leading up to Hal's death, then it would be well worth the effort.

I just couldn't let it go. Maybe the problem was I wasn't writing at present. Maybe this was my mind's way of telling me it was time to plunge into my next book, to channel my overactive imagination onto the page. Solve a crime in fiction, when I clearly wasn't going to be able to solve this one in fact, assuming a crime had even been committed. Eugene Labine, after all, seemed the sort who left no shortage of enemies in his wake. And it wasn't too much of a stretch to imagine that one of them followed him to Cabot Cove and murdered him for reasons entirely unrelated to Hal's death or his misadventures on a dating site.

But I had to know, had to be as sure as I possibly could, and so I resolved that tomorrow, after the funeral, I would suggest that Mort indeed interview all the guests who'd attended Hal and Babs's Labor Day party, that being the only way—

I froze in midthought, my quivering hand snatching the phone from my bag and redialing Mort's number, willing him to pick up fast.

"Already? Please don't tell me someone tried to kill you again."

"Not yet anyway. I think there's a way we can figure out if Hal was murdered or not."

"Divine inspiration strike you again, Jessica?"

"Not exactly; I just remembered something about the party."

Chapter Sixteen

We wouldn't be able to act on what I told Mort until after the funeral. He wasn't certain how early he'd be able to get to the church, so Seth Hazlitt picked me up instead. I was never sure what to wear to such things and opted for a plain black dress, content to lose myself in an endless shroud of darkness that enveloped such occasions.

As expected, a big portion of the town showed up, packing the mass, where Father Donald Barnes presided over a majestic service, highlighted by his stirring sermon that was more of a eulogy, a fitting testimonial to Hal Wirth and all he had meant to Cabot Cove. I caught Babs weeping through much of it, Alyssa squeezing her mother's hand, while Chad, looking awkward in a rumpled sport coat, held Alyssa's.

After the service concluded, and attendees were

filing into the aisles to make their exit, I crossed paths with none other than Deacon Westhausen, Cabot Cove's resident tycoon.

"Nice to see a fellow author in attendance," he greeted, managing a smile that looked painted onto his face.

Fellow author? Westhausen had written a single motivational business book, which had shot up the bestseller list, number one for months. I remember Hal mentioning that they'd met at one of Westhausen's book events and had hit it off to the point where Hal had taken credit for introducing the technology superstar to Cabot Cove.

"Thank you," I said.

"Hal mentioned he was trying his hand at writing a book," Westhausen said, with an uneasy edge creeping into his voice. "He ever share that with you?"

"Not personally. But I stumbled onto it while helping Babs sort through his things," I said, having no desire to offer anything further.

"Any good? As one writer to another."

"It needs some work," I commented, wondering about the source of his interest.

"Maybe I could give it a read."

"You'll have to ask Babs, Mr. Westhausen."

"Please, Mrs. Fletcher, call me Deacon."

"Only if you call me Jessica."

He smiled brightly this time, displaying a glimpse of the charm that had won him such celebrity and fame while still in his mid-thirties. Wearing his trademark jeans and sneakers even to a funeral, though he'd opted for a sport coat as rumpled as Chad's as a kind of compromise.

"I'm not a mystery fan, Jessica. If I was . . ."

"No reason to apologize," I told him.

"Anyway, it's not like you're at a loss for readers."

"I could always use another."

"I'd like to sit down with you sometime," he said, continuing up the aisle alongside me. "See if there's something I can do to aid the Cabot Cove Library's Friends group that you're a part of."

"We'd love the help, and the support. As one writer to another. And how's your estate coming, Deacon?"

He seemed surprised at my description of his home. "It's just a house."

"But the biggest one Cabot Cove has ever seen."

"Everything's relative, Jessica. I'll put you on the guest list for the housewarming."

"I'll be sure to bring a gift."

"How about some signed first editions? I've built quite a collection I'd love to show you."

"I thought you didn't read mysteries."

"Maybe I should start."

I could have left things there, but I couldn't help myself. "I've heard you've had some problems with the construction of your amphitheater."

"The Westhausen Garden?"

I had to stop myself from shaking my head. "Is that what you're going to call it?"

"It's one of the possibilities. Should prove a boon to the local economy, don't you think, Jessica?"

Again, I couldn't help myself. "If you get past those

problems. A shame some supplier sold you substandard lumber."

Westhausen stiffened, surprised I was privy to such information. "Replacing it did set us back a bit."

"I'm glad to hear the rumors that the choice was intentional are unfounded."

Westhausen grinned, an odd gesture under the circumstances. "You've been reading too much of Evelyn Phillips's writing in the *Cabot Cove Gazette*."

"Well, she's always been a much better gossip than a journalist," I said, recalling my own unpleasant exchange with Evelyn from the other night. "When there's nothing there, she has a tendency to—"

"Make it up," he completed for me. "Sounds like we've both been victims of her keyboard's wrath. Something else we have in common."

I cringed at the very notion of that. Fortunately, Westhausen spotted someone else he knew in the crowd ahead and started to sift through the aisle toward him, after casting me a final smile. I didn't know what to make of him. There was something unquestionably charming and disarming about Deacon Westhausen, but there was also something that felt, well, off. I couldn't quite put my finger on it and had pushed the notion aside by the time we got to the cemetery. Maybe it had been his interest in Hal's memoir, and I resolved to give the lot of those pages a more thorough read to see if I could find something I'd missed that might explain his curiosity.

I saw Westhausen nowhere amid the crowd flowing toward the grave site. The church graveyard where

Hal was being buried was the oldest in town, dating all the way back to the eighteenth century. Neither he nor Babs had much family they still talked to, so there weren't a lot of new faces in the cortege. Listening to Father Barnes's words over Hal's coffin outside, I thought of how many mysteries featured the killer showing up at the funeral of his or her victim. Such things make great fodder for a novel, but in my experience, when they happen, it's because a close relative or friend turns out to be the murderer. The general statistic is that ninety percent of all victims know their killers, and most of those crimes end up getting solved.

Mort arrived for the tail end of the service, then joined Seth and me at the grave site for the burial. My eyes strayed about the crowd, as I made use of the very mythology I'd just denounced, wondering if a face my gaze passed might yield a revelation. All I saw, though, were the flat, somber expressions worn by all funeral goers. For some, the tears were real; for others, not so much, as if they felt obligated to show emotion, to make the most of what for them was just another social occasion.

My eyes fell on Evelyn Phillips from the *Cabot Cove Gazette*, and I again recalled our terse conversation from the other night. She must've felt me looking and met my stare. Instead of jerking my gaze away, I exchanged a nod with her. The gossip about Hal and Babs was already flying, but so far, none of the scandalous rumors Evelyn had spouted at me had come to light.

Is it true that Hal was acting strangely? Not as if he was sick—more like he was worried about something?

She'd been referring to his behavior at the party,

now explained by the financial hole he'd somehow dug for himself. But Evelyn, I now recalled, hadn't stopped there.

My sources tell me he was known to have engaged in affairs with several women.

That's how she described Hal before pulling me into the rumor.

I was hoping you might shed some light on the details. For instance, how many women, how many of these affairs, were there?

Hal was a successful, good-looking man who spent a lot of time away from home, a combination that made great fodder for gossipmongers even when there was nothing to back up their charges. But recalling my conversation with Evelyn made me think again of Nan, the mystery woman with whom Hal had connected on LOVEISYOURS. What was I to make of the fact that her profile had been wiped from the site as well, almost surely by a "cyber ghost" like Chad? There had to be a connection there, but it had vanished into the ether of cyberspace.

I had only one hunch left to act upon, the one I'd shared with Mort the previous night and that we intended to follow up on after the reception at Babs's house. Cabot Cove Catering had taken that much off her hands, as the company was well versed in staffing such events thanks to the spate of deaths in the village I often found myself investigating. I'd heard once that a news commentator in Boston had referred to our village as Killer Cove or Murder Cove. Fortunately, the names hadn't stuck.

The reception was exactly what you'd expect it to

be: people milling about, trying to appear casual as they balanced their plates of food with their silverware and drinks. For this kind of thing, the food was wonderful, highlighted by elegant dessert trays, and Cabot Cove Catering further relieved Babs's burden by supplying all the plates, trays, coverings, and utensils. A truly full-service operation.

As I said, they've had a lot of experience.

"Ready, Jessica?" Mort asked, suddenly by my side.

I laid the tea I'd been sipping from a paper cup down on the nearest table. "Let me just say good-bye to Babs."

"Eve Simpson?" Mort had said the night before, after I told him what I'd remembered. "You really think Eve Simpson can help us?"

"Not her, actually—the footage she shot from all those interviews. She said something about a video chronicle of the party, like a yearbook or something. She spent the whole day going around with her camera, asking guests to say something about Babs and Hal for their anniversary."

"Sounds like a decent gesture."

"And I'm sure it came with an ulterior motive, since everything Eve does has an ulterior motive."

"So what do you expect to find in all this footage?"

"Well, I doubt we'll see somebody coming up and killing Hal Wirth on camera, but maybe there will be something to indicate whether he was murdered or not."

Eve Simpson had stayed at the reception only long enough to put in the proverbial appearance in a fashion befitting our town's premier real estate agent. Others had moved in and put up their shingles since Cabot Cove became trendy, but locals still preferred using Eve, because her supercilious manner got results. She was just phony enough to make you think she wasn't, and who could argue with the fact that she invariably reaped the full asking price? She was a whiz at creating majestic brochures that could make a seaside cottage look like a waterfront estate capable of impressing the likes of Deacon Westhausen, and she had in fact rented him one while he waited for his own estate to be completed.

As soon as Mort parked his squad car, I spotted Eve through the plate glass window of Simpson Realty, on the phone as always. Her office was located diagonally across the street from Mara's, which looked strangely empty now that the summer season had ended. I was about to climb out when Mort took a call and then looked across the seat at me apologetically.

"There's something I have to attend to back at the station, Jessica. I'm afraid you're going to have to handle this alone."

I climbed out of the car but peeked back in, instead of closing the door. "Tell me the truth, Mort: Was that a real call or did you just do something to make the phone ring, so you wouldn't have to deal with Eve?"

He put the car into gear, even though the door was still open. "I'm going to take the Fifth on that." He winked, then pulled away after I'd finally closed the door.

"Now, this is a surprise," Eve said, after she'd hung up the phone.

"I need to ask you a favor, Eve."

She perked up. "Tell me, does it involve a mystery?"

"It might."

"Murder?"

"You never know."

She actually clapped her hands at the prospect. "What do you need? Just tell me."

"I'd like to see the footage you shot at the Wirths' Labor Day party."

She came out of her chair and sat down on the edge of her desk, kitty-corner to where I was standing. "The interviews?"

"Yes."

"All of them?"

I nodded.

Eve's eyes gleamed. "Can you tell me what this is about?"

"You already know."

"Murder?"

"Maybe."

It was strange to see someone perk up at the mere mention of murder, but that's what Eve did. "Something to do with Hal's death?"

"We'll see. If there's something to it, you'll be the second to know—I promise."

"Second?"

"Sheriff Metzger needs to be the first."

She frowned. "I don't think he likes me."

"Whatever gave you that idea?"

Eve Simpson set me up at the currently unoccupied desk of one of her associate agents, logged on to his or her computer, and inserted a thumb drive onto which she'd transferred all the footage she'd shot at the Wirths' Labor Day party. I didn't bother asking what her actual intention was in filming all those interviews, because I assumed it was nothing more than a device to make her stand out at the party amid all those potential clients gathered in one place. I also figured Eve, being such a gossipmonger, might have hoped to get at least a few juicy tidbits from Cabot Cove residents, especially as the day wore on and they ingested more alcohol.

Eve wasn't about to let her attention stray too far from my task, but she left me alone to sort through the footage. I even heard her cancel at least two appointments in a hushed voice to avoid having to either leave me here by myself or kick me out. In all, she'd conducted somewhere around sixty interviews, the average length of which was two or so minutes. Many of those interviews involved couples or were done as a group; more people speaking meant a few of the interviews went longer and the total number of people she actually spoke with might've been closer to a hundred.

I kept the sound very low, since I wasn't interested in the actual interviews as much as what was taking place in the background. I focused especially on the parts of those recordings that contained Hal as he stood various distances away from those being recorded. Amid all this, black-and-white-clad Cabot Cove Catering personnel bobbed and weaved through the throng, hand-passing tiny hot dogs tucked into miniature buns, pizza strips, bite-sized sliders, and those famous lobster rolls it took only two bites to wolf down. Comfort food that had proved perfect for the occasion, not to mention those luscious bite-sized desserts I never could resist.

After an hour, I'd uncovered nothing of note, nothing to suggest anything nefarious had caused Hal Wirth's death later on in the day. I didn't actually know what I expected to find, and ninety minutes in, I began to see this whole idea as a fool's errand that I was nonetheless committed to completing. This in spite of the fact that seeing Hal alive and entertaining his guests this way left me feeling like a voyeur, spying on a departed friend. I felt particularly guilty when I saw a quick shot that included Hal and Seth seated on the bench, engaged in the conversation during which Hal had confessed some of his financial plight. I did notice several places where Hal didn't realize the camera was on him as he clenched his jaw and a worried expression settled over his features. He was clearly trying to put on a good show for Babs and their guests, but in the rare private moments the party afforded, his demeanor was strained with worry over the financial calamity hanging over his head.

His worry was so palpable that, at one point, Eve Simpson pointed the camera at him and said, "You look like you ate something that disagreed with you, Hal. Any comment for the masses?"

Hal had politely demurred and slipped away.

I continued my scrutiny but still found nothing awry as the end of the footage, and the party, neared. Nothing that made me think twice about what I'd just seen. Nobody appeared to slip anything in one of Hal's several drinks.

"I'm going out for coffee," a clearly bored Eve Simpson said, rising from behind her own desk. "Want anything?"

I looked outside and saw dusk had fallen. I'd lost all track of time and my search had yielded nothing so far.

"I'd love a tea," I said gratefully. "Not the herbal kind. Something as close to Lipton as they've got."

"Are you okay on your own?" Eve asked me, her tone one of measured concern.

"I promise not to steal or break anything."

She smiled and took her leave.

I realized I'd gotten to the part of the footage that contained my own interview, after the completion of which the camera followed me joining Babs en route to the kitchen, where we'd found Hal on the floor. I slid the bar back a few minutes and tightened my gaze on the screen, focusing on the door leading into the kitchen that Hal must've passed through not long before us. And, sure enough, there he was, entering the kitchen maybe seven minutes before we discovered him on the floor. This was footage taken before Eve had even approached Seth and me to record our own congratulatory videos.

I switched to slow motion then, to make sure I didn't miss a single thing. At first, I thought there was nothing, nothing at all. But then I saw a shadow I hadn't noticed before, and rewound the recording, freezing it in the spot where I thought I'd glimpsed the shadow.

That shadow turned out to be a male shape wearing the black-and-white uniform of Cabot Cove Catering, slipping unnoticed into the kitchen. I brought the recording back another thirty seconds and let it run. Sure enough, Hal entered the kitchen, followed fifteen seconds later by the man I'd first taken for a shadow. The camera twisted in another direction, but resettled on the area of the French doors leading into the kitchen around fourteen seconds of real time later.

What I saw next left me reaching for the phone, unable to get a dial tone until I finally pressed nine, followed by the number for the sheriff's station.

"Mort," I said after his receptionist got him on the phone, "I've found something you need to see."

Chapter Seventeen

"There!" I said, freezing the screen again so Mort could see what was revealed from his position standing over my shoulder.

"What?"

"You didn't see it? Watch again."

"What am I supposed to be seeing?" he asked as I pushed the bar just slightly backward again.

I'd felt a cool rush of air when he stepped into the offices of Simpson Realty, the first scents of fall trailing Mort inside. Amazing in these parts how nature seems to know that summer really ends with Labor Day. I thought I even detected woodsmoke in the air beyond, someone nearby having lit a fireplace, perhaps to welcome autumn. Before you knew it, we'd be talking about foliage and the looming first snow.

"You need to see it for yourself," I told him, stopping at just the right point before starting the video again.

I figured having him come straight over to Eve's office made the most sense, since the sheriff's station was just down the street and I knew Eve wouldn't have stepped out just for a coffee. She'd linger and loiter about, talking to as many passersby as she could, as was her custom.

"Stop the picture!" Mort exclaimed suddenly.

And I did so at the very point the man in the Cabot Cove Catering outfit emerged from the kitchen, seeming to tuck something back into his pocket.

"Can you zoom in, Jessica?"

I think that's called a "spot shadow." It took me a while to position the mouse properly and click while holding the correct keys down. But soon the screen around the man's torso filled the entire square, and when I ran the few seconds of footage again in slow motion, both Mort and I could clearly see him tucking *something* back into his pants pocket.

"By golly," Mort said, utterly deadpan, as if unaware he was probably the last person on earth to use that expression.

"That was my thought, too."

"Can't see exactly what it was he put in his pocket there."

"No. I tried a bunch of times before you got here." I shook my head. "Nothing. What we're looking at is all there is."

I enlarged the picture captured on the screen to include a not quite front-on shot of the man who'd slipped something into his pocket. Blown up much beyond this, it would be too grainy to be of any use to anyone.

"Can you sharpen the picture up a bit, give us a better look at him?"

"I can't, but somebody better versed and who has the software certainly could."

"Come to think of it," Mort said, standing up straight again, "I think the station has the software, courtesy of Homeland Security."

"You're kidding."

"We were allocated twenty thousand dollars a few years back. The software was part of the package we purchased. Now, if I can only remember who trained on it . . ."

My gaze wandered back to the screen as Mort pondered. I pictured the man captured only in a blur following Hal into the kitchen and doing *something* to him that induced his heart attack. But what Eve had accidentally recorded would be useless if we couldn't get a better look at him.

As if on cue, the front door opened, dragging more of the fall air with it, and Eve Simpson returned with a cutout tray containing her coffee and my tea. She smiled at the sight of Mort, then fixed her eyes upon me.

"Did I miss anything?"

Mort called Becky Thayer, owner of Cabot Cove Catering, and asked her to meet us at the station in an hour, enough time, we hoped, for Mort to make use of that magical software Homeland Security had supplied to get a better look at our potential suspect. It turned out that Billy Simms, the town's youngest deputy, had been the one trained on the software, and Mort called him in from patrol to take a seat in the sheriff's office behind the computer Mort used as little as possible.

Billy was still fiddling and diddling when Becky Thayer arrived, giving Mort and me a chance to explain to her what we needed. Becky had started to respond when Billy burst out of Mort's office, fresh color printout in hand. Mort snatched it from his grasp and I joined him a few steps from where Becky was seated to get a look at his handiwork.

"The software first sharpens the fragment as best it can," he explained to us, "and then extrapolates the rest. So what you're looking at is maybe half actual footage and half fill-in-the-blank."

"Extrapolate," Mort said as he studied the picture. "You learn that word at the training seminar down in Boston?"

"As a matter of fact . . ."

The face of the man revealed was utterly flat, the complexion somewhere between pale and sallow, the expression quietly intense in a way that made him appear scary. He had black hair combed straight back, his features meshing in a way that made me think of a Halloween mask. I wondered if this was really the man we were looking for or whether he was indeed wearing some kind of disguise.

Mort and I looked at each other, exchanging a shrug, after which he moved back toward Becky Thayer and laid the picture down before her.

"Do you recognize this man from the crew that staffed the Wirths' Labor Day party?"

She looked at the picture, then shifted it about to take better advantage of the light sprayed by a single desk lamp in addition to the overheads. "I'm afraid not, Sheriff, but we were so busy that day, I contracted out some jobs to the temp agency we use in Boston. We could certainly send the picture to them to see if they could be of more help."

"Why don't you leave their name and number with my receptionist? I'll contact them first thing in the morning."

Becky rose from the desk chair. "Tell them I referred you. They'll be cooperative if they want to continue getting my business."

"I appreciate that," Mort said. "Truly."

Becky looked as if she was about to take her leave, then didn't. "Tell me, Sheriff. Might this have anything to do with . . ." She let her voice trail off and then shook her head. "Never mind. I don't think you can tell me."

"You're right. I can't."

"What now?" I asked, back in Mort's office after Becky Thayer was gone.

He laid the picture down on his desk. "I run this through the national criminal databases to see if we can get a match. If this man's ever been booked and fingerprinted for anything, anything at all, he'll be in the system."

"Could you make a copy of that picture for me?" I asked him.

Instead of complying, Mort snatched up the picture from his desk. "Simms has already inputted this electronically through the proper channels. Unlike the cases on television, it'll take some time to see if there are any results." He started to hand me the picture, but stopped short. "Care to tell me what you need this for?"

"No."

"That's what I figured," he said, and handed it to me.

I arrived unannounced at Babs's house, one of Mort's deputies having dropped me off. Babs greeted me, clearly exhausted after such a long, draining day. The house was otherwise empty, save for Alyssa and Chad, who were seated in the kitchen, still wearing the more formal clothing they'd donned for the funeral, except Chad's shirt was missing its tie. Babs was more than happy to retire upstairs, so I had them to myself.

"I need something else," I said, taking the chair next to him, opposite Alyssa.

He flashed that wry grin of his at me. "What are you paying your research assistants these days?"

"With the favor of not telling the mother of your girlfriend that the guest room bed wasn't slept in last night."

Chad and Alyssa exchanged a nervous glance, one that seemed to say, *How did she know that?*

"Gotcha!" I said.

They relaxed immediately, Chad breathing an audible sigh of relief.

"Your secret's safe with me," I added, patting Alyssa's forearm.

"So what can I do for you in return?" Chad asked me.

I eased the computer-generated picture from my bag and unfolded it, thinking that Chad looked kind of naked without his laptop in front of him, and then laughed inwardly at the quip I was glad I hadn't shared.

"Is there any way you can find out who this man is?" I asked, sliding the picture in front of him.

"What's wrong with his face?"

"Computer enhanced."

"The computer needs its software updated," he said, studying the picture carefully.

I shrugged, wondering how long ago Homeland Security had actually provided it to Cabot Cove. "You didn't answer my question."

"I've got a few tricks up my sleeve."

"I don't suppose you'd care to share them."

Chad's eyes flashed their familiar glint. "They might not all be exactly legal."

"Wise choice, then," I said, pushing myself up out of my chair.

Alyssa's eyes followed me. "Jessica?"

"Yes."

"Does this have something to do with what happened to my father?"

I wasn't about to lie to her, but the last thing she needed right now was to hear my suspicions. I tried to look as reassuring as I could.

"That's what we're going to find out, dear."

Chapter Eighteen

My wake-up call the following morning came from Mort, a good thing since I'd somehow managed to oversleep. I'd decided to walk home the night before from Babs's house to clear my head and enjoy the crisp, cool air. A bad idea, as it turned out, since I kept hearing footsteps and car engines at every turn, sharp memories of being knocked off my bike bringing the throb back to my head.

"I spoke to the temp agency Becky Thayer uses in Boston," I heard Mort say, as I shook the grogginess from my mind. "And guess what?"

"You e-mailed them the picture," I started, clearing my throat, "and they've never seen the man before. Have no idea who he is."

"How'd you know?"

"Because you're so predictable. Whenever you say 'Guess what?' it's not good."

"And that makes me predictable? Have you read your own books lately?"

I sat up all the way and stretched my free arm. "I think we're missing the point here."

"I was waiting for you to say that."

"And I've said it. Because we now have a very real indication that Hal Wirth was murdered."

"Guess what?"

"More bad news, Mort?"

"The man pictured drew a blank with all the criminal databases, too. He's clean as the driven snow."

"It wasn't a very good picture," I reminded. "A little light on features."

"I've sent it to the FBI to see what magic they might be able to work."

"Don't hold your breath."

"Never do. I think when they see a request stamped 'Cabot Cove,' they cringe, given our murder rate."

"Must be something in the air."

"I actually have another explanation, Jessica: We're all characters in one of your books and none of this is really happening. It only exists in your mind."

"Then I should be able to tell you how it ends, but in this case I can't."

"How about just the next chapter?"

"Already working on that, Mort," I said, wide-awake at last. "What do you suppose that man was tucking back in his pocket? Do you think it could've been a syringe?"

"You're reading my mind again."

"Because you're such an open book."

"One of yours is sitting on my night table, by the way."

"Which one?"

"I don't remember. But they're all the same anyway, right?"

Since I lacked Alyssa's cell phone number, I called Babs to ask her if Alyssa and Chad were still there.

"I need to ask you something, Jessica," she said, after confirming they were. "What's going on?"

"I don't know what you mean," I said, lamely crossing my fingers.

"Yes, you do. Something's going on about Hal and Eugene Labine that has to do with whatever you've been talking to Alyssa and Chad about. You think I didn't notice?"

"I was hoping you didn't," I confessed.

"I need to know."

"Do you trust me, Babs?"

"Of course I trust you."

"Then believe me when I tell you there's nothing you need to know, at least not yet."

"On one condition, Jessica—that you answer a question for me. Was Hal murdered?"

"I'm . . . n-not sure," I stammered.

"What can you tell me? You need to tell me something. You can't put me through this. It's like losing him twice."

"Has Lawrence Pyke been able to learn anything about those loans Hal took out?"

"Not a thing. The money seems to have vanished.

Lawrence suspects gambling debts or some shady business dealings Hal managed to keep secret all these years that he finally had to settle. It makes no sense."

"No, it doesn't," I agreed.

"You have to get to the bottom of all this, Jessica. I don't have anyone else I can turn to."

"Count on it, Babs. Count on it."

"I haven't been here in years," Alyssa said, her eyes agape as she took in the sprawling first floor of my home.

Much too large, I knew, for a single person, and requiring constant maintenance. But I couldn't bear to part with it. Too many memories, and I never considered myself the type to move to one of those fancy waterfront condos or single-level, cookie-cutter homes in a fifty-five-plus community. This was *home*, where I'd done the bulk of my writing and where my memories of Frank were the strongest. As much as anything, I couldn't bear entertaining the notion of giving it up because it felt like I'd be betraying him, making me keenly aware of what Babs must be struggling with over the loss of Hal. That sense of kinship between us redoubled my resolve to get to the bottom of what was going on, as the pieces of the puzzle kept falling together without revealing a discernible picture.

"Is this where you write your books?" Alyssa continued.

For a moment, her youthful enthusiasm made me see the little girl I remembered, instead of a nearly grown-up, beautiful young woman. She had the boundless enthusiasm and youthful imagination that were part and parcel of being a writer, and in that moment I wanted nothing more than to guide her on that path. I found myself envisioning her rushing over with her first published book in hand, the two of us celebrating a moment she'd cherish for the rest of her life.

"Can you show me your office?"

Alyssa's question lifted me from my trance. "I call it a study."

Chad, meanwhile, was gazing about more absently, as if disappointed by the visible lack of technology. I thought he was smirking at my old RCA Victrola record player I'd had painstakingly restored, but he broke into a smile.

"That's real, isn't it? Not one of those new ones you can buy on Amazon."

"Oh, it's real, all right," I told him. "And I've got the bills to prove it."

"Man," he said, running a hand over its smooth wood finish, "this is something." He spotted my collection of LPs battling for space with books in my built-in bookshelves and lovingly eased one of the cardboard sleeves out. "This is incredible. You like jazz?"

"My late husband did; I inherited my love of it from him."

Chad traded that LP for another, then put that one back, too, and removed a folded-up piece of paper from the pocket of his jeans. He unfolded it, revealing a much more detailed image of the man pictured at

the Wirths' barbecue who I was convinced had murdered Hal. The image had been sharpened to a significant degree. The man's face didn't look like a
Halloween mask anymore. But his skin looked more
like smooth ceramic than flesh, almost like flesh-
toned porcelain, fragile and ready to crack. And whatever program Chad had used had swallowed the
whites of the man's eyes and left them totally black.

"I think I've figured out a way for you to pay my
consulting fee, Jessica," he said, eyeing my albums
again.

"That's good," I told him. "Because I find myself in
need of your services again."

I asked Alyssa to let me speak with him alone, not
bothering to explain that I didn't want to risk making
her an accessory to what might be a crime. She didn't
look happy to be left out of whatever I wanted to discuss with her boyfriend, but respected my wishes and
traipsed upstairs to the office I called a study, while
Chad and I adjourned to the kitchen.

"Are you able to hack into government databases?"
I asked him, positioned so I could see if Alyssa strayed
close enough to hear our conversation.

"Depends on which ones you mean."

"Homeland Security, TSA specifically."

"As in airports?"

"As in airports." I nodded. "Both Logan and Portland, Labor Day or the Sunday before."

He still hadn't affirmed whether he could. "And
what would I be looking for?"

I slid in front of him the picture he'd given me of

the man who hadn't been hired by Cabot Cove Catering at all. "Can I trust you, Chad?"

"You just asked me to commit a felony, Jessica," he said, matter-of-factly.

"I think this man may have killed Alyssa's father."

He tried not to look surprised, but couldn't hide it. He brushed the long hair from one side of his face, then the other, and looked at the picture with what passed for a snarl spreading across his soft features.

"I won't tell her. I promise." His eyes met mine again as he tapped the picture. "You want to know if this man came into either airport on his way to Cabot Cove."

"Is it possible for you to find that out?"

Chad thought for a moment. "Well, it would be easier if we knew the originating airport, as opposed to the destination one. Plenty of security cameras are focused on the security lines, where people are often standing still, providing the perfect opportunity for facial-recognition software to kick in. But security cameras are also trained on every single flight arriving at major airports. Trained on the exits to jetways."

"I didn't know."

"Very few people do. I only know from swapping stories with hackers who've managed to penetrate Homeland Security's firewall."

"Should I be hearing this?"

"You knew what you were getting into when you posed your initial question."

"Then let me ask you another: Is Portland considered a major airport?"

Chad drummed his fingers atop the face of the

man who might have murdered Hal Wirth. "I don't know. I've never had reason to find out."

"And now that you do?"

"If you don't hear back from me, it means I found nothing. I'll only contact you if I find something you need to see."

"I understand," I said, trying to convince myself I was doing the right thing here by asking an innocent young man to commit a crime.

Then again, Chad wasn't really so innocent, was he? He might never have used his hacking skills for truly nefarious means, but that didn't mean his efforts sometimes didn't come very close to crossing a dangerous line. And his clear affection for Alyssa told me he wanted to help her as much as I did, Babs, too.

"And something else," Chad said, tapping on the picture he'd enhanced to crystal clarity. "However this goes, I never saw this picture, because it never existed."

"What picture?"

Chapter Nineteen

I hated waiting. I'm exceedingly patient when it comes to my books, never rushing and making sure I get every detail correct. People who've been writing as long as I have may bemoan the changes in the industry and the way books are sold, but no one can dispute the magic of the Internet as a research tool. I'd spent countless hours during the formative years of my career, and well beyond, in the company of library shelving and card catalogs, searching for what was now a mere keystroke or two away. I'd like to tell you that I missed those days mired in the dusty stacks, but I don't.

Nostalgia carries only so far.

I knew I was too distracted waiting to hear back from Chad to get any worthwhile writing done, so I busied myself instead with returning e-mails and other correspondence, and also managed to review the page proofs for an upcoming paperback reprint.

As a writer, I've never tired of the feeling of seeing my name on the front cover. And I believe that having success come to me later in life has made me appreciate it all the more. I also don't know what I would've done without my writing. It got me through Frank's death and has provided the means to live as I wish, which now included upgrading my ruined bicycle.

As I stared at my cell phone, hoping to receive a call from Chad, I also reviewed in my mind the meeting Mort and I had had the other day with Sean Booker at LOVEISYOURS down in Boston—well, Chestnut Hill. He had been helpful and cooperative to an extent, but something was nagging at me about our exchanges and I couldn't quite put my finger on it. Had it been something he said? A gesture or a look maybe? Something was there all right, but I couldn't identify what it was.

Almost on cue, my phone rang with "Mort" lit up on the screen.

"I was just thinking of you," I greeted. "Sort of."

"Sort of?"

"Our meeting with Sean Booker."

"I've been looking into him. As best I can."

"What's that mean exactly?"

"He founded LOVEISYOURS five years ago. Built it into one of the top sites of its kind, from what I've been able to learn."

"Okay. And before?"

"That's what I'm calling you about. There is no before."

"What do you mean, Mort?" I said, pressing the phone tighter against my ear.

"I can't find any trace of him prior to his establishing

the company. Almost like Booker and LOVEISYOURS were both born the same day."

I tried to make some sense of that. "What's your next move?"

"I'm checking if the federal databases have anything on him in all those years prior and I have a call in to the Boston office of the FBI. You wouldn't happen to have something with his fingerprints on it, would you?"

"Why would you think that?"

"Because your suspicions have led you to do stranger things in the past."

"I had no reason to be suspicious of Mr. Booker."

"So nothing with a fingerprint?"

"And that's why you called, to ask me that?"

"Well . . ."

"Let me know if you find out anything more."

"Will do. And make sure you keep your doors and windows locked, Jessica."

"Mort?"

I heard him ruffle through some pages on the other end of the line. "That man in the picture, the man who pretended to be a temp out of Boston for Cabot Cove Catering, is still out there."

I felt something like a feather slide up my spine. "Are you in your office?"

"Where I always am when I'm not out fighting crime in our bucolic town."

"Can you pick me up? We need to pay a visit to Hill House."

"Why?"

"I'll explain when you get over here. And bring a copy of that picture, Mort."

* * *

I climbed into his squad car ten minutes later, closed the door, and slid down the window.

"Okay, what's this about?" Mort asked me.

"You bring the picture?" I asked, not about to display the even better one Chad had created for me.

"Of course I did."

"We need to show it to the hotel staff, because what if—"

"—the same man murdered Eugene Labine?" Mort completed the thought for me.

Unfortunately, none of the staff on duty at Hill House at the time remembered seeing anyone who looked like the man in our picture. Neither the front desk manager nor the hotel's general manager did either. The same held true for the housekeeping staff. Labine's having been murdered at night meant far less staff were about at the time, and the absence of security cameras didn't exactly help our cause either.

"Hold on a sec," I said to Mort after we'd given up and started to take our leave.

He followed me back to the front desk, where the manager, Thomas (not Tom) Wilkerson, was still sorting through reservation cards of upcoming guests— Hill House was old-school that way.

"Excuse me," I said to rouse his attention. "Was anyone doing landscaping work here the day Eugene Labine was murdered?"

"That would have been late Monday, Labor Day, or early on Tuesday."

Wilkerson flipped open a day planner, perhaps to refresh his memory. "They normally cut the grass on Saturday. But the landscaping company is here right now, doing some pruning and trimming back the trees."

"Where can I find them?"

"You think he was watching the place during the day?" Mort ventured, as we walked outside and around the oddly shaped building to the area where the bulk of the landscaping crew was concentrated.

"For a while anyway. Long enough to familiarize himself with the surroundings, the logistics. Entrances and exits—that sort of thing. And the positioning of his target's room."

"So he could plan the least visible way in and out."

"You're learning."

"It comes with the job."

Mort's uniform was all we needed to get the gardening staff to talk to us. The man in charge, Jesse, introduced himself as the brother of the company's owner and professed to have never seen the man in our computer-enhanced picture. Neither did any of the members of his crew, until we came to the final man, who'd been up on a ladder cutting back an elm tree.

"*Sí,*" he said, nodding when Mort showed him the picture.

The worker didn't speak English, but Jesse was more than happy to serve as translator for us.

"He remembers seeing *this man* on the grounds?" Mort said.

"*Sí,*" the worker said, without waiting for the translation.

Then he spouted off some more Spanish, which Jesse translated. "He says it was Monday night."

Mort and I looked at each other.

"It was nighttime," Jesse continued. "He says his cousin drove him back to pick up some tools he left behind on Sunday; we mowed that day because it rained on Saturday. He thinks he saw this man standing by the woods over there, almost hidden by the trees."

"And this would've been Monday," Mort followed, the same day that Hal had been murdered and I had run into Eugene Labine in Mara's.

"He's almost positive," Jesse said after an exchange with the worker.

"What time would this have been?"

The worker shrugged and responded again without waiting for a translation. "Eight o'clock maybe."

"*Gracias*," Mort said to the man, drawing a polite smile.

"I didn't know you spoke Spanish," I said as we walked away.

"You just heard the extent of my vocabulary."

"The man in the picture was watching Labine around sunset. I ran into you and Labine at Mara's near closing, at midnight."

"So we can assume the killer may have followed him there."

"And wherever else he went before ending up there," I added.

"The Sea Breeze bar," Mort elaborated, "where he had several bourbons. On the rocks."

"You forget to mention that before?"

"Must've slipped my mind," Mort told me, "what with you running me ragged around town."

"Just so long as you're not holding out on me."

He stopped in his tracks and shot me a stare. "You mean, like you're holding out on me?"

I felt something sink in my stomach. "Really, Mort?" was all I could think to say.

"You want to tell me what else you've got on your mind?"

"Why do you think there's anything?"

"You keep checking your watch and your phone."

"Maybe I'm waiting for a call from my publisher," I said, not about to tell Mort the truth.

"That's not your waiting-for-a-call-from-my-publisher look."

"Got all my looks catalogued, do you?"

"You're an open book, Jessica," he smirked, "no pun intended. You'd make a lousy detective."

"Really?" I said again, hoping Mort would let it go.

"Why don't I get you back home and you tell me whatever it is you've got brewing when you're ready?"

"Maybe I'm just working out a problem with a book."

"I thought you were waiting for a call from your publisher."

"I can do two things at once, you know."

He nodded, not bothering to argue the point further. "Like I said, Jessica, whenever you're ready."

Which I hoped would be soon, thinking of Chad.

Chapter Twenty

When the doorbell rang just after Mort had dropped me off, I thought it must be him, having forgotten something. It wasn't.

It was Chad.

I could see one of the Wirths' cars, an SUV, in my driveway. Alyssa was nowhere to be found.

"Chad," I said, trying to make sense of his expression, which looked like a suit that didn't fit right. Then I added lamely, "Where's Alyssa?"

"Can I come in, Jessica?" I noticed the laptop tucked under his arm. "There's something I have to show you, something you need to see."

I felt my heart skip a beat and opened the door all the way so he could enter. Then I closed and locked it, remembering Mort's advice.

Letting Chad into the house left me wondering what my neighbors might make of me having such a handsome young visitor. I cringed at the thought of someone like Evelyn Phillips catching wind of what she might well proclaim to be some tawdry, illicit affair. We moved into the kitchen and took the same seats we'd occupied earlier in the day. I watched Chad fire up his laptop and then turn to look at me.

"You think this man killed Alyssa's father." A statement.

"Did you find something on those airport security cameras, Chad?" I asked him.

"I'm getting to that. But I wanted to show you something else first," he said, tilting the laptop's screen so I could better see a blown-up shot of the man in question's entire body from Eve's original video, not just his face. "He's putting something back into his pocket— that's what the picture shows. I think it's a syringe, Jessica. You can just make out the top of it. I know because I was always scared of needles as a kid."

He looked scared now, too.

"That's how he killed Alyssa's father, isn't it? Injected him with something that gave him a heart attack."

I nodded, because that's all I could do. By then, the computer had come to life and Chad moved over to the chair next to mine, so we could watch the screen together. He hit a few keys, then clicked on the built-in track pad, and the picture of the man filled the screen, remarkably clear in comparison with what the sheriff's station software had managed.

Chad pointed at the man, his pants pocket. "You can see it here. The plunger of a syringe. I'm sure of it, Jessica."

Suddenly, Chad didn't look so boyish anymore.

"That accident Alyssa told me you had on your bike. You think this man was the one who caused it, don't you?"

I didn't respond, so Chad picked up on the same thought.

"Or someone else working for the same people."

"I never suggested there were other people involved."

I could tell Chad wasn't buying it. "What does that dating site you asked me about, LOVEISYOURS, have to do with this?"

"I don't know. Not yet."

"But they're involved. I mean, you wouldn't have asked me to do this if you didn't already have your suspicions, maybe a theory."

"Suspicions, yes, but no theory."

"Then maybe this will help."

Chad worked a finger agilely atop the track pad again. The man whose face looked like porcelain appeared in a different pose, a different setting, the world around him lost to a soft blur, while his torso and face were captured in a clarity comparable to that of the photo Chad had enhanced from the party.

"Logan Airport. This was taken just after six p.m. the Sunday before Labor Day. I was able to use footage from other security cameras to track him outside the terminal, but I lost him before determining where he went from there. But we know where he was the next day, don't we?"

"Yes." I nodded. "We do."

"There's something else I need to show you, Jessica," Chad said, his voice cracking a bit.

He worked a few keys, then the track pad again,

and the laptop's screen separated into six equal segments, each of them picturing the same man in different settings—all of them airports, I guess.

"Denver, Houston, Miami, Charlotte, Tampa, and San Francisco. All of these were taken in the past ten months. So our guy's been busy racking up the frequent-flier miles."

"Can you tell when these pictures were taken?"

Chad nodded. "Yes, thanks to the time and date stamp. I wrote it all down for you. Jessica, do you think—"

"Stop."

"But it's possible this guy—"

"I know what you're suggesting. Stop," I repeated. "I started reading another of your books last night. I know you're thinking the same thing I am."

"Is that what's got you frightened?"

Chad shook his head. "No, I'm worried about something else. I think I was pinged," he continued.

"What's that mean?"

"Something I did attracted the wrong kind of attention."

I felt my stomach flutter. What had I done—what had I been thinking, involving an innocent young man in all this? Not only had my single-mindedness subjected Chad to possible federal scrutiny; it might well have endangered his life.

"I'm sorry," I said lamely. "I need to fix this. I need to fix this somehow."

"There's nothing to fix, Jessica. I did what I did because I wanted to, not because you asked me. I did it for Alyssa."

I felt myself nod. "But if hacking these airport security databases has made you a target or something . . ."

"It wasn't that, wasn't the airports," he said, leaving it there.

"The picture," I realized. "But why would that result in your . . . What did you call it?"

"Being pinged." Chad turned his gaze back on the screen, six different views of the man I now genuinely believed had murdered Hal Wirth. "And the answer is because somebody who knows who this guy really is must've caught wind of the fact that somebody else was trying to find out."

"Can he, or she, trace it back to you, your computer?"

"No, Jessica, I'm safe there. At least, I think I am. I use the Dark Web. Tracing my intrusion would lead them there, and maybe to the general area of Cabot Cove, but not back to me. At least, I don't think so. I'm safe."

"You mean you *think* you're safe."

"Reasonably."

"Reasonably, Chad?"

He shrugged his narrow shoulders. "This has never happened to me before, so it's hard to know for certain."

I didn't want to look at the screen, at the man. "But what would have alerted someone to what you were doing? Why would they have noticed you running our man through facial-recognition software?"

"I have no idea. Could be somebody's protecting him or maybe it's his file and identity that are protected, as in classified, or flagged, at some governmental level."

I took a deep breath and settled back in my chair. "Can you erase all evidence of what you found and how you found it?"

"If I wanted to."

I leaned forward and clamped a hand on his shoulder. "You want to, Chad. You most certainly want to."

"I'd need to dump the entire hard drive to be sure."

"Then do it. Or leave the laptop here."

"So if whoever did the pinging manages to trace its location . . ."

"This is my fault. I'm the one who put you up to this."

"I can't let anything happen to you, Jessica."

"Just as I can't let anything happen to you."

"I wanted to help, and I want to keep on helping." Chad eased the laptop closed. "It was worth it. If it gets you closer to whoever killed Alyssa's father, it was worth it."

Chapter Twenty-one

I can't remember another time when I felt more un-settled. My heart was in my mouth as I watched Chad back out of the driveway, half-expecting an armada of big black SUVs to close in on him as he pulled away. But he edged up the street, picked up speed, and was gone.

I realized I'd been holding my breath and quickly inhaled. Then I closed the door, locked it again, and paced the living room while I tried to plan my next move. I'd been overlooking the fact that nothing of substance had been found in the murdered Eugene Labine's hotel room. Nothing besides clothes and toiletries. Not a briefcase, a satchel full of papers, nothing containing any documents at all. Labine had come to Cabot Cove for the express purpose of confronting Hal Wirth with his financial malfeasance. It stood to reason, then, that Labine would've brought proof in the form of documents to make his point.

But there was nothing.

What had I stumbled onto? What had *Hal* stumbled onto?

I tried to settle my thoughts, compartmentalize them to make sense of everything. But my mind was racing too fast, the disparate pieces of the puzzle hanging before me like cobwebs.

Hal registers on a dating service site, his entire profile made to disappear after a single date.

Not long after that date takes place, he opens several lines of credit totaling more than ten million dollars, which has remained unaccounted for.

He hides all that from Babs and his former business partner and is murdered at his annual Labor Day party.

Then his business partner shows up in town and gets murdered, too, albeit in far less subtle fashion. A bullet to the head instead of a syringe jabbed . . . somewhere.

Whom might Hal have owed money to? What had he gotten himself involved in that led to his murder and what did it have to do with LOVEISYOURS?

That was as close as I could come to assembling the pieces, because I was still missing too many of them. But Chad had served up my next step on a silver platter, I thought, walking back into the kitchen, where he'd left the piece of paper listing the time and date stamps of all the cities in which Porcelain Man, as I'd come to think of Hal's potential murderer, had shown up in the past eleven months.

My phone rested next to it. I checked the screen

and saw I'd missed a call from Mort while I'd been pacing the living room. Since he hadn't bothered to leave a message, he must not have anything new to tell me. It was I who had something new to tell him.

But I wasn't ready yet.

There was something else I needed to check first.

Cabot Cove's library was located on the other side of town from my house, not far from the Hill House, where Eugene Labine had been murdered. As the last of the day's light burned from the sky, I wheeled the old bicycle I'd put out with the trash a thousand times but never got rid of, because of the memories it carried. It's the one I used for bike rides with Frank, and though I'd discarded his bike long ago, I'd hung on to mine. A good thing, since I'd need it while my newer one was being repaired.

The bike was wobbly, the tires low on air, conspiring to make the ride to the Cabot Cove Library miserable in all respects, even before rain dotted the air with the promise of a late summer storm. I reached the library just as the skies opened up, ushering in a premature night.

I'd been a supporter of the library and member of the Friends group ever since I came to Cabot Cove. It's a quaint old one-story building, surprisingly spacious for a town of our size and crammed with books from floor to ceiling, and in every nook and cranny where more could be squeezed. This in spite of the fact that at any given time a third of the entire inventory was checked out. Our librarian, Doris Ann, hated parting with any book, no matter the space requirements; she grew attached to them as if they were all her own children.

I parked my bike beneath the overhang set directly before the entrance and leaned it up against the railing. I had forgotten to bring along a chain, which made me reflect fondly on the time when nobody in Cabot Cove would even think of using one, or of locking the front door at night, for that matter. All that has changed now, what with the influx of new people and development. Used to be you could walk along Main Street and know everyone you passed by name—or at least three out of every four. Now that ratio seems to have reversed amid demographic changes and an aging populace's inability to afford the cost of living here. When I'm pedaling about our pristine village, there are days where it seems to have barely changed at all, and other days where I can barely recognize it. I neither bemoan nor lament the change, given that there's nothing I can do about the likes of Deacon Westhausen altering the town's nature, as well as its footprint.

But I could do something about making sure Hal Wirth's killer was brought to justice.

Given the hour, and the old bike's weathered condition, I wasn't worried about leaving it unchained no matter how much Cabot Cove had changed. Doris Ann smiled at my approach from her lonely perch at the checkout desk.

"Research for your next bestseller, Jessica?" she posed.

"I guess you could say that," I said, forcing a smile. I'd relied on the library for all my Web-based research for years, after stubbornly resisting switching from a typewriter to a computer. I'd been unwilling to give up the familiar and comforting clack of the type-writer keys hitting paper, and when I finally climbed out of the Stone Age, I wondered why I hadn't done it sooner. That said, force of habit left me doing the bulk of my Web-based research on the library's computers to this day. And it also gave me an excuse to get out of the house and clear my head.

Amazing how much the space and the machines had evolved over the years. The computer area had once been a ratty old closet. Now the cubicled stations filled the library's periodicals room. My Friends of the Library group had endowed the building fund with a special stipend to purchase new machines at regular intervals so as to never be caught behind the times, once a familiar refrain here in Cabot Cove until our tiny town became trendy and fashionable. "A Hamp-tons of the North," Evelyn Phillips had recently pro-claimed in the *Gazette*, a headline that made me cringe, loathing even the suggestion of such a thing, given what I knew about those fabled Hamptons. It was hard to stomach the thought of turning the town's identity over to the likes of Deacon Westhausen.

As expected, at this hour, and with the weather, I was the only one about in the periodicals room, as well as in the library itself. I sat down in the middle of three computers on the long table divided into cu-bicles, glad to see the machine was already on, saving me the bother of booting it up. I removed the sheet of paper Chad had printed out for me that contained the times and dates of all the cities where Porcelain Man had landed, in addition to Boston's Logan Airport.

I had a plan as to how I was going to proceed, but my expectations that it might actually yield anything of promise were low. My thinking, thanks to that overactive imagination of mine, was wildly specula-tive, but this was where the trail had brought me and I intended to follow it for as long and as far as I could. I figured I'd waste a few hours and would ultimately come up empty.

I couldn't have been more wrong.

I started with Denver, making careful scrutiny of the obituary pages for the week following Porcelain Man's visit. The fact that Chad had managed to find him present in at least these six other cities in approxi-mately a one-year time frame suggested the possibil-ity of a pattern that could fit with Hal Wirth's murder. It was a long shot, especially given we still had no actionable evidence that Porcelain Man had killed Hal in the first place. The fact that he hadn't worked for the Boston-based temp agency Cabot Cove Catering employed, coupled with his happening to be in the kitchen right around the time of Hal's apparent heart attack, even pocketing what appeared to be a syringe, didn't amount to very much from an evidentiary standpoint. Even though he had been identified on the grounds of Hill House the night of Eugene Labine's murder, and that further strengthened his status as a suspect, there was still no firm proof.

The *Denver Post* was one of the numerous papers

that Doris Ann subscribed to, and its online obituary listings were voluminous. As I began perusing the listings, I made a mental check-off list of what I was looking for, based on Hal's profile: successful, middle-aged men who'd died suddenly of a heart attack. I pulled a pen and pad from my bag and rested them on the table next to me on the other side of the computer mouse and added a few more items:

RECENT FINANCIAL SCANDAL OR ISSUES
DIVORCED OR WIDOWED
DATING SERVICE?
STRICKEN IN A PUBLIC PLACE

Sure enough, on the third day following Porcelain Man's arrival in the Denver area, a fifty-three-year-old successful real estate entrepreneur died unexpectedly while attending a retirement party for a friend. He'd collapsed after reportedly feeling ill.

There were four other possibilities reported in the *Denver Post* obituary listings, but the real estate entrepreneur checked the most boxes, and I decided to Google him to see what I could find before proceeding on to the next city. And—wouldn't you know it?—a headline immediately caught my eye:

REAL ESTATE SCION ACCUSED OF FRAUD

Details in the article were sketchy, but bore a remarkable resemblance to Hal's financial plight. Specifically that the man had leveraged virtually his entire fortune to borrow millions of dollars that were unaccounted for at the time of his death.

Just like Hal.

The money, by all accounts, had disappeared without a trace.

Again, just like Hal.

I jotted down the man's name and a few notes, then hit Print to make a copy of the article so I could show it to Mort to prove whatever case I was trying to make.

I moved on to Houston, the *Houston Chronicle* specifically, and found on its obit pages a name that jumped out at me because of the boxes it checked. A recently divorced lawyer had suffered a heart attack while attending a Houston Rockets basketball game. I Googled his name as well and clicked through to an article in the same newspaper, featuring the headline LAWYER ARRESTED ON CLIENT CHARGES HE BILKED THEM OUT OF MILLIONS.

I couldn't help but lean forward to read the rest of the article, the bright screen seeming to flutter as I got close. The lawyer had died the day after Porcelain Man had been recorded by a security camera arriving at Houston's Hobby Airport.

So right now I was two for two, when I had initially expected to come away empty-handed. For all I knew, that was still the case. Maybe if I studied the obituary section of any daily big-city paper, I'd find someone recently deceased who fit Hal's pattern perfectly, but who'd died without any nefarious means involved. Then again, it was getting to the point where the emerging pattern couldn't be so easily dismissed.

Miami was next on my list, where the profile that best fit the pattern belonged to a woman. I hadn't been expecting that. But there it was, a victim who checked each and every one of my boxes, with the one glaring distinction that it was a she.

Shelby Lynn Dietrich was actually a single woman who, the obituary made a point of saying, "died suddenly and unexpectedly." It said nothing about a heart attack, but said plenty about her entrepreneurial successes and her obsession with feats like climbing the tallest mountains in the world and sailing the globe.

Not what you'd expect from someone stricken so suddenly and unexpectedly.

I imagine suicide might've been suspected by some, since, according to the *Miami Herald*, Shelby Lynn Dietrich had recently been arrested on charges of wire fraud and misappropriation of funds from a successful start-up she'd launched eighteen months before her death. In the article she wholeheartedly proclaimed her innocence and insisted she'd be exonerated.

I looked at the phrase "misappropriation of funds" again and thought of Eugene Labine, Hal Wirth's murdered former business partner, uncovering the fact that Hal had squandered a vast fortune in a remarkably fast period of time.

Listening to the printer purr to life after receiving another article to spit out, I was convinced that I'd indeed locked onto an inexplicable pattern of potential murders and that Hal Wirth perfectly fit the mold. What I'd been intimating to myself and others had now been lifted from the shadows of pure speculation into the light of likelihood. I needed to share this with Mort. I needed to find out what else these other victims had in common with Hal. Might they have registered on the LOVEISYOURS matching site, too? Could this all be as simple as that?

A difficult question to answer, given that their profiles had likely been wiped off the site, just as Hal's had been.

I rose, moved to the printer stand set against the wall, and had just retrieved the three printouts when all the lights in the library died.

Chapter Twenty-two

My first thought was Doris Ann had forgotten I was still in the library and had turned the lights off without alerting me. But my watch read only eight forty-five, still fifteen minutes until closing.

"Doris Ann?" I called out. "Doris Ann."

I could hear my voice echoing through the cluttered stacks of books.

"Doris Ann!" I called louder when no response followed.

I couldn't help but think of the brilliant *Twilight Zone* episode called "Time Enough at Last," which starred Burgess Meredith in the role of a timid bank clerk who loves only to read. He has his ultimate wish fulfilled when the end of the world finds him aglow over the possibility of reading unencumbered for the rest of his life . . . until he breaks his glasses.

No power outage had triggered the emergency

lighting, meaning the lights had been manually turned off. The sole illumination came from what little light could sneak through the windows.

I heard a soft clack, as if someone pawing through the library's darkness had accidentally kicked something. I shuffled back to the table, lifted my bag from the floor to my chair. Then I fished my phone from my bag and hit 911. I buried it back deep inside my bag without waiting for my call to be answered, not wanting to speak even in a whisper to further advertise my presence. Then I switched the monitor off, plunging the periodicals room into almost complete darkness, and pressed my shoulders against the far wall.

A slight scraping sound, like shoes dragging over the library's original wood floor, found me, growing louder as it neared the periodicals room, set farthest back in the building. The three crank windows that looked out over a small garden were vertically aligned, much too narrow to squeeze through even for someone as slight as me. That left . . .

Left *what*?

In my books, when my characters got boxed into corners, they always found something to make use of, forging weapons from ordinary objects. With my heart pounding and no sirens screaming this way yet, I quickly catalogued what I recalled of the room in intricate detail.

Clack.

Whoever was coming had struck another obstacle, not nearly as familiar with these surroundings as I was. I'd often joked that I knew this place so well that I could walk about the stacks blind, a claim that was now being sorely tested. I longed for the days when heavy ashtrays abounded in places like this, making for the perfect weapon.

Thud.

Louder this time, the intruder almost to the entrance to the periodicals room. I glanced at the doorway as I backed up toward the magazine stacks, no shape or movement yet breaking the plane of my vision. I raised my hand to grab the end of the stacks for support, brushing against one of the sleeve bookends I'd personally donated, having amassed too many of them for my own book collection.

A realization struck me and I eased one of them free, and then another. Each weighed a pound at least. I recognized these to be the brass lion set that had once resided in my office. I took one of the lions in my right hand and the other in my left, concealed in the darkness of the stacks when a glint of motion flashed in the doorway.

With no time to aim, I threw one of the lions and then the other. I heard a loud thud, as one of them struck a wall, but the second drew an *uggghhhhhh*, followed by an audible gasp.

I lurched out from the stacks without waiting to ascertain the level of damage the strike had done. I moved swiftly and as quietly as I could, glad riding a bike kept me in sneakers as opposed to more formal shoes that would've rendered movement like this impossible. I felt a hand grab for my shoulder, grazing it and coming away with the light sweater I relinquished to make a mad dash for the library's main door.

All I remember was the sound of my sneakers

against the wood, no echo when it seemed there should be. Then that sound was buried by the louder thumping of feet pounding my way, drawing closer.

I had no choice but to bypass the door for the main stacks of books in the library's single large reading room, angling for one of two emergency exits, their red signs glowing in the near total darkness. Our library's stacks were a labyrinth of warrens and aisles, battling for space with the nooks and crannies where books waited on wheeled carts to be reshelved.

I couldn't hear the steps at my rear anymore as I wove my way amid the stacks, the scent of the pages and glued bindings heavy in my nostrils. But I could hear the sound of a siren, distant but growing louder by the moment, evidence that the Cabot Cove Sheriff's Department had managed to trace the origins of my 911 call.

Still slicing an irregular path through the stacks, I let myself hope the intruder had heard the siren, too, and might even have fled. But I soon realized that he'd anticipated my move and was positioned to intercept me when I essentially stormed right into him.

I backpedaled and grazed one of the wheeled, book-laden carts. I ground my feet to a halt, squeaking against the hard wood. I couldn't see the intruder coming at me through the darkness, but I knew he was, all the same.

I worked myself in behind the cart and shoved it into motion, gathering as much speed as I could manage as I was swept into the utter blackness. A dizzying impact rattled my bones and jammed the cart painfully against my pelvis. I heard a loud gasp and a *whooooooshhhhh* of air that could only have meant I'd hit my target.

But I kept the cart going, books flying everywhere, until the wheels caught on something and sent it toppling over, scattering the rest of the books in all directions. They partially blocked my way and I tried to surge past them, convinced the wheels had caught on the intruder's frame after he'd gone down. The siren was really screaming and I detected the faint glow of revolving lights through a window overlooking the library's front.

I could practically reach out and touch them, almost safe when I felt a hand with an iron grip clutch at my ankle, tightening like a vise. I tried to kick free and then grabbed hold of an end of metal shelving for leverage. That section teetered ever so slightly and instinct almost made me release my grip, until judgment won the day.

As a second hand joined the first trying to yank me downward, I grabbed hold of the shelving with both hands, and pulled with all my strength. It rocked, but didn't fall, so I pulled harder.

And harder.

Then harder still, as I felt my leg starting to slide and give, the rest of me soon to succumb to my assailant's violent tugging, when the shelf finally began to topple over. Books sprayed everywhere, a few volumes striking my cheeks, nose, and head. But they must've distracted my assailant enough for me to pull free of his grasp and lurch away just before the entire shelf came tumbling down.

I caught a fleeting glimpse of a shiny, bald pate before I looped around the refuse and angled for the main entrance, heaving for breath, my path lit dimly by the revolving lights now spilling through all the nearest windows, like landing lights illuminating a runway. I reached the door to the sound of my own panicked wheezing and threw it open.

To the sight of Mort Metzger and one of his deputies.

Chapter Twenty-three

I recognized Deputy Andy before I registered the gun in his hand. I saw it from Mort's arms, into which I'd collapsed.

"He's inside!" I managed to rasp. "He's inside!"

Deputy Andy charged into the library, pistol in one hand and flashlight in the other. The beam carved up the darkness, turned every chair and floor plant into monstrous shadows cast against the walls.

I realized in that moment I'd just thrown the door open, meaning it hadn't been locked, meaning . . .

Doris Ann!

I pulled from Mort's grasp and scurried back inside, hearing him yell, "Hey!" after me. He rushed inside in my wake, his flashlight beam illuminating me as I ran to look behind the circulation and check-out desk. The beam reflected off Doris Ann's glasses, which rested on the floor alongside her downed form.

She looked pale, seemed to be breathing fitfully, but was, thankfully, alive.

"Call an ambulance!" I cried out.

I heard the approach of a fresh siren in the next instant.

"I wasn't born yesterday, you know," Mort said. "It pays to play it safe."

"You thought I was hurt."

"We get a nine-one-one call from your number at this location with no further information. What did you expect me to think?"

Deputy Andy approached from the area where I'd spilled a section of shelving atop my assailant, his flashlight beam seeming to duel Mort's in the darkness.

"Nothing," the deputy reported, holstering his pistol. "He's gone. Emergency exit door is still open."

Mort addressed me as he moved to tend to Doris Ann. "Did you recognize him, Jessica?"

I shook my head. "Not in the darkness. He was big, though. And bald. I remember he was bald."

"The man pictured at the Wirths' barbecue had a full head of hair." He eased Doris Ann up to a seated position, leaned her gently back against some drawers so she could breathe better. "But Ansell Hodges is bald."

"This wasn't Ansell Hodges," I insisted, referring to a local homeless veteran Cabot Cove did its best to take care of.

"He might have snuck into the library to avoid the storm that's coming."

"And attacked Doris Ann? Then me?"

"Thunder does that to him, thanks to all the post-traumatic stress he suffers from. I've let him sleep in one of our cells a few times when a storm blows in."

"It wasn't Ansell Hodges," I repeated.

"You said you didn't get a good look at him."

"Maybe not good enough to see who it was, but plenty good enough to see who it wasn't."

Mort didn't look convinced, as he continued checking Doris Ann's vital signs. His flashlight illuminated a nasty bruise to the side of her throat.

"Someone must've squeezed off her air," he surmised.

"Sound like Ansell Hodges to you?"

"The man was a Green Beret or something, Jessica," Mort said, climbing back to his feet to greet the just-arriving Cabot Cove rescue squad. "You tell me."

"I think it was the same man who tried to run me over, Mort."

"You said you didn't get a good look at him either."

"It's the same man. I'd bet anything on it."

Mort held the door for the paramedics, who wheeled a gurney past him toward Doris Ann. "You want to tell me what brought you here?" His gaze through the open door found the old bike I'd pedaled over on. "On that old thing, with a storm in the forecast? You want to tell me what was so important?"

"Research."

"For a book?"

"Not exactly."

"What's that mean?"

I swallowed hard. "I was following a new lead about Hal's death."

"Without telling me?"

"There was nothing to tell. That's why I was here, to find something."

"And did you?"

"I'm not . . . sure."

"Not sure you found something or not sure you were going to tell me about it?"

My mouth was bone-dry, but I wasn't thirsty. I wasn't anything but scared and realized I was still shaking.

"I think Hal Wirth was murdered, Mort."

"We both do."

"But there's a pattern."

"Pattern?"

"I think there were other victims. I think we may be onto something much bigger here."

Additional deputies arrived to search the library more thoroughly. The same crime scene techs who'd scoured Eugene Labine's room in Hill House were en route as well, to check the library for the man's fingerprints and perhaps DNA, too. I'd already alerted Mort to the presence of my bag in the periodicals room and asked him to make sure a deputy fetched the last pages spit out by the nearby printer as well.

Doris Ann, meanwhile, had regained consciousness while the paramedics were tending to her and asked them groggily what had happened. She told Mort her last memory was checking in some of the books deposited through a wall slot. Then finding herself on the floor between two able-bodied young men poking and prodding at her.

"Maybe I should pass out more often," she said, smiling at them, as the paramedics eased her atop the gurney for transport to Cabot Cove Hospital to be given the once-over.

"You don't remember anyone choking you?" Mort asked her in the last moment before the paramedics hoisted her gurney into the back of their rescue vehicle.

"Choking me? Certainly not. One minute I was checking in books and the next I was waking up on the floor."

I followed Mort to his car and climbed into the passenger seat, while he took the driver's. He switched on his windshield wipers to better view the comings and goings of his deputies. As soon as they swiped the rain away, more drops collected to obscure his vision again.

"Tell me more about this lead you were following," he said, "this pattern you think you've found."

I sketched out the broad strokes for him, leaving out any mention of Chad's involvement.

"So you were following one of your hunches."

"That's right."

"And this particular hunch just happened to lead you to these recently deceased who fit the same general profile as Hal Wirth. Notice I said 'deceased,' and not 'murdered.'"

"I noticed. And I also noticed that these potential victims were mostly recently divorced or separated. Hal and Babs were sorting through some problems, but it fits the same pattern."

"What pattern is that?"

"Vulnerability, which made them more susceptible

to not realizing they were being taking advantage of. Like Hal, they were all very successful entrepreneurs who became embroiled in financial scandals shortly before their deaths."

"Thank you for not saying 'murders,'" Mort groused, and turned the windshield wipers up another notch.

"Also like Hal, by all accounts they squandered vast sums of money in a short period of time. Went from the front of the line to financial ruin virtually overnight."

Mort eyed me skeptically. "And you just *happened* to pick these cities and time periods."

"A writer never reveals her sources."

"I thought you said this wasn't for a book."

"Perhaps I was mistaken."

Mort shook his head, his gaze scorning me. "How am I supposed to protect you if you won't tell me everything?"

"Protect me from me what? Ansell Hodges? He's mostly harmless, remember?"

"Jessica . . ."

"Mort."

He gazed toward my bag, which was lying on the squad car's passenger-seat floor between my legs, those pages his deputies had retrieved from the printer poking out from the top. "What say you let me take a run at those?"

"I say we can make copies when you get me home. There were others, Mort," I told him, thinking of the three cities Chad had provided that I hadn't had the opportunity to look into yet. "As many as six possible victims at the very least, and the man pictured outside the kitchen where Hal died was in each of the cities around the time of their deaths."

Mort's brow furrowed. "That's what you were following up on?"

"Yup."

"And you found a pattern in their deaths that fits Hal's profile, too?"

"Like a glove."

"But you're not going to tell me how you came by this information."

"Nope." I paused. "But it wasn't Ansell Hodges."

"That's not funny, Jessica."

"No more than him being the man who attacked me."

Mort started the engine. "I better get you back home. I'll have one of my guys drop off your bike in the morning."

"I'm fast running out of transportation."

"Well, you do have your pilot's license. . . ."

"Not much room for parking planes in Cabot Cove."

Mort jammed his squad car into reverse. "But plenty of room for murder."

Chapter Twenty-four

I didn't want to make copies for him of the printouts I'd made at the library, but I knew I had no choice when Mort insisted on coming inside to make sure my house was safe. I almost joked about the possibility of finding Ansell Hodges asleep in my bed, but then opted against it.

I didn't think Mort would be able to do much more with the printouts covering the stories of the victims from Denver, Houston, and Miami than I had already done. Discerning whether any of the three potential victims I'd managed to trace had had occasion to use the LOVEISYOURS dating site would be difficult at best and likely impossible, if truly nefarious ends were behind this and their profiles had been wiped completely clean, as had been the case with Hal's.

What I knew, what sentenced me to a fitful sleep that night amid the storm that finally arrived, was that someone would kill to protect whatever it was I'd uncovered, which meant I had to get him before he got me.

Mort had gotten no further with the background of Sean Booker, owner of LOVEISYOURS, of whom no record seemed to exist prior to his establishing the site. And he agreed with my supposition that Eugene Labine would never have come to Cabot Cove empty-handed, that whatever documents he'd brought with him to support his claims about Hal Wirth, his former business partner, must have been scooped up by his killer.

I tossed and turned through the night, my mind refusing to quiet, finally nodding off, only to oversleep yet again. I was roused by a determined knocking on my front door after ringing the bell must not have claimed my attention. I fetched my cell phone from the night table as I sat on the bedside and saw what looked like a dozen missed calls and texts from Babs. I climbed into my bathrobe and held fast to the railing while descending the stairs to avoid any more calamities. I threw open the door to find Babs standing there, Alyssa and Chad standing sheepishly behind her.

"What were you thinking, Jessica?" She glared at me. "Involving my daughter and her boyfriend in this."

"Why don't you come inside, Babs?"

She did so after hesitating briefly, seeming to forget Alyssa and Chad were even there until they followed her through the door, each casting me a shrug.

"Don't look at them," Babs snapped. "They haven't uttered a word, other than to say I needed to hear it from you. So, Jessica, should I be blaming them for your being attacked last night or you?"

"Me, Babs. It's all on me."

"I knew you'd say that."

"Because it's the truth. Alyssa and Chad helped me because I insisted."

"No," Alyssa broke in, "we helped because we wanted to. Because this was my father."

But Babs's attention was still rooted on me. "Why didn't you share this with me, Jessica? Why didn't you talk to me?"

"Because I wasn't sure."

"About what?"

"Hal."

"That you suspect he might have been murdered?"

"There's . . . more," I managed to utter, not feeling like going into the whole dating site business, which smacked of cheating.

Babs didn't need to hear that about her late husband. A friend would never tell her such a thing.

Alyssa positioned herself physically between us. "Chad and I volunteered our help, Mom."

"And your help almost got as good a friend as I've got in the world killed. I'm not fragile. I don't break so easy. I could've handled whatever you have to say."

I found my voice again. "This is about Hal, Babs. This is about finding out what brought Eugene Labine to Cabot Cove," I continued, "and what led to both of them being killed."

"And you don't trust the professionals to do that?"

"Mort's been working with me every step of the way."

"You're a writer, Jessica, not a real detective. If you want to keep playing one on the side, dabbling in these real-life mysteries you keep stumbling upon, go right ahead—so long as they don't put my family in danger."

"Your family's already in danger, Babs. What they did to Hal," I went on, trying not to say too much, "maybe I can fix it. Maybe I can help."

I guess I had said too much, because Alyssa's reaction was to get face-to-face with her mother, no longer the little girl in a young woman's body. "The house, the bills, my *school*—what are we supposed to do?"

"I don't think your father lost all his money, Alyssa," I said when Babs was stymied for an answer. "I think it was stolen somehow. I think maybe somebody was threatening him, or the two of you. I think he paid them everything he had to make them go away. Because he was scared."

"And now I'm scared."

"We're all scared."

I could see Alyssa's features tighten. "You could've been killed last night."

"But I wasn't. I'm still here and I'm not going anywhere, not until I get to the bottom of this."

"No," Babs said, storming toward me. "Leave it to the professionals this time. We'll wait this out. We'll go away for a while."

"With what, Mom?" Alyssa shot at her. "We're broke, remember?"

Babs lapsed into silence. I could feel how much Alyssa's remark had stung her, just as I could feel the air leave the room. Chad seemed to be edging back toward the door, as if to make a break for it, given his clear discomfort. But I was struck by something else entirely:

Determination.

Someone had turned the lives of my friends upside down—had murdered a husband and father and drained all the resources his family was now counting on. Depending on how deep the problems went, I had no idea how Babs was even going to pay for the funeral expenses, and I wasn't about to sting her pride by offering to pay them myself or loan her whatever she needed. Because there was something else I could do that was far more fitting and relevant:

Find who was behind the crime.

"I need a few minutes alone with Chad," I said, breaking the silence in the room. "If the two of you don't mind."

"I do mind, Jessica," Babs protested. "I very much mind. No more going behind people's backs, no more sneaking around—we've had quite enough of that. And if you're so sure about where this is headed, call Mort, or the FBI. Tell them what you know and let them handle it."

"Mort knows everything I know, but not how I know it, Babs. That's a risk I'm willing to take. It's a risk *Chad* has made plain he's willing to take. But it's not a risk I can let you or Alyssa take, not under any circumstances."

Babs looked visibly shocked by the forceful nature of my comments. She'd never heard me speak that way before, because, truth be told, I never did. I can't even remember the last time such firmness had crept into the tone of my voice. But I knew she understood it was due to how much I cared and how much I wanted to make this right.

And make whoever was behind it pay.

I'd gotten myself involved in any number of real-life mysteries over the years, but never one of this scope and, apparently, conspiratorial nature, stretching from coast to coast and potentially including such a cross section of victims. Almost like some crazed, high-tech serial killer had used LOVEISYOURS, or comparable dating sites, to make a date with murder.

That stopped now, I thought, my resolve rooted in the conviction to make Hal Wirth his, or their, last victim, while making Hal's wife and daughter whole again.

I hugged Babs tight. She stiffened, but then slowly relaxed and hugged me back just as tight, until I eased away.

"You need to trust me, Babs."

She tried to take a deep breath, but it caught in her throat. "I know you're doing this for me."

"And Alyssa," I told her. "And Hal, too."

"What now?" Chad asked, the two of us alone after I closed the door behind Babs and Alyssa.

I fished the printouts from my bag, where I'd left them overnight, and sat down next to Chad on the couch. "We need to determine if the profiles of these three people were ever included on the LOVEISYOURS site. The circumstances of their deaths otherwise match Hal Wirth's to a T."

Chad shuffled through the printouts, shaking his

head in disbelief at their contents. "All this from those airport security photos I isolated for you?"

I shrugged. "I had a hunch."

"Of course, if you're right, then we can assume the profiles of these three victims were wiped clean off the site's server, just like Mr. Wirth's was."

"Yes, but—"

"Relax, Jessica," he interrupted, flashing that trademark smirk I now found strangely reassuring. "I got it covered."

"Another way in?"

The smirk remained. "Something like that."

My cell phone rang as Babs pulled out of my driveway with Chad and Alyssa as her passengers.

"Why don't you ever call me on my landline, Mort?" I greeted.

"Because I always figure you'll be out fighting crime somewhere. You know, doing my job for me."

"Are you calling to criticize me?"

"No, to see if you want to take a ride."

"Where?"

"Boston. The FBI has Sean Booker in custody."

I felt something shift in my stomach. "Is he talking?"

"No."

"Then why are we—"

"Because he says he'll only talk to you."

Chapter Twenty-five

Sean Booker was being interviewed, again without success, by a trio of assistant United States attorneys when we arrived at the Moakley United States Courthouse. The official address, located amid a constant construction zone, was 1 Courthouse Way. I couldn't recall the actual street off which the building was tucked, only that the sprawling, modern, seven-story structure backed up almost square against Boston Harbor, making it likely one of the few waterfront courthouses in the nation.

Mort had plenty of friends in the FBI and the Justice Department from the earlier days of his career, before he was appointed sheriff of Cabot Cove in what he'd probably intended to be a soft retirement. That is, before he realized I lived there. He had already alerted those friends in federal law enforcement of our interest in Sean Booker, and it was they who'd determined that the man's life on paper went back only a few years. Apparently, he had lawyered up and wasn't saying a word about his actual identity, or what had led him to concoct his current persona around the time he founded LOVEISYOURS five years earlier. He was being held in an interrogation room on the seventh floor, where he'd remain until the authorities settled upon exactly what to charge him with.

Mort and I went through the airportlike security. I had to check my cell phone with the deputy at the reception desk before proceeding to the elevator and riding it to the seventh floor, but Mort was allowed to keep his.

"Are his lawyers with him?" I asked the FBI agent who was Mort's friend, after pleasantries were exchanged.

"They're already writing and filing motions," the man said, a sour expression spreading across his face.

"So he's alone." I was going to add the man's name, try to establish a bond between us, but I couldn't remember what it was for the life of me.

"And not saying a word, on advice of counsel. I think asking for you was a ruse, a stall tactic. Sorry you wasted a trip, Mrs. Fletcher. For what it's worth, my wife loves your books."

I get that a lot, I almost said, aware my audience was dominated by women.

"Well, then I suppose there's no harm in honoring his request to see me."

The man—Castner or something, I now remembered—looked toward Mort.

"Welcome to my world," Mort said, making himself look equally sour.

"Does she know how unusual this is?" Castner or something said, addressing his remarks toward Mort.

"Oh, she knows, all right," Mort told him.

The agent nodded. "I'm still waiting for clearance on this."

"From whom?" I asked him.

"It's such a rare occurrence, I really don't know."

"Here's something Mort and I know, Agent. This isn't about a single murder anymore."

Mort shot me a glare, about to speak when Castner or something beat him to it.

"No?"

The same resolve I'd felt with Babs and Alyssa rose again. "I believe I've uncovered a pattern suggesting Hal Wirth is one of what could be many, many victims in cases that fit the same profile," I said.

"I'm still listening, Mrs. Fletcher."

"But I'm not talking, not without you giving me something in return."

Castner or something started to smile, then stopped, ended up shaking his head instead. "You do know I'm a federal agent?" Then, to Mort, "She does know I'm a federal agent, right?"

"Oh, she knows."

"I want you to honor Sean Booker's request to talk to me."

Castner or something looked toward Mort again. "Should I trust her?"

"Oh, you should trust her."

* * *

"Booker's real name is Larry Dax," Castner or something said before letting me into the interview room. "Committed a number of low-level computer crimes out of Washington State that would have stayed off our radar if he hadn't gotten greedy and come up with a bank fraud scheme. We nailed him for mail fraud and about sixteen other counts, but he skipped bail before the trial. After we located Sean Booker, thanks to Mort, we ran his fingerprints and lo and behold."

"Larry Dax."

"The kind of guy who'd scam you in three-card monte before the Internet age. Between cyberspace in general, and the Dark Web in particular, we're dealing with more outlaws than ever roamed the Old West. We've started throwing the book at these bastards, no more going gentle, to make examples out of as many as we can. Larry Dax is looking at considerable time behind bars, and nothing he tells you is going to change that. So I'm wondering why he's bothering to make the effort."

"I'm sure he has his reasons."

Larry Dax looked significantly smaller and less important than Sean Booker had behind his big desk when I'd seen him just a few days before. His shoulders were hunched and his expression carried the stiff resignation and plaintiveness of a man who knows he's got no cards left in his deck.

"Nice to see you again, Larry," I said, closing the door behind me. "I wanted to speak to you, too."

Dax kept looking, as if certain someone else was going to be following me through. "You're alone?"

"Just you and me," I said, taking the chair across from him.

"Seems strange."

"Murder always is."

His eyelids fluttered. "I didn't kill anyone. Not my style or Sean Booker's."

"That's not what they're accusing you of."

"They might add it to the charges if you turn out to be right."

"I'm right. I'm more convinced of that than ever. Someone tried to kill me last night."

Larry Dax, aka Sean Booker, chuckled humorlessly. "Well, at least you can't blame me for that. I've got an alibi."

"Too bad you got caught. You had a good thing going with LOVEISYOURS."

"Guess I can thank you and that sheriff for ruining it for me."

"You could be charged as an accessory in as many as four murders and probably plenty more. That has to be the reason you wanted to see me, although I can't for the life of me figure out why."

Dax's flat, cold stare turned desperate and pleading, just for a moment. "Because I think you might be the only person who can get me off."

"Me?"

He nodded. "It's what you do."

"I'm a writer."

"And real murders keep finding you. I read all

about you after you and that sheriff paid me a visit. It's like you're a magnet for murder."

"Can I use that as a title?"

"You think this is funny?"

"A friend of mine was the most recent of the victims somehow involving your dating site. What do you think?"

Dax shifted in his seat, a man starting to come to grips with the fact he was about to lose his freedom for a long time. "I already told you. You might be the only person who can help me."

I decided to get to the point. "Was it Denver, Houston, Miami?"

"Was *what* Denver, Houston, or Miami?"

"Three of the other victims who used the LOVEISYOURS site came from those cities," I embellished, hoping my expression didn't give me away. Writers are great liars on the page, not so much in person. "I'm guessing someone else got wise to what had happened, someone who would've led us straight back to you."

"It's not like that at all."

"Then what is it like, Larry?"

"Just after you and the sheriff came to see me, the site went down."

"LOVEISYOURS?"

He nodded. "I don't mean a glitch, a hack, or an overload. I mean down and done, as in every scrap of data lost. We couldn't even refund our clients' money if we wanted to, because we don't know who they are. Don't you get it?"

"Somebody got spooked."

"By you, by your poking around. So they shut me down to avoid leaving a trail for the great Jessica Fletcher to follow. That's why I asked the Feds to call your sheriff. Because if you follow that trail, you'll be able to prove to them that I had nothing to do with these murders."

"You're still going away."

"Five years in a federal pen with walk-around privileges?" Dax moved his head from side to side, as if to consider the prospects. "I can live with that. Life without parole is something else."

"So you need my help."

"That's why you're here."

"Then you're going to need to help me."

Dax looked down at the table for a long moment, then back up at me. "Just tell me how."

"How does your site actually work?"

"What do you mean?"

"The matching. How's it happen?"

"Algorithms."

"Algorithms?"

Dax nodded. "Micro-bits of random data assembled into a cyber profile. Our software extrapolates out the best fit possible by finding two people whose algorithms come closest to a match."

"How?"

"What you're going to do next is predictable based on what you've already done. Can you explain compatibility, Mrs. Fletcher, what it is exactly that makes two people the perfect fit for each other?"

I thought of my late husband, Frank, how we'd both

been struck by what could only be called love at first sight. I'd never bothered to look deeper than that.

"No, Larry, I can't. I don't think anyone can."

"And that's where computers come in, because they *can*. They put the pieces of who we really are together in search of placing us with someone who best fits those pieces. That's the definition of compatibility. And LOVEISYOURS has taken that a whole bunch of steps further. Our software, through our app, tracks you. It knows where you go, what television shows you watch, what you order for lunch, your favorite muffin, how fast you drive. It's constantly updating itself on a quantum level, following every move those registered on our site make, in search of someone making similar moves. It's not just a simple questionnaire anymore. Give us ten answers and thirty-nine ninety-five a month and we'll give you love. The strange thing is that the algorithms we use today really do work, and they're remarkably good at achieving compatible matches."

I tried to get my hands around what I was hearing, the utter intrusiveness of it all, how much people were willing to sacrifice in search of love.

"Isn't that illegal?" I asked Dax.

"It would be, if our clients didn't pay us to do it. The software isn't looking for an exact match—that would be like dating yourself. Instead, it looks for the *right* match, like the pieces of a jigsaw puzzle. Our goal is to fit two people together the same way you try to find the pieces of a puzzle that mesh. We find round pegs for round holes and square ones for the square holes." Dax stopped, then started again almost immediately. "Is this helping at all?"

"I think it does," I told him, starting to put something together for myself. "Quite a bit, maybe."

Dax's expression turned pleading once more. "You need to prove I had nothing to do with that man's murder. Or any of these others."

"It's not easy to prove a negative, Larry."

"I'll give you whatever you need."

"Which isn't much, given that somebody wiped your slate clean."

Dax leaned closer to me, lowering his voice. "What if they left a trail?"

"A trail?"

"A *cyber* trail, plain as bread crumbs."

"Are you working with them, Larry?"

"No, I already told you that. No!"

"But you know who they are?"

Dax looked like he wanted to nod but didn't. "I've got an idea, an inkling."

"How?"

I could see from the tightening of his expression that he'd said as much as he intended to.

"This trail you mentioned," I said, instead of waiting for him, "I'm supposed to follow it?"

He stretched his hands across the table and I noticed a glimmer of white protruding beneath one of them, his palm hiding a small scrap of paper that might have been a Kleenex. As casually as I could, I stretched my own hand out and captured it beneath my palm.

"And see where it leads," said Larry Dax.

Chapter Twenty-six

I didn't even glance at what was written on the scrap of paper until I was back in the front seat of Mort's department-issued SUV emblazoned with CABOT COVE SHERIFF'S DEPARTMENT in white letters across blue paint.

"He really thinks you can get him off?" Mort quizzed me, as I unfolded the tattered piece of paper on my lap to keep its contents from Mort.

"He thinks if I get to the bottom of this, he'll be exonerated."

"He's a con man. He's using you."

"I don't think so," I said.

I looked down as unobtrusively as I could at the scrap perched on my lap. It contained a series of numbers and letters that made no sense at all to me.

Hmmmmmmm . . .

I assumed *ME* referred to Dax, or Sean Booker, himself. Given the presence of the *Y*, 2006 seemed to indicate a year.

So Larry Dax had done something in 2006 that somehow held clues to what I was facing today and who was behind it.

Hmmmmmmm . . .

"What's that?" Mort asked suddenly.

"What's what?"

"Whatever it is you're reading."

"Just a note I made to myself," I said, pocketing the crumpled husk of paper I realized was a piece of commercial toilet tissue doubled over, as if Dax had written this note inside a bathroom. I knew if I told Mort the truth, he'd make us head back into the federal building, turn the note over to the investigators, and tell them everything Dax had told me. But I couldn't let that happen, couldn't let their investigation hamper my search for the truth behind Hal Wirth's murder. They'd laugh me out of the office if I told them everything I knew—that is, if they didn't arrest me instead, which meant I'd also be endangering Chad.

"Something that explains why Dax thinks you're the only person who can help him? What exactly did he tell you?"

"I think you were right. He didn't say much of anything really, other than to proclaim his innocence. But he's scared, Mort. He told me somebody wiped the LOVEISYOURS server clean. I think he sees himself as a target."

Mort shook his head. "When was it exactly that you became a magnet for this kind of thing?"

"I honestly can't remember. But also I don't remember somebody trying to kill me twice either. So maybe Dax has a point."

"And maybe he really is in danger. Is that what you're suggesting?"

"More like desperate."

"Jessica Fletcher," Mort said melodramatically. "Patron saint of lost souls."

"I believe that's already Saint Anthony's job."

"Well, you're giving him a run for his money. And speaking of money, how exactly do you expect any of this to help get Babs's back?"

"I haven't thought that far ahead yet."

"I should say not." Mort took a deep breath and squeezed the steering wheel harder. "You don't outline your books in advance, right?"

"You know I don't."

"Why?"

"You know that, too, Mort."

"Refresh my memory."

"Because I know the story will take me where it needs to go."

He nodded, as if I'd made his point for him. "Well, here's the thing, Jessica, and I'm sorry to be the bearer of bad news. But life doesn't always work that way. There are plenty of detours along the route and sometimes things just don't work out."

"You think you need to tell me that?"

"Apparently, I do," Mort said, his tone remaining

firm. "I've seen you use that magical mind of yours to solve plenty of real-life crimes, murder included, but this is different."

"How?"

"You've never let it get to you this way before. You've never taken it so personally."

I wanted to argue the point with him, but I couldn't. I'd been involved in other cases that hit home. When my friend Martha was accused of killing her husband in Las Vegas, and I flew out to her aid, for example. Or when another friend's death in her beloved retirement community turned out to be murder. Or when the foster son of my friends the Duffs, out in Arizona, was accused of killing a teammate on his minor-league baseball team. I've even helped my own charming but ne'er-do-well nephew, Grady, out of countless scrapes, including one in New York when he was making television commercials featuring celebrities. But Mort was right:

This *was* different.

It wasn't so much about solving Hal's murder as it was doing whatever I could to make sure Babs could keep her beloved home and Alyssa wouldn't have to drop out of college. The fact that the basis of my resolve, that I could somehow recover Hal's stolen fortune, was hardly rooted in reality swayed me not one little bit; after all, the number of victims swindled out of their money who ever get a dollar of it back can best be described as zero.

"Do I have to remind you why, Mort?" I asked him anyway, because if I wasn't going to help Babs and Alyssa, then who was?

"No more than I have to remind you that someone tried to run you down on your bicycle and then attacked you in the library. And it wasn't an unhappy member of the Friends group."

"It wasn't Ansell Hodges either."

Mort nodded again. "My point exactly."

"You want me to lay low."

"I think I made that clear already."

We stared at each other across the front seat, neither ready to give.

"I have to see this through, Mort," I said, my tone as close to conciliatory as I could make it. "I have to."

Mort settled back, sighing in what I took for resignation, but he wasn't done with me yet.

I thought of the jagged scrap of paper I'd tucked into my pocket. "I need one more day, Mort. If I haven't found a way to proceed, I'll give up the hunt."

"Promise?"

"Promise."

Mort looked less than convinced. "Can I take you for your word on that?"

I nodded.

He continued to grouse. "Because there's one murder you'll never be able to solve, Jessica: your own."

Chapter Twenty-seven

"Do you know what it is?" I asked Chad as he ran his eyes over the line of numbers and letters that Larry Dax had clandestinely passed me in the interrogation room. "Does anything about it strike a chord?"

ME2006Y

I'd phoned him as soon as Mort and I returned to Cabot Cove, eager to have Chad take a look at what I was certain would be a key clue to breaking the case.

He looked up at me, shaking his head, stymied for the first time since I'd met him. "Sorry, Jessica. I can't help you with this one. Maybe I should do some digging around this Larry Dax guy, see what he was up to in 2006."

"The *Y* could be throwing us off," I suggested. "Maybe it doesn't stand for 'year' at all."

"That might help," Chad said, hardly enthusiastic about the prospects.

"I shouldn't have gotten my hopes up."

"Don't give up yet. I'm pretty good with this stuff. Just give me a day."

Same thing I'd said to Mort, I remembered.

Chad stretched his hand forward and retrieved the scrap of paper from where I'd laid it on my kitchen table, once again our de facto office.

"Maybe 2-0-0-6 isn't a year," he said suddenly.

"Then what is it?"

"I don't know yet, Jessica."

Maybe I was being selfish and shortsighted by continuing to involve Chad, since I might be subjecting him to the same danger. But his fondness, if not love, for Alyssa was obvious, and I knew he wanted to help her as much as I did, and that he would continue doing so whether I enlisted his services again or not.

A bit of rationalization, I know, but as I said, time was running out. And the longer Hal's fortune was missing without a trace, the higher the likelihood it would never be found again. Just like a kidnapping victim, only more so.

"It gets worse," I told Chad. "He also told me somebody wiped the entire LOVEISYOURS site clean."

"I noticed that." Chad nodded.

He attempted to bring the site up on the laptop he'd already switched on, drawing the message *Cannot find site*.

"I guess whoever the man in our picture is working for is trying to cover their tracks, eliminating any potential links back to them."

"Only through the front door, Jessica," Chad said, flashing that mischievous grin of his that I'd already come to appreciate so much.

"Is there a back one in this case?"

"Not per se, as far as the LOVEISYOURS site is concerned, but I got to thinking."

"Something that seems to always get me in trouble," I told him.

"Anyway, I figured LOVEISYOURS wouldn't necessarily be the only dating site the four victims we know of would have used."

"You mean three," I corrected.

"I was including Alyssa's father," Chad told me, and swallowed hard. "Turned out I was wrong about him, but right about the others. All three, the two men and one woman, still had their profiles up, each on other dating sites that are rivals of LOVEISYOURS."

"And there must be some pattern in their profiles that led to them all being targeted," I theorized.

"You think that's the key to all this, to what happened to Hal Wirth?"

I shrugged. "All four victims suffered financial calamities of varying degrees before their deaths. And we know they were all successful entrepreneurs."

"You're reading my mind," Chad said, "particularly the entrepreneur part, because all four victims worked for themselves."

"Meaning they managed their own money. Larry Dax, the man I knew as Sean Booker when I met him for the first time, boasted about the advanced algorithms LOVEISYOURS employed."

"All the sites use algorithms—it's how they match

people with each other, essentially looking for areas of commonality beyond simply favorite color and zodiac sign."

"And those algorithms would key off certain elements in a profile that made Hal and these three other people targets."

Chad nodded. "The killers, whoever the man who attacked you last night worked for, must've created their own algorithm to isolate profiles of potential victims."

"Then what?"

"That's what we don't know."

"But if we could figure out these same areas of commonality, then we'd know exactly what the killers were keying on."

Chad flashed me a look, as if he thought he'd figured out where I was going with this. "You mean, so we could isolate other potential victims?"

"I was actually thinking so we could create a potential victim."

"Who?"

"Me," I told Chad.

Chapter Twenty-eight

I thought the lights might have flickered when I said that, but it was just the product of my imagination as I studied Chad's expression for a reaction.

"Alyssa would kill me if I helped you do that," he said after a pause.

"Somebody already killed her father, Chad. And this might be the only chance at all she and her mother have of getting their money back."

"That is, if you can catch whoever was behind it before they vanish into thin air."

"That's the idea," I said, nodding.

"You're talking about a sting operation."

"I suppose I am. Of sorts anyway."

Chad looked at me, his expression drained of its typical confidence and swagger, his gaze one a stranger would give another, as if he were meeting me for the first time. Which, in one sense, I suppose he was.

"What do you think your friend the sheriff's going to think of this?"

"We're not going to tell him."

"We're *not*?"

I held the boy's stare. "We're not going to stage this in Cabot Cove. It wouldn't work." I let that sink in a bit before I continued. "Because the victims we've managed to identify all come from big cities. Even Hal had his single, disastrous date in Boston. And it just so happens I keep an apartment in New York."

"Alyssa mentioned that."

"So I'll relocate there."

"You mean, *we* will."

"Once the die is cast, there's no reason for you to miss any more school."

"You really think we'd let you do this alone?"

"We?"

"Alyssa's coming, too. That's from her, not me. She told me to tell you she doesn't want to be left out of this anymore, that she wants to learn from the master firsthand."

"This has nothing to do with writing, Chad."

"I guess she wants the total Jessica Fletcher experience."

I hesitated. "I can't accept putting either of you in any more danger. You were pinged, remember?" *Whatever that means*, I almost added.

"I've got it under control."

His strident tone surprised me no end, the veneer of a boyish computer genius receding in the face of a mature young man. Even his hair looked shorter, probably a trick of that kitchen light I'd thought I'd just caught flickering.

"And there's something else," Chad said suddenly.

"Is this your last condition, or are there more?"

"Nope, this is the last one. Whether we tell the sheriff what we're up to is your call. But I assume you know some New York City cops."

"I do," I said, thinking of Lieutenant Artie Gelber. "But what chance do you think we've got of convincing the NYPD to have our backs without being laughed out of One Police Plaza?"

"That never stopped you in your books, Jessica," Chad said, the familiar gleam back in his eyes.

"Do I really need to explain the difference to you?"

"I was just kidding—about that, but not about trying to do this without professional backup. Alyssa and I are of one mind on that."

"You haven't even told her about this plan yet."

"But I know how she thinks. We bring someone else into this, or it's a no-go."

"No problem." I nodded. "I've already got someone in mind."

Chad had managed to find the profiles of the Miami, Houston, and Denver victims on dating sites other than LOVEISYOURS. Not Hal Wirth's profile, though, since apparently the midlife crisis he was experiencing extended only as far as Larry Dax's now downed site.

While Chad toiled away at assembling a fake profile for me, based upon the traits that would hopefully lead to my being targeted just as at least four others had been, I went upstairs to my office and dialed a number from memory I hadn't used in quite a while.

"You still owe me from the last time," private investigator Harry McGraw greeted.

"How much is it?"

"A lot."

"You'll have to be more specific, Harry."

"How about alimony for an ex-wife and tuition for a couple of kids I'm trying to put through college?"

"Help me with the latest case I'm working on and you'll be well on your way to that."

"Case or book?"

"Case. Since when do I consult you for books?"

"Meaning you must not trust my PI skills as much as you claim."

"I called you, didn't I?"

"Because, I'm guessing, I'm the only one you know will answer his phone."

"You haven't been working?"

"I used to charge for what pretty much anyone can get off the Internet these days, my dear Jessica. I quit drinking, by the way."

"You're kidding."

"Yes," Harry said from the other end of the line, "I am."

"You still have your New York office?"

"I moved to a floor without a bathroom to save on the rent. But I've got a water view now."

"In Manhattan?"

"Sewer construction for three new office towers

going up around the dump I'm renting in. When I'm there, I have to wear earplugs, which doesn't matter since nobody calls anyway."

"I'm calling, Harry."

"And to what do I owe the privilege?"

"That job I've got for you."

"Doing what?"

"Watching my back."

"Something I'm well versed in. Did I tell you I gave up drinking?"

"You tried."

"Sorry. All that booze has given me memory problems."

I chuckled. "Haven't changed at all, have you, Harry?"

"No more than you, my dear Jessica. When trouble doesn't find you, you're bound to go looking for it."

"Oh, it found me, all right; I'm just looking for more."

"What's in it for me?"

"Your usual fee."

"Sounds like an offer I can't refuse."

"You built a profile for me?" I said when Chad completed his work several hours later.

"Uh-huh. To post on the same sites used by the other three victims, besides Alyssa's father. I'm glad he hadn't posted on those other sites, since I wouldn't have felt right about looking at him this way."

"What way is that?"

"As an assemblage of data. You want to find the right match, you tell the truth in your profile. I'm not sure I'd want to see that for Hal Wirth. A lousy way to meet somebody, to say the least."

"You never met him in person?"

"He wasn't home the other time I came to visit. The point, Jessica, is that Alyssa would never want me to see that side of him."

"A side she'd never seen herself, you mean."

"Yeah," Chad said, nodding, "exactly."

"Now tell me more about my profile."

"The good news is you fit a lot of the algorithm's components without me needing to change a thing."

"What's the bad news?"

Chad flashed that smirk, back in his element again. "I just gave it to you."

I didn't understand all of what he went on to explain to me, but I was able to focus on key words and phrases.

"You're not poor," Chad said for starters, "just like the victims you uncovered."

"Meaning, like them, I'm rich."

"I didn't want to put it that way. In addition to being of means, you're widowed. Lonely, in other words."

"I'm not lonely."

"No, but the victims in Denver, Houston, and Miami were."

"They listed 'lonely' on their profiles?"

"Nobody lists it that way. They might say looking for companionship or romance. There's a ton of phrases they use that boil down to the same thing that the algorithm keys off of."

"And I imagine that describes pretty much everyone who registers on these sites."

"True enough, but whoever's using them to target their victims must have written code capable of identifying other tangential and contributing factors to pare down their lists and choose potential victims most vulnerable to the overtures of the bad guys who want to match with them."

"In other words," I picked up, "the profiles of these bad guys fit exactly what their victims are looking for."

"Exactly."

"I don't even know what I'm looking for."

"I don't think anybody can know that as well as this software they've written can. The kind of algorithms these sites use, even at the rudimentary level, are meant to pinpoint things we don't even know about ourselves in order to find the right match. Because they're guessing that what you're really looking for is distinct from what you think, or may say, you're looking for."

"In other words, the software knows more about you than you know about yourself."

"These sites aren't just trying to match people who both enjoy skydiving, or follow the same sports, or even enjoy the same TV shows or movies," Chad explained. "They're matching people based not so much on what they said in their questionnaires, or even interviews in some cases; they're matching them based on what can be extrapolated from their answers. It's kind of like, well, remember the other day when I used enhanced facial software to bring to life the features of the man who may have killed Mr. Wirth?"

"Of course."

"Well, Jessica, what I did to give the man a face on the outside is pretty much what the best dating sites do on the inside. Their algorithms sharpen what's already there, add clarity to the blurriness in finding potential matches for your profile."

I thought for a moment, trying to assemble everything I knew. "So whoever's behind this must be crafting fictional profiles to match the ones of their targets."

Chad nodded. "Using reverse engineering, pretty much, just like I did when I crafted a profile for Eileen Vogel."

"Who's Eileen Vogel?"

"Your alias."

"Have you posted my—I mean *her*—profile yet?"

He shook his head. "I wanted you to see it first."

"Maybe I'd rather not see it at all."

"It's a fabrication, Jessica, concocted to contain as many of the factors and attributes Miami, Houston, and Denver possessed. Kind of like the way you must create your characters. No more real than that."

"My characters are real to me."

"Just like the profile I've built for you will hopefully make you seem real to whoever's responsible for four murders and probably a whole bunch more." Chad's expression lost its boyish glint. "You realize," he continued, his tone serious, "that once we put this profile up on those sites, you'll be painting a bull's-eye on your forehead."

"That's precisely the idea."

Chapter Twenty-nine

Harry McGraw looked as rumpled and ragged as ever, a cheap suit with arms and legs hanging out of it and a face that looked like he washed it with coffee grounds. We met at the Tick Tock Diner in Manhattan, located on Thirty-fourth Street not far from Penn Station. And, from the number of torn Sweet'n Low packets, he was well into his third or fourth cup of coffee.

"You're late," he groused, ever-present scowl etched onto his features. "I was hoping you changed your mind."

I slid into the opposite side of the booth. "I haven't."

He took his mug in hand and leaned forward. I noticed a small plate with a crumpled-up muffin wrapper surrounded by any number of stray nuts with pieces of batter clinging to them, evidence that Harry had pulled out the nuts prior to ingesting the muffin.

"So let me see if I've got this straight, Jessica. Four men—actually three men and one woman—whose profiles were up on these dating sites were murdered shortly after they'd gone on dates with someone the sites had matched them with."

"Potentially just one site—LOVEISYOURS. But it's been taken off-line, so we'll have to hope the killers are still using the others."

"Let me ask you another question. You mentioned four victims *that we know of*—your exact words, I think. So how many other victims do you think there are?"

I hedged. "I have no idea."

"A few?"

"For sure."

"Ten?"

"At least, I'd say. Beyond that, it's anyone's guess."

I watched Harry considering the ramifications of that. "You mentioned Hal Wirth," he said.

"A good friend of mine"—I nodded—"and the one victim I was personally acquainted with."

"And judging by what you told me about him, your working theory is that there's a direct link between whoever he was matched with on LOVEISYOU and—"

"LOVEISYOURS," I corrected.

"Whatever," Harry said, frowning. "A direct link between his LOVEISYOURS match and the financial calamity that followed."

"Almost immediately," I added.

"And you intend to find out exactly how they did it, their modus operandi, as you call it."

"I don't call it that, Harry. I've never used that term in my life."

I'd told Mort I was leaving town for a few days to teach some classes I didn't want to cancel at New York University, where I was a visiting professor of criminology, meaning I appeared on campus irregularly. Mort didn't bother questioning me on that and was probably glad to have me out of his hair for a few days anyway. Of course, we really had no idea how long it would take for the profile Chad had created of me to yield its desired results. He hadn't used my real name for anything, including billing, and the profile he created fit all the parameters of that algorithm the people behind Porcelain Man had employed to select their targets.

"You've got to admit, Jessica," Harry was saying, after the server refilled his mug, "that all this is a little extreme, even for you."

"Hal Wirth was a friend of mine, Harry. I can't let this go."

"You mentioned the FBI was involved."

"Through the shady owner of LOVEISYOURS. When I met him after he'd been taken into custody, I knew he wasn't telling me everything. But he told me enough to convince me he'd gotten in well over his head. Somebody had taken down his site and I got the feeling he was afraid they were going to take him down as well. That's why he contacted me, and to give me this clue," I finished, handing Harry a full-page copy of Larry Dax's hand-scrawled message.

"M-E-two-zero-zero-six-Y," he read out loud, before handing it back to me.

"Mean anything to you?" I asked him.

"Nope, not a thing. Can I assume you said nothing to the FBI about the note?"

"You can."

"So by helping you do this, I'm helping you further obstruct justice."

"Worried about your PI license, Harry?"

"What license?" he joked from behind the steam rising from his fresh mug of coffee. "And what exactly do you want me to do?"

"I was hoping you could tell me."

"Well, I'm thinking protection mostly. Another set of eyes on wherever these dates that may or may not happen take place." He laid his coffee mug down. "Can I ask you another question, Jess?"

"Of course."

"Besides me, have you dated anyone else since Frank died?"

"I wasn't aware that I dated you."

"All things being relative, I mean, and given all the quality time we've spent with each other in places like this."

"Is this a date, Harry?"

"No, because you're paying. I'm expensing lunch to you."

"The answer is no," I told him. "I haven't dated anyone since Frank died."

"Unusual circumstances to jump back in."

"I intend to act natural, which means nervous."

Harry nodded, weighing what I'd told him. "It might be hard to be inside wherever you end up. So I'll be listening from a short distance away. I've got people who could handle the technical side of things, although I think we can probably wire you up unobtrusively through your cell phone. You do have a cell phone, right?"

I fished the big one from my handbag and flashed it at him.

"Whoa, state-of-the-art. Now I'm impressed."

"Don't be. I miss my flip."

"Which wasn't even Wi-Fi-enabled."

"I'd never have noticed."

"The way my listening in works is the phone doesn't have to be on—it just has to be somewhere it can pick up what's being said, so I can keep ears on you, if not eyes. People place them on the table a lot these days, but we'll test it from inside your handbag as well."

"I usually leave my handbag on the floor."

That drew some concern from Harry. "How about in your lap? Or next to you in your chair?"

"That could work."

"And we'll need a signal, something to tell me you need help right away. A word or phrase."

"How about, 'Harry, I need help!'"

"I was thinking of something more subtle."

"Just 'Help!' maybe?"

"I was thinking, 'I love you.'"

"Keep thinking," I said, when my phone rang and I started to fish it from my bag.

"See," Harry said, "it works."

I saw Chad's number lit up in the caller ID and greeted him.

"Your profile got a hit, Jessica," he told me.

Chapter Thirty

Harry McGraw accompanied me back to my apartment, where Alyssa and Chad were eagerly awaiting my return.

"I've already responded for you," Chad said.

"Making me seem a bit overeager," I noted, as if it mattered under the circumstances.

"That's the point," he told me, "because overeager also means vulnerable."

"Vulnerable or desperate?"

"Both, I guess, add up to loneliness."

"You think my father was lonely?" Alyssa said to Chad, her tone a bit biting.

Part of me regretted letting her and Chad accompany me to New York. But another part was grateful for her presence, the same part that believed she had the right to be involved. This was about her father, after all. I guess I could have thought the same thing about Babs, except I knew her well enough to be sure she'd never have approved of such a crazy scheme. As crazy as it might have been, though, it was all I had.

"Let me take this one," Harry offered, "having tried my hand with several wives. Didn't mean I still didn't love them. It just meant I wasn't sure about myself anymore."

"Are you the private detective?"

"Well, little lady, I'm not sure about being *the* anything. Always been more comfortable just being an *a*."

Alyssa didn't look like she quite grasped what Harry was saying, but nodded anyway. "So long as you can help us."

"If by 'help,' you mean coming to the rescue of my favorite amateur sleuth, then count me in."

"You know about my father."

"Yes." Harry nodded. "Yes, I do."

"It could have happened to anyone."

Harry nodded again. "I've been a detective about as long as I've had teeth, and the phrase I keep coming back to when it comes to victims like your father is 'wrong place, wrong time.' You're right, it could've been anyone. But you can bet I'm going to do everything I can to make sure whoever did this to your dad never does it again."

"Are you going to shoot them?"

"I'd have to carry a gun to do that, little lady." Harry smiled.

"Your date's confirmed for tonight," Chad proceeded to tell me.

"Tonight? Already?"

"I answered for you. Details to follow."

"I'm not ready."

Harry squeezed my arm tenderly. "Er, it's not a real date, Jessica, remember?"

"It's the closest I've come to one since Frank died."

"You're not counting your time with me?"

"Didn't we cover this at the diner? That was all coffee out of foam cups and take-out pizza."

"You like coffee out of foam cups and take-out pizza."

"I never had to worry about how I looked around you, Harry."

He rolled his eyes. "Thanks, Jessica, truly. I'll remember that when you need me to save your life."

"I think I just came up with our code phrase."

"What?" Harry asked me.

"Shut up."

Chad brought up my would-be suitor's profile on a dating site that had been a rival of LOVEISYOURS.

"He's not bad looking," I commented.

"His looks might be the only thing about him that's real. His profile's got holes in it big enough to drive through."

"Any way of telling whether he's cut from the same cloth as the woman Hal Wirth dated?"

"You mean, a murderer?" Alyssa asked, so much bitterness and repressed rage lacing her voice that I began to regret including her in all this.

"Accessory, anyway," I conceded.

"No," Chad finally answered, "but I wouldn't have expected the signs to be obvious, any more than the profile I built for you is."

"Where'd you come up with the name 'Eileen Vogel,' by the way?"

"Alyssa has an aunt named Eileen and I've got an uncle whose last name is Vogel," Chad explained.

Which drew a smirk from Harry McGraw before his expression settled back into its perpetual scowl. "How much are the two of you paying for college again?" he asked as he shook his head.

"Do I have time to get my hair done?" I blurted out. "How long do I have before I need to meet . . . what's his name?"

"Phil Tabor, on the site anyway," Chad told me. "Maybe no more real than Eileen Vogel."

"What should I look for? How will I know if he's one of them?"

"You won't," Harry said, before Chad had a chance to respond. "From what you've told me, these people are meticulous in the way they go about their business. I'm figuring the little lady's dad was a pretty smart guy, and they took him for everything he was worth. Same thing they're gonna try with you, Jessica. If I'd have to guess, I'd say blackmail. Second choice: hypnosis. Wave some pendulum in front of your face and get you to hand over all your passwords, security questions, and account numbers. Maybe get you to sign over power of attorney while they're at it."

"I'll be ready for anything," I told him.

Harry's perpetual snarl lengthened. "Nobody's ever ready to die, dear lady."

I have no idea why it was so important for me to look good on my fake date, but it was. Fake date or not, I wanted Phil Tabor to see me as more than just an aging widow, a schoolmarm masquerading as a bestselling author. Except tonight I was indeed playing the role of the aging widow, though in the profile Chad had constructed for me, I'd inherited a ton of money a few years back and I was finally ready to get back into the dating world. Although I wasn't privy to the details of what he'd done in making my profile match the algorithm conjured by the other victims, and wouldn't have understood them if I did know, I found myself fascinated by the sophisticated nature of this crime.

I started writing, and sleuthing on an amateur level, before the era of *CSI,* DNA evidence, AFIS, and other sophisticated criminal databases. A time when law enforcement bodies shared almost nothing with one another, allowing criminals to evade capture by simply moving their crimes across state lines. All that had changed with computers and the Internet age, of course, but with that change had come a new kind of criminal, one equally adept at using technology as the detectives committed to catching him.

Harry's "wrong place at the wrong time" quote stuck in my mind, because my sleuthing could best be described the same way, or, perhaps, *right* place at the *right* time. But this was different. My involvement this time wasn't random or accidental; it was by conscious choice and duty to a friend. I'd long believed my obsession with catching criminals, in fact and fiction, was rooted in an insatiable desire to see justice done, and that was the case more than ever this time.

My regular New York City hairdresser was off, but

I managed to snag an appointment with another stylist for that afternoon ahead of my fake date. A blessing, as it turned out, since it better allowed her to alter my appearance as much as possible from the publicity shot on my book covers. The last thing I needed after all this preparation was to be recognized by someone I was trying to entrap. So the stylist trimmed, coiffed, and blow-dried me, working a mirror about my head to reveal a fresh hairdo that made me look different enough from the Jessica Fletcher who appeared on book jackets. Then again, neither that Jessica Fletcher nor this one was particularly glamorous, so it hadn't been a difficult task.

I was to meet Phil Tabor at Novita, a restaurant not far from my apartment on the East Side, a restaurant I'd heard wonderful things about but, thankfully, had never dined at before tonight. I filled the rest of the afternoon pondering alone, and with Harry, how a man like Phil Tabor or a woman like Naomi, Hal Wirth's date, figured into the rapid financial ruin and ultimate murder of targeted victims. I'd spent my writing career in search of the perfect crime and wondered if I'd finally stumbled upon it.

"How long you think this has been going on?" Harry asked from alongside me on my terrace, which overlooked Park Avenue.

"You must be reading my mind."

"More interesting than reading your mail."

"The answer is, I have no idea, any more than I've got any idea how many victims have been claimed or how many people there are behind the curtain."

Harry's scowl deepened once more. "So they knock

off their marks before those marks can figure out how they got taken and report it. Smart."

"That was my thought."

"I'm glad you called me, Jessica. Seems like the only fun I have is when I get to work with you."

"You call this fun?"

He shrugged playfully. "You're the one going out for the fancy dinner."

"With you ready to storm the restaurant if things go bad."

Harry's expression turned somber. "What do I have to say to get you to call Mort or the FBI?"

"Nothing. I'm determined to see this through myself."

"It's not a book, Jessica. You can't write the ending."

"Watch me, Harry. Just watch me."

He looked at me across the terrace, groping for words he couldn't find, while I fretted about the breeze messing up my freshly styled hair. I moved through the sliding door ahead of him, and noted Chad looking up from behind his laptop.

"Whoa, Jessica, you look . . ."

"The same?"

"I was going to say 'dressed to kill.'"

"Odd phrase to use, under the circumstances," I said, managing a chuckle.

"Glad you're enjoying this, Jessica," Chad told me. "Because I just confirmed a new date for tomorrow night."

Chapter Thirty-one

Phil Tabor looked exactly as he did in his profile picture, to the point where I wondered if his registration was only a few days old, just as mine was. Chad had explained that there was no point in bothering to ascertain how long his profile had been up, because if he was a plant, those behind it would've taken elaborate steps to make it seem as if he'd been registered for a long time.

He was already seated when I arrived at Novita, where a hostess named Melissa escorted me to the table where he was waiting. Harry McGraw had parked his beat-up old car in a no-parking zone across the street, prepared to listen in on everything that transpired. I'd already switched on the surveillance app he'd asked Chad to install on my phone, available only on sites like the spy store he frequented to buy or borrow his "toys," as he called them.

Phil Tabor rose when I reached his table, a prime one set before a mirror and against a partition for reasonable privacy.

"You must be Eileen," he greeted, smiling.

"And you must be Phil," I said, taking his extended hand. 'But if you're not, I think I'll stay anyway."

The joke sounded so lame when I uttered it, but the man who may or may not have really been Phil Tabor chuckled anyway. "I'll take that as a compliment."

He moved to pull my chair back and eased it in again once I was seated.

"Been a long time since I've done this," he said, retaking his spot alongside me on a bench seat set against the wall beneath the mirror.

"Me, too."

"Well, we have that much in common."

"And plenty more," I offered, "given that we're a match."

"I hate that word."

"Me, too."

"I'm sorry you lost your husband," Phil said, sounding as if he genuinely meant it.

"And I'm sorry you lost your wife."

"Well, truth be told, I didn't actually lose her."

"No?"

"We're divorced. Sorry if my profile may have been a bit misleading. I've found the sympathy factor makes me more appealing."

"Not enough maybe," I heard myself say, too late to stop the words, "given that you're still trying."

"Ouch."

"Oh, that came out so wrong."

"No reason to apologize," Phil Tabor said with a smile that seemed as genuine as his expression of sympathy.

"It's just that, like I said, I'm new at this."

"The truth is never anything to apologize for." I watched him place a cell phone that looked like mine onto the table. "I'm not being rude. This thing controls my hearing aid, believe it or not, and sometimes crowded restaurants require adjustment."

I slipped on my glasses. "I can't read the menu without them."

"So I can't hear and you can't see. Guess we make quite the pair."

"I'll drink to that," I said, toasting him with my water glass.

"Why don't we order something more appropriate? Wine?"

"One glass, unless you want me to fall asleep."

He looked at me like an old friend instead of a fake match made on a dating site. "Wouldn't be the first time, Eileen."

I almost didn't respond to my name, until I remembered the alias. Our banter and exchange of smiles left me wondering if it had been like this for Hal Wirth the night he'd gone out on a date with the woman he called Nan in his memoir. His words intimated that he'd tired of the whole thing almost from the time the date began. Absent the circumstances, I could have actually enjoyed being out with a man of suitable age who might have been here on pretenses as false as my own.

What might the experience have been like if there were no pretenses, if this weren't about the murder of a good friend by forces the charming Phil Tabor might well have been working for? That thinking made me ask myself for the first time why I'd never dated again, or sought even the most rudimental male companionship beyond the friendships I maintained with Harry McGraw, Mort Metzger, and Seth Hazlitt since Frank's death. Was I afraid of feeling guilty? Afraid of building a new life for myself outside the pages of my books? My output had doubled, almost tripled in the wake of Frank's passing, as if I'd willingly plunged into a world of fantasy because reality was too harsh. I never thought I could enjoy another man's company, much less one I met on a dating site, until now.

I tried to remind myself the whole thing was a ruse, that I was never going to see Phil Tabor again no matter how well tonight went. Still, even the inkling of enjoyment I was taking from our encounter made me question exactly why I'd rejected male companionship like this ever since Frank had died.

Besides using his cell phone to adjust the volume on his hearing aid a few times, Phil Tabor otherwise did nothing but eat his breaded swordfish while I wolfed down my Chilean sea bass, which I'd learned long before didn't actually come from Chile. Being nervous inevitably heightens my appetite, and I was a nervous wreck, not just over the fact I was out on a date with a man who might be an accessory to murder, but because I was on a date, period.

"You're no better at this than I am," Phil Tabor said over cappuccino.

"Maybe we're just too old for this kind of thing."

He nodded, as if weighing my words. "Our demographic is the fastest growing when it comes to dating sites."

"Demographics are a rationale for anything these days, aren't they?"

He looked at me, as if unsure what that meant exactly. "Well, there's nothing wrong with a friendly dinner, is there?"

"A dinner between friends is different from a friendly dinner," I said, surprising myself with a remark that sounded biting, my discomfort with this whole "dating" thing starting to show through.

Phil Tabor sipped his cappuccino. "I'll make you a deal, Eileen. If we decide to do this again, we agree to tell each other our real names."

"Deal," I said, extending my hand across the table so we could shake on it.

Harry McGraw was still laughing when I climbed into the passenger seat of his car, the door sticking and grinding so much I had trouble closing it.

"You know, instead of yukking it up at my expense, maybe you should get your door fixed."

"I don't use that door."

"Your passengers do."

"You're my first passenger in months. And that was your first date in . . . how long exactly?"

"A long time."

"Since Frank died."

"What, you think I was dating while we were married, Harry?"

He started laughing again. "That's the same tone you used on that poor guy in the restaurant."

"Was I that mean?"

"Let's say, considerably less amiable than your usually charming self."

"You hear anything that raised any eyebrows?"

"I was laughing so hard through most of it, it's hard for me to say. How about when you insisted on splitting the check?"

"When was the last time *you* dated, Harry?"

"Had dinner with one of my daughters last week."

"That doesn't count," I told him.

"Everything's relative, Jess."

Chapter Thirty-two

As of the next morning, Chad had found no attempts of forced entry, so to speak, into any of the fake bank and brokerage accounts he'd opened in my name. The elaborate financial history and holdings he'd built for me would stand up to the closest scrutiny until any attempts to drain the money, or borrow against the assets, revealed the ruse.

This was hardly a comfort, given that Phil Tabor had done nothing to stoke my suspicions. He'd had no opportunity to fish through my handbag in search of pertinent information, nor had he asked me any prohibitive questions that may have led me to reveal anything personal, like my password or something similar. In fact, he had done nothing at all that had even remotely raised my suspicions, including either blackmailing or trying to hypnotize me. And when I recounted the highlights of my evening to Chad, the only thing he seemed to take note of was Phil's use of his cell phone to control his hearing aid, though he didn't say why.

I'd fallen behind on my latest book and thought the day leading up to my second "date" might offer opportunity to do some catching up, but I couldn't keep my focus on fiction when so much was swirling around me in fact. I'd always looked at the process of writing as a refuge to which I could retreat and shut out the demands of the real world. In stark contrast to that world, my writing universe was mine to control. I was the puppet master, as opposed to just another puppet.

The one exception to this proclivity seemed to be when I found myself embroiled in an actual mystery. During those times, I found it difficult to write at all, as if the intrusion of reality on my fictional world made it impossible to linger there or produce anything worthwhile. It wasn't writer's block per se, so much as the strange aura a real-life mystery cast over a fictional one. Not only was I not the master; I was barely a puppet. Real life had infringed on my fictional world in a way that rendered the musings of my characters and their actions irrelevant, moot. It had happened before, but never quite like this, because never before had I taken on a real-life mystery with so many personal overtones. While going "undercover" wasn't totally new to me, I'd never done so in a way that subjected me to such risk, and could only imagine what Mort Metzger would say if word ever got back to him.

I was also taken aback by the degree to which I remained unsettled by last night's so-called date. The fact that it had been a sham didn't stop the experience from illuminating the path my life had taken. I wasn't questioning that direction so much as wondering how things might've been different if I'd opted for other choices. Spending so much time around Chad and especially Alyssa left me pondering an alternate existence where Frank and I had managed to have kids of our own, who today would be filling my life with what it otherwise lacked. It's easy not to miss something you've never had, until the slight taste of it fills you with angst over roads not traveled.

Increasingly discomfited by that line of thinking, I turned my attention to my date with one Richard Fass. According to his profile, which could've been as fake as mine, he was a corporate attorney and litigator, and listed his hobbies as model shipbuilding, painting, and poetry. He'd been married once, but his profile listed him as single for some seven years. We were to meet for coffee at a trendy East Side coffee shop that catered to the non-Starbucks crowd at five o'clock that afternoon. And, after last night, I was ever so glad to forgo dinner in favor of something less formal and, well, less lengthy.

I tried to nap. Failed.

Tried to read. Failed there, too.

Tried to watch the news. Failed again.

I started to fear I'd never be able to do anything again until all this was resolved, which left me wondering what would happen if it never was. If this whole assemblage of algorithms, profiles, and dating data was the product of folly and nothing more.

I was still pondering that when Harry McGraw drove me to the coffee bar and found another illegal space to park his beat-up wreck in. This time I could barely get the passenger-side door open until I put all the heft of my shoulder behind it.

"Thanks for the help, Harry," I said, from the sidewalk.

"How much are you paying me again?"

I recognized Richard Fass immediately from his profile picture. He was seated at a back table facing the door and waved to me as soon as I entered. A stately, handsome gentleman with a shock of dazzling white hair, he bore a slight resemblance to Seth Hazlitt. He waved me over with a smile and I started for the table, wondering why he hadn't risen, as was the gentlemanly custom. And I didn't get my answer until my second date in as many days pushed his wheelchair out from beneath the table, stretching a hand up to greet me.

"I know," he said with an easy smile. "Something I left out of my profile."

"You think it would've mattered?" I asked, taking the seat across from Richard Fass as he pushed his wheelchair back into place.

"Makes me less of a catch, don't you think?"

I shook my head. "Not really."

"My ex-wife begs to differ."

"Car accident?"

"Persian Gulf War. We didn't suffer a lot of casualties in that one, but I was one of them. I was thirty-five at the time. Thought I had my whole life ahead of me. Know what I learned?"

"What?"

"That it was still ahead of me, just a bit lower."

"Your wife didn't agree?"

"I think she would've left me even if I could dunk a basketball. We had issues that had nothing to do with the chair."

I had no idea why, but I immediately felt comfortable in Richard's company, stoking thoughts in me again about the choices I'd made, or didn't make.

"You didn't mention serving in the army in your profile either."

"It turns some women off," he told me, "and others on, for all the wrong reasons."

"Like?"

He leaned forward, his wheelchair rocking with him. "Let's save that discussion for the next date. Over alcohol."

"It's a deal," I told him. "And to tell you the truth, I prefer coffee."

The shop was self-service and I had every intention of fetching our orders when Richard rolled his chair out from the table before I'd had the chance to offer.

"What can I get you?"

"How about a tea?" I replied, not bothering to argue the point. "Something fancy. Your choice."

"The fancy ones tend to be weak. I'll make sure to bring you two bags."

He rolled on, his thick hair remaining in place the whole way to the counter. The sneakers he was wearing curled over the footrests, affixed with some neon strips runners used to keep them safe at night. They shone brightly under the spill of the coffee bar's fancy lighting.

Richard rolled back to our table with his coffee and my tea tucked into cup holders built into the arm of his chair. "Hey, if cars can have them, right?"

I smiled and accepted my tea from him—two bags, true to his word, and of my favorite flavors.

"How did you know?" I asked him.

"It's in your profile."

I knocked myself in the head. "You'd think I'd remember that."

"What's my favorite beverage?"

"Craft beer," I recalled. "I remember it clearly because it's called Frank—something. Frank was my late husband's name."

"How long ago did he die?"

"Some days, it feels like yesterday; others, a hundred years ago, to the point I wonder if he was even real."

"You miss him."

"Desperately," I said, surprising myself with my candor.

"I wish I missed my wife." He took a sip from a mug overflowing with some foamy concoction. "The truth is, I was glad when she left; it freed me from having to please her, from trying to be the man I was before Iraq. Anyway," he said, lifting his mug in the semblance of a toast, "here's to happiness."

I felt myself smile, hoping Richard Fass had nothing to do with whoever was behind Hal Wirth's death, because I was already considering a second date with him.

"I'll drink to that," I said, toasting him in return.

Chapter Thirty-three

Harry McGraw pretended to be sleeping when I got back to the car, not popping an eye open until I slammed the door to rouse him.

"Sorry, listening to the banter between the two of you must've knocked me out. You know, Jess, for an author who writes page-turners, you're pretty dull."

"Tell me something I don't know, Harry."

"How about this could be the most boring case we've ever worked on together? How many more dates are you expecting to go on?"

"As many as it takes to get targeted." I waited for Harry to pull out into traffic before I resumed, not wanting to distract him. "What do you suppose it's like to wake up to the realization you're flat broke?"

"I wake up that way every morning. You get used to it."

"Not if you were rich the night before."

"Yup, the good ole World Wide Web has created a whole new cast of criminal characters."

"Who are a lot harder to catch than the old-fashioned ones."

I checked my phone to see if there was anything from Chad while I'd been having coffee with Richard Fass.

"Oh, jeez," I said.

Harry looked at me across the seat. "Something wrong?"

"Yes, you not keeping your eyes on the road."

"Besides that," he said, and let the scowl return to his face.

"A text from Chad telling me I've got a third date set for tomorrow."

Lunch this time, as it turned out, with a man named Max Gladding. I arrived at the restaurant first and didn't recognize him when he got there, because he looked quite different from his picture.

Younger, much younger. By as much as twenty-five years maybe.

"I hope you're not offended," he said, after we exchanged the usual greetings and pleasantries.

"Well," I said, still at a loss for words over having been matched with a man closer in age to Chad and Alyssa than me.

"My shrink tells me I'm trying to date my mother."

"I'm sure she's a fine woman."

"Was. She died when I was a kid."

You still are a kid, I almost said, but didn't.

"I've never been happy with women my own age."

I swallowed hard, noticed Max Gladding was wearing something on his wrist in addition to his watch. A dull glow seemed to be emanating from it, but that could have been a trick of the restaurant's lighting. I almost asked him about it but stopped short, not wanting to appear overly suspicious.

He must've caught me looking, though, and maneuvered his arm to hide that wrist from my sight.

"Have you ever dated a younger man?" Max asked me.

"You mean, someone young enough to be my son?"

He nodded.

"I haven't dated anyone in a long time."

"Your profile lists you as a widow."

"And I haven't dated since my husband died. I'm thinking around the time you were born."

I was expecting any number of responses from Max Gladding, but not the laughter he broke into. "Age is in the eye of the beholder."

"I think you mean 'beauty.'"

"Everything's relative, Eileen."

I suddenly found myself comfortable in his presence, due to the fact that he was unabashedly open about whatever frailty led him to seek out the company of older women.

"What was your mother's name?" I asked him.

"Paula."

"What do you remember most about her, Max?"

"The way she smelled after taking a bath. I've tried to find whatever it was she used on her skin, but I haven't been able to."

I pictured him scouring the women's perfume

section of department stores in search of the right scent.

"Thank you for not turning around and walking out when you saw me."

"Actually, I'm feeling rather flattered."

"It's not like that," Max said, suddenly sounding shy, shifting his shoulders the way a boy might.

"Like what?"

"You know."

"Okay," I managed.

"I'm looking for what I lost as a young boy. I know I can't keep it, but moments like this, spending time with women like you, make me feel whole again. As if I've never lost anything."

"I'm not sure that's healthy, Max."

"That's what my latest therapist keeps telling me, just like the other ones did. I try their prescriptions for happiness, but always end up back in the same place. Is that wrong?"

"The only thing wrong is the deception. Pretending to be much older than you really are. Have you ever tried telling the truth?"

"That's what I'm doing now."

"I meant in your profile, Max."

"Young man looking for his mother?"

"Young man looking for an older woman."

"Because he misses his mother."

"I think you need to get past it," I told him. "I think you need to grow up."

Tears welled in his eyes and then began to pour out. "That sounds just like what my mother would have said."

Then he buried his face in his hands.

"Oh, boy," I muttered.

This time, Harry McGraw was laughing hysterically when I got back to his car, unable to contain himself.

"Enjoying yourself, Harry?" I asked, settling into the passenger seat and feeling the duct-taped vinyl squish beneath me.

He laughed some more. "I wish I'd taken a picture," he managed finally.

"For posterity?"

"To sell to the tabloids. I can see the headline now . . . 'Bestselling Author Caught Dating Her Son.'"

"You're a barrel of laughs, Harry."

He slammed the steering wheel with both palms and laughed even harder, stopping only when the horn engaged and wouldn't shut off, no matter what Harry did.

And now it was me laughing.

"Very funny, Jess. Yuk it up at my expense."

I laughed some more.

I slept through the night peacefully for the first time since Hal Wirth's death, and felt freed, as if the whole afternoon had unbridled me from the burden I'd been bearing. I couldn't remember the last time I'd laughed as hard as I had in Harry's car, which also made me realize how much I enjoyed his company. His gruff briskness was camouflage for his warm heart and compassion for people, especially crime victims who had no one else in their corner. Harry was like a knight-errant coming to their rescue when the system had abandoned them, caring nothing about his fee and willing to sacrifice his own lifestyle if it meant others could live better.

So maybe we'd both needed a laugh.

The upshot of my so-called date with Max Gladding was to make me realize all at once the folly of this pursuit. The fact that I had actually entertained the thought that I could infiltrate an elaborate criminal network by simply posting a fake profile online was so absurd on its face, I wondered how I'd let myself be so deluded. I guess this whole case had confronted me with the evils of technology to the point where I thought those same evils could be used to turn the tables.

Like snapping my fingers to make magic happen. Make a killer appear instead of a rabbit disappear. I had become my own fictional character, believing real life could be manipulated as easily as fiction, where the world moved at the pace of my choosing, and life unfolded in neat, convenient chapters kept short to please the digital audience. I was so glad neither Mort Metzger nor Seth Hazlitt was around to witness the extent of my silliness, and imagined they would've gotten a laugh at least as big as Harry McGraw's at my expense. Maybe someday I'd have the courage to share this story with them, but I doubted it.

I emerged from my bedroom in my bathrobe and headed straight for the kitchen to enjoy breakfast and the newspaper before plotting my route back to Cabot Cove, where I could put this entire experience behind me.

Alyssa and Chad were both seated at the kitchen

table, studying his laptop screen. And there was Harry McGraw, gulping down a huge polystyrene cup of coffee while standing at the counter.

"If you came here to laugh at me again, Harry, go right ahead."

"Not this morning, Jess. I'm not in a laughing mood."

I followed his gaze toward Chad, who tilted his laptop toward me as if I could see it from so far away.

"Your bank accounts were accessed last night," he said.

Chapter Thirty-four

"Not the real ones," he added. "The ones I set up for you."

I breathed a sigh of relief. "You're telling me somebody tried to steal Eileen Vogel's fake money."

"No, this was a data mining operation. They accessed your accounts, and your financial records, to determine how much you were worth, pulling passwords and any other info needed to prove that they were you."

"Prove to whom exactly?"

"No one in the flesh, that's for sure. Less-than-scrupulous Web-based loan outfits that masquerade as official, pretending to offer small business loans, that sort of thing."

I moved to the table and sat down without making myself tea or pouring a cup of coffee from the old drip percolator Chad and Alyssa had somehow figured out how to work.

I couldn't believe what Chad had just said and could tell neither could Alyssa nor Harry.

"And once they have all this information," I started, my thoughts forming as I spoke.

"They'd be able to use it to do pretty much what they did to Alyssa's father," Chad picked up before I could continue. I noticed he took Alyssa's hand in his when he got to the part about her father. "Open lines of credit on these unscrupulous lending sites that are the very definition of fly-by-night—literally, since they change their Internet identities on a weekly or even daily basis. And once those lines of credit are opened, secured by your assets, they could immediately draw the lines down to nothing, essentially bankrupting their targets. Because by then the unscrupulous sites have placed the deals with foreign lenders who've placed liens on the target's real accounts by the time that target realizes he's been taken to the cleaners."

"Or she," I added, needing to remind myself again this was happening to Eileen Vogel and not Jessica Fletcher.

"Wait a minute," Harry said, in what sounded more like a growl than a voice, "are you telling me that's all it takes? No signatures, no handshakes in person, to borrow millions of dollars?"

"That's exactly what I'm saying," Chad told him. "A lot of business these days accept e-signatures and e-verification. And if you had the kind of information whoever's behind this was able to accumulate on Alyssa's father, and now the fictional Eileen Vogel, you'd have everything you need."

"Banks have lost their minds," Harry groused, shaking his head.

"Not the legitimate ones, Mr. McGraw."

"Ha-ha!"

"What's so funny, Harry?" I asked him.

"Nobody ever calls me 'Mr. McGraw.'"

"What do they call you?"

"Jackass a lot. Harry sometimes. These days, there aren't many calling me anything. Not like my phone is ringing off the hook with PI work." He looked back toward Chad. "You were saying, kid?"

"I was about to say there are plenty of—let's call them less-than-reputable lenders that are mostly shells for off-shore holding companies that charge exorbitant fees for borrowing and take them all up front." Chad focused his attention back on me. "Here's how it might work in the case of our dear Eileen Vogel. They secure her account numbers, passwords, personal information—pretty much everything. And with that information, they go to these less-than-reputable lenders and open a line of credit for, say, a million dollars secured against Ms. Vogel's assets. All the institution knows is that the loan or line of credit is adequately collateralized with assets she either can't touch or doesn't want anyone to know about. The institution takes maybe a ten percent fee off the top and whoever's behind the crime pockets nine hundred thousand dollars. By the time Ms. Vogel learns she's effectively broke, it's too late. That is, if she's still alive to notice."

"You're saying all this can be done *online*?" Harry said, shaking his head in disbelief.

"Pretty much all of it, with willing partners," Chad

explained, clearly on comfortable turf here. "Sometimes online means the Dark Web, the identities of the online lending partners changing by the day, even hour. But the bottom line is that by the time someone like Eileen Vogel, or Hal Wirth, realizes they've been taken, the money's gone and there's no way to get it back. No trace back to who took it, and the actual lender might already be in the wind, still operating but under an entirely different alias."

"Will somebody pinch me?" Harry sighed. "I thought I'd seen everything. Gotta love progress, right, Jess? I was a beat cop back in the days when people were still robbing banks with guns. Now all you need is a finger."

"And a keyboard," Chad added.

"Okay," I started, "I think I'm getting a handle on this part of the crime. But how exactly did one of the three men I dated in the past couple days steal all this data from me? It wasn't like I handed over any information, and none of them even had a phone number— well, a phone number for Eileen Vogel."

"Glad you asked," Chad said, sounding like he was getting to the best part. "Your phone," he followed.

"What about it?"

"That's how they got your information. I synced your fake profile to your phone, just in case."

"None of them even touched it. It was in my bag the whole time, that new surveillance app Harry loaded open so he could listen in."

Chad seemed to think of something. "You have your phone on you right now?"

I felt about the bulky pockets of my bathrobe. "Must've left it in the bedroom. Just give me a sec."

I retrieved the phone from my night table and handed it to Chad back in the kitchen. He jogged through a few screens, looking for something.

"You keep track of your apps?"

"Pretty much. I don't have too many of them."

He tilted the screen toward me, pointing at the icon for an application I'd never seen before. "Recognize that one?"

"No."

"Of course, you don't. Because you didn't load it onto your phone; one of Eileen Vogel's three dates did."

I was beyond confused. "Chad, I told you none of them even touched my phone."

"They wouldn't have to. Reasonable proximity is plenty close enough for them to clone a program from their phone onto yours. Do you remember if the restaurants you met these dates at had Wi-Fi?"

"No."

"Because that's all you'd need. Both phones pull signals from the same cell towers, transmitted over the same Wi-Fi network. In the past couple years, there's been a twentyfold explosion in the theft of financial details from mobile devices. Not many people realize just how open and vulnerable to hacking their cell phones are. It's not so much hacking as hijacking," Chad continued. "Smartphones are like minicomputers, full of data, e-mails, and other personal information users like to keep private. That app they managed to put on your phone was like a sponge that sucked up every bit of the fake financial data I loaded onto your phone and then sent it to the cloud to be retrieved later."

I gazed again at the flaming red icon for the app I didn't recognize on my screen, trying to remember again why I traded in my flip. "What about the encrypted data, passwords, and the like?"

"I was getting to that. An application, like this one here, is software. To get everything they'd need, these guys would've also needed to employ hardware, like an advanced offshoot of the Stingray."

"Stingray?" I said as Harry rose to refill his polystyrene coffee cup from the percolator.

"Like a whole bunch of these devices, it sprang from devices built for intelligence agencies. On the surface it's a listening device—but a listening device that functions like an electronic vacuum cleaner, sucking up thousands of phone ID codes. The next step is to use those codes to track the users of all those phones. Where they go at what time of the day."

"That sounds like a long way from stealing data and private information."

"Like I said, the latest versions are offshoots capable of doing just that. Going from tracking, monitoring, and listening in isn't as far as it sounds from stealing a phone's data. Once somebody's in your phone, they're in your phone, free to roam around for as long as they want to take what they came for."

"Kid," Harry started, swirling his cup about in his hands, "you're saying we have good old Uncle Sam to blame for all this, that the government invented this technology these space-age thieves have now corrupted."

"The government opened the door, yes." Chad nodded. "But criminals like the ones we're looking for built the room beyond it. Giving them the benefit of the doubt, spooks might've had the best of intentions when concocting these machines, maybe not thinking ahead to what else they might be used for."

"Maybe?" I repeated.

"I'm thinking that was their intention to begin with. The bad guys just beat them to it."

I looked toward Harry. "Do you understand any of this?"

He frowned. "Not a word."

"I wish I didn't either."

"There's more," Chad said. "It's called the Gossamer. Super, super expensive and requires a degree of expertise to operate, but, man, can you do some crazy stuff with it. It's much smaller than the Stingray, but is even more capable of targeting all mobile phones within range and stealing the unique codes that keep their content private."

"You said small," I noted. "Small enough to fit into a man's jacket or pants pocket?"

"Jacket, for sure. I've heard there's a version of the Gossamer that's no bigger than a thumb drive. Think of it like a magnet, drawing all the personal information on your phone to it. The smaller Gossamer works on proximity and may have to actually come into contact, or close to it, with your device in order to be effective."

I racked my brain trying to think if there'd ever been an opportunity for something like that to happen while I was with any of my three dates, one of whom was part of the same conspiracy that had cost Hal Wirth his life. But I didn't recall ever even lifting my phone from my handbag, which had never left my sight. I thought of Max's odd bracelet, started to wonder if his whole older-woman fetish was nothing but a ruse to make me lower my guard. He'd seemed so sad and milquetoast that I, or some other potential victim, would never have felt threatened by him. Annoyed maybe, but not threatened.

"Then there's the Kingfish," Chad was saying, totally in his element. "A classic mining device."

"Don't tell me," I chimed in. "Because it mines data from phones."

"Which isn't nearly as difficult as it may seem. Everyone is obsessive about the data stored on their phones, so almost invariably that data is automatically backed up to the cloud. Devices like the Kingfish trick targeted phones into thinking they're actually the cloud. They don't have to steal the information because the phone willingly hands it over to them."

"A classic mining device, in other words," I said, repeating the words Chad had just spoken.

He nodded. "And there are even more elaborate, though larger, devices like the Harpoon that are essentially amplifiers capable of drastically boosting the signal of a Stingray or Kingfish, expanding their range, and giving them the ability to mine a phone's data in a much faster fashion."

"How large?" I wondered aloud.

"The size of an old-fashioned computer tower, or at least as big as a laptop computer. But you could custom design one to resemble, or be hidden inside, pretty much anything."

"Look," Harry said, finally breaking in, "I come out of an era where we used the Tin Ear, old-fashioned bugs, transmitters planted in the lairs of the bad guys we were trying to catch. That was real surveillance, traditional surveillance. What you're describing is modifying the latest version of the Tin Ear so it can lift the contents off any cell phone within a certain proximity."

"That's right. And I made sure to load the kind of apps and programs on Eileen Vogel's phone to make these bad guys think they'd hit the jackpot."

"What happens when they realize they've hit a dead end?" I asked Chad. "Will they know they've been had?"

"Maybe, but it won't matter because the only trail they've got leads back to Eileen Vogel, not Jessica Fletcher."

"Go back to what you said a second ago," Harry said, "about how you loaded the right apps and stuff on Eileen Vogel's phone. Wouldn't Jessica Fletcher's information be on there as well?"

"No, because I deactivated it during each of the dates and replaced the real Jessica with a second user identity for Eileen Vogel."

"What if you hadn't set the trap that way? What if these had been real dates and one of them had intended to do to me, Jessica Fletcher, what they'd done to Hal?"

Chad nodded, as if ready for the question. "When you pay for an app, the phone's software charges the credit card it has on file for you. So they'll have that credit card. Let's say you use your phone to make purchases on Amazon—they'll have all the credit info on you, including credit card numbers that Amazon has. Since your e-mail program runs on your phone, they'll have access to all your e-mails that are still archived. And they'll be able to figure out your password for that, and since most people actually use only one password, it's like a golden ticket into the rest of your life."

"What about Eileen Vogel's Social Security number?" I raised. "How could they get that?"

"Once they have all this other info, they'll be able to go into the profiles you set up with various vendors or access your original credit card application documents that contain it. Everything they do opens the door into your life another crack, until it's open all the way."

"Back in the day," Harry started, "I worked some bunco and vice. What you're describing reminds me of scam artists, con men, and grifters. That's what this all boils down to, doesn't it?"

"With advanced principles of technology applied, absolutely," Chad acknowledged. "Instead of conning you out of your money, they use proximity technology to steal it. That's what they did to Eileen Vogel." He took Alyssa's hand again. "And Hal Wirth."

I weighed that in my mind. "So these three dates I went on . . ."

"One of them was a plant, just like the woman who dated Hal. Their role is nothing more than to mine your data. The rest is handled in a dark room somewhere by people behind computer consoles rigged to a powerful central server."

Harry uttered what sounded like a low growl. "You know what that means? It means there are layers of insulation between the various levels. By its very nature, this operation's grunts never come into contact with each other. The levels remain separate, like different floors in an office building."

"Or different buildings altogether," Chad corrected, "because they wouldn't even pass in the elevators."

Harry looked toward me. "I feel like Rip van Winkle. I wake up from a nap and it's a whole new world out there. What am I still doing in this business, Jess? Can you tell me that?"

"Do you have an alternative?"

"I don't even have a pension. Didn't stick with the department long enough."

"So what do we do now?" I said, turning back toward Chad. "What's our next step?"

He sighed and let go of Alyssa's hand, crossing his arms. "That's where it gets tricky. We may have figured out how they mine for the data, but we still don't have a notion as to where it goes. So the next step would be to follow the digital trail of the intrusion into Eileen Vogel's personal data and—"

The doorbell ringing cut him off. I rose stiffly from my chair and traipsed across the room to answer it, serenaded the whole time by the chime sounding over and over again.

"All right," I called out, "I'm coming!"

I yanked the door open to the sight of a familiar face.

"Aren't you going to ask me in?" asked Mort Metzger in greeting.

Chapter Thirty-five

"You sold me out!" I snapped at Harry McGraw, who'd followed me into the foyer from the kitchen.

He didn't bother denying it, nodding in a way that made his jowls look bigger. "I let this go as far as I could, Jess," he said, his worn expression taking on the contours of a wet dishrag.

Mort stepped inside the apartment and closed the door behind him. "What did you think you were doing?"

"What I always do."

"As in sticking your nose in where it doesn't belong? Even for you, this is a new level. Setting yourself up as a mark? Really, Jessica?"

I looked toward Chad and Alyssa, who had joined us in the apartment's combination living and dining room. "I had to."

"That's the best you can do?"

"What would you have done if I'd just dumped all this onto your desk?"

"Not put myself, or anyone else, in any danger, I can tell you that much." His gaze drifted over my shoulder toward the kids. "Does your mother know you're here, young lady?" he asked Alyssa.

She shook her head.

He turned his eyes on Chad. "And who are you again?"

"Her boyfriend. We go to school together."

"You should get back there, both of you."

"I can't, Sheriff," Alyssa said, with a firmness bordering on obstinacy. "Because whoever killed my father stole all our money first. We can't afford the tuition anymore."

"I'm going to get it back," I said, immediately wishing I hadn't.

"*You're* going to get it back?" Mort shot at me, shaking his head. "From what I'd already figured out for myself, and what Harry here told me, we're dealing with a national, or international, ring of high-tech thieves who effectively steal everything their victims have and then murder them. We don't know who they are. We don't know where they are. We don't know how many of them there are, or how long they've been at this, or how many victims they've claimed. Tell me, does that sound right so far?"

I nodded and left it there.

"And you were going to get Hal Wirth's money *back* from them. Why not just walk right up to their offices, knock on the door, and ask them to write you a check?"

"Because I don't know where their offices are. That's what I was doing. Trying to flush them out."

"And how's that going for you?"

I glared at Harry. "I guess we'll never know now."

"All those mystery books you've written," Mort sneered, claiming my attention again, "got any ideas what I should charge you with?"

"Not off the top of my head, and it's out of your jurisdiction anyway."

"You want me to bring in the NYPD on this, just say the word," Mort said, in a tone like none I'd heard him use before. "Anything to get you off the street. Jeez, I might just arrest you for reckless endangerment. Yup, that should work."

"Who am I endangering?"

"Yourself, Jessica." He stopped, scratched his head, and gazed about as if still in disbelief over the circumstances that had brought him there. "And, hold on, I've saved the best for last. Harry also tells me that Sean Booker, a prisoner in federal custody—"

"Larry Dax, Mort. His real name is Larry Dax."

"—Larry Dax, a prisoner in federal custody, slipped you some message you neglected to turn over to the proper authorities. So I guess we can add obstruction of justice to that reckless endangerment charge. Imagine the field day Evelyn Phillips at the *Gazette* is going to have with this. . . ."

"Do I have to?"

"Relax, Jessica—maybe she'll go easy on you for keeping her so busy all these years by turning Cabot Cove into the murder capital of the country."

"You're blaming me for that, too?"

"I can't even go to conventions anymore because of all the questions about statistical anomalies and the like."

"You never went to conventions, Mort."

"But now I couldn't even if I wanted to." He stopped and held his stare on me, as if waiting for me to respond, then resuming when I didn't. "This message Larry Dax slipped you, can I have a look at it?"

"It's probably nothing. I think he wrote it on toilet paper, maybe never got to finish it."

"Do you have it or not?"

I fetched the photocopy from my bag and handed it to Mort and watched him mouth the sequence of letters and numbers I'd been unable to make any sense of:

ME2006Y

"The best I've been able to come up with is Dax was talking about himself because he wrote *ME*. Two thousand six must refer to the year, something that happened back then that he's trying to draw my attention to. Or maybe *ME* stands for medical examiner and there's some case somewhere I'm supposed to find to bring me closer to who's responsible for Hal Wirth's death. It's the *Y* that's got me baffled. That's why I don't think he got to finish the message. Or maybe there was another piece of doubled-over toilet paper he thought he'd passed me, too, containing the rest of the message."

Mort was staring at me, his expression utterly flat. "Figured all that out by yourself, did you?"

"I'm working on it."

He shook his head, a bemused look settling over his features, as he flapped the piece of paper in the air. "You should've showed this to me earlier, Jessica. I could've saved you the trouble."

I felt my eyes widen, my breath catching briefly in my throat. "Wait, you know what it means?"

Mort nodded, looking no less bemused. "It's not 'me,' Jessica. It's 'M-E,' which is short for 'Maine.' You know, the state in which you currently reside."

"Maine," I repeated, utterly dumbfounded over how I'd missed that.

"And the two-zero-zero-six-Y that follows the M-E? You don't spend a big chunk of your life as sheriff of a coastal town like Cabot Cove without knowing a boat registration when you see one."

Chapter Thirty-six

"Stay in the squad car, Jessica," Mort ordered me, as a blanket of fog swept in over Cabot Cove. "I see you out of it and I might just shoot you."

It turned out that the boat with Maine registration 2006Y was currently berthed in a Cabot Cove Marina slip and had been under watch since a few minutes after Mort had deciphered Larry Dax's message. So Larry Dax had clearly known plenty more than he'd let on to me or the federal authorities, obviously a participant in the plot instead of just an accidental accomplice. He might not have known the identity of whoever was behind all this, but whatever he knew was somehow connected to this boat: a thirty-five-foot cabin cruiser registered to some shell company that Mort could find absolutely nothing about, almost as if it didn't exist.

I felt like an idiot. Not so much for being confined

to the passenger seat of the squad car, not even for recklessly endangering myself, as Mort had put it. He'd given me time to shower and dress hours before shepherding me out of New York City, insisting on driving me back himself to make sure I didn't stray again. It was a quiet drive, made worse by the awful traffic, accident after accident on Route 95, which turned a difficult five-hour trek into an interminable seven-hour one.

And people ask me why I never bothered getting my license.

Night had already fallen by the time we'd made it back to Cabot Cove, trailed by the Wirths' SUV, which Alyssa had borrowed for the occasion. Mort insisted she and Chad follow us every inch of the way, promising to put out an APB on the kids if they ever lapsed from his rearview mirror. Toward that purpose, he actually deputized Harry McGraw to ride with them to make sure no further hijinks ensued. Upon arrival in Cabot Cove, Harry's revised orders were to see them home and "sit on them," to make sure they stayed right where they were, while we proceeded to the marina.

Cabot Cove Marina was undergoing a substantial renovation, adding a sea (no pun intended!) of new docks and slips, along with that five-thousand-seat amphitheater, the Westhausen Garden, where concerts and other performances would be held. As a result, the smell of fresh lumber mixed with the salt air blowing in from the sea. The large area of new construction was barely visible through the fog carried by a thick swath of humidity that had settled over the region, and it was all I could do to catch a glimpse of the cabin cruiser docked in Slip 41 under the boating registration ME2006Y.

Before we'd left my New York apartment for the long ride home, Mort had put the young man I referred to as Deputy Andy in charge of surveillance of the vessel. The sheriff's orders were explicit: Watch the boat, but don't be seen doing so. I gnashed my teeth at that a bit, but held my tongue, refraining from commenting on the Cabot Cove police department's lack of experience surveilling anything other than the streets for a missing dog or cat. Especially since the harbormaster and several dockworkers said they recognized Porcelain Man meandering about the marina, from that picture lifted off Eve Simpson's Labor Day video assemblage. None, though, could say they saw him anywhere near the cabin cruiser docked in Slip 41.

Meanwhile, I sat in the passenger seat of Mort's squad car, stewing. The windows on both sides had been rolled down, doing little to relieve the increasingly fetid conditions inside the cab. I was roasting, starting to perspire through my clothes, and wondering why I hadn't asked Mort to just drop me at home. I was exhausted. My first three dates in twenty years had worn me out. The last few days had left me with a clearer picture of the circumstances surrounding Hal Wirth's death, but no real resolution or comfort. That wouldn't come until the true perpetrators were caught. This was no longer about solving a puzzle, as involving myself in real-life crimes normally was. It was about making sure whoever was behind this could claim no more victims and destroy no more lives.

I gazed out the open passenger-side window toward the docks. The fog and the night sky conspired to strip away my sense of perspective, stealing the blue and white cabin cruiser docked in Slip 41 from my sight. I had no idea where Mort and his deputies were posted for their vigils—a good thing, since the fact that I couldn't see them suggested the boat's owner wouldn't either, should he return.

I thought I caught a dark shape moving through the fog, outlined briefly by the LED lights shining down from a series of telephone poles. I thought it might be a trick of the eye, an illusion, until the movement, black against the grayness of the night and fog, flashed again. I wished I knew how to operate the police radio in order to inform Mort, warn him of the figure skulking about.

I still wasn't entirely sure of what I'd seen, so I wiped the sweat from my eyes and climbed out of Mort's cruiser, careful to close the door quietly behind myself. All I could picture was Porcelain Man descending on Mort and his deputies, catching them unaware.

Even if I was overreacting, I had to find Mort, had to alert him.

But I couldn't spot him anywhere amid the shroud of fog and darkness and hadn't caught any further glimpse of what I'd thought was a man's shape since I'd stepped out of the car. I moved a few steps to my left toward the general direction of where all the new construction was happening and found a fissure through the fog, a clear path carved by a cooling breeze coming off the water. I glimpsed the dark shape again, wondering if I should cry out a warning, when the figure stooped as the cat he must've been looking for leaped into his arms.

Phew! I breathed an audible sigh of relief and started back toward Mort's cruiser.

That's when a dank, sweaty, soiled hand closed over my mouth.

Chapter Thirty-seven

I knew it was him, Porcelain Man, from a smell I'd detected rising off him in the library. Something more stale than odorous, a man whose lifestyle didn't always include good habits of hygiene.

"Make a sound and I'll kill you," he said, his voice slightly above a whisper.

I felt something poking at my back—a gun barrel, I thought at first, but a sharp sting as it ripped into my blouse told me it was a knife instead. He pushed me past the row of cars still in the parking lot, heading toward all the unfinished construction, and I caught enough of his reflection in window glass to recognize him all too well: It was Porcelain Man, all right, though with what must've been a wig of thick hair restored.

"What a pain in the ass," I heard him huff out in more of a rasp, uncertain that his words were directed at me, until he repeated them. "What a pain in the ass you are."

The way he was cupping my mouth, so my head was cocked backward from pressure beneath my chin, kept me not only from crying out but also from biting into him. Not that I would have done so given the chance, not with that knife poking at my spine. The best I could do was hope Mort or one of his deputies spotted us— unlikely, given their focus on the boat in Slip 41. I guessed the man had been hiding out there when not killing, or trying to kill, residents of Cabot Cove.

I could see he was pushing me toward the unfinished Westhausen Garden. We were weaving in and out of the labyrinth created by piles of lumber layered amid construction equipment and vehicles. I could hear the currents lapping gently against the shoreline, caught glimpses of the docks bobbing lightly up and down under their force. As soon as we reached the unfinished structure, currently with tarpaulins flapping where the finished roof would eventually reside, I knew he was going to kill me, because that's what he did. To Hal Wirth and Eugene Labine in Cabot Cove, not to mention who knew how many people in cities across the country.

I cursed myself for involving Chad and Alyssa in this whole sordid episode, realizing with choking fear that I had endangered their lives, too. It was a safe bet Porcelain Man knew of their involvement, and once he finished with me, he'd be going for them next.

That meant I had to find a way to overcome my assailant. If I didn't survive, then neither would they.

Porcelain Man pushed me past a myriad of construction vehicles en route to the future Westhausen Garden, and my eyes searched for anything I could use as a weapon. I caught sight of something beneath the fog, an object resting on the soft ground near where construction workers had begun to lay a stamped concrete walkway that would lead from the area of the docks to the sprawling new structure. I recognized from a book I'd once researched the rakelike tool that was used to smooth out the concrete prior to the stamping process. The object I had glimpsed had to be that—this thought unfolding in two seconds, maybe, three at most. I'd have to time my move perfectly and hope fortune was on my side, but what choice did I have? If I died, then likely Alyssa and Chad would, too, and probably Babs. I'd go from musing about becoming their savior to causing them to follow Hal Wirth from this world.

Unacceptable, I thought, just a step away from the smoothing rake.

My next awkward, lunging step brought my soft shoe down on its head, launching the rake's broom-handle-like base into the air. It whistled past me as I twisted sideways, the move having the added benefit of distracting Porcelain Man from the handle making a beeline for his face.

I heard the *crack* of impact against his cheek and nose, and chose that moment to pull from his grasp, relieved he was wielding a knife instead of a gun, which he would've otherwise used to shoot me, as I scampered away deeper into the labyrinth of construction vehicles and neat stacks of lumber. Weaving my way in and out of the rows, I was afraid to cry out for help for fear of alerting Porcelain Man to my position. My intention at that point was to work my way circuitously back toward the general area of the docks where Mort and his deputies were concentrated.

Bang!

A gunshot split the night and a section of lumber just over my head showered wood splinters into the air, some lodging in my hair. I gave up trying to work my way to Mort's position; surely he and his deputies had heard the gunshot and would be working their way toward me instead. In the meantime, I had to keep moving, out of Porcelain Man's sight line and aim.

I emerged from the mazelike confines to find the unfinished Westhausen Garden straight ahead. I charged through ground littered with refuse that had been torn up by the heavy construction vehicles. I nearly tripped when another bullet whistled past me, a miss only because I was doubled over.

There were no stairs leading up to the shell of the future Westhausen Garden, so I tried to leap the meager rise, only to find it much steeper than my first glance had revealed. I didn't make it and had to hoist myself through the eventual multidoored entry, pulling myself across the floorboards as another two bullets whizzed over my head.

A powerful odor burned my mouth and filled my lungs, nearly overcoming me. I recognized it as varnish or stain, not from research but from work I'd tried to do around the house to hardly favorable results. The walls looked shiny under the glow of numerous heat lamps set up to make the stain dry faster to prevent construction on the amphitheater from falling further behind schedule.

I reclaimed my feet and launched back into motion, but then tripped on a thick orange extension cord rigged to one of the heat lamps and I went down hard. As I pushed up to rise again, I felt a hand close on my hair and yank me painfully upright, jerking my head back enough so that I could glimpse Porcelain Man just before he closed his free hand over my throat. I flailed wildly, desperately, anything to free myself from his grasp. I sucked in as deep a breath as I could while we wheeled across the floor, banging into one of the heat lamps, which teetered and then toppled over.

I heard the crackle of its bulb exploding and felt Porcelain Man's grasp slacken enough for me to use the nearest weapon I had at my disposal: my teeth. I sank them into the back of his hand as hard and deep as I could, and he gasped and jerked his hand away. Stumbling a bit as he groped for me again, he banged into a wheelbarrow piled high with rags soaked in the same stain that coated the drying walls. The wheelbarrow toppled over, the pile of rags covering the fallen heat lamp like a blanket.

I'd already twisted around to run away by then, hearing Porcelain Man's feet thud after me across the wood flooring just before a *poof!* sounded. I felt an intense surge of heat blast by me and I swung back to find the pile of rags had erupted into an inferno that overtook Porcelain Man. The amphitheater's darkened interior was suddenly awash in a brilliant flash of flame that swallowed him from head to toe, turning him to little more than an indiscernible shape trapped behind a fiery curtain.

Then I heard the screams, high-pitched, deafening

wails that made my ears ring. Porcelain Man had vanished altogether inside a blanket of orange crusted with a reddish hue. I'd never heard, nor could I have imagined, anything like the screams that continued to split the sudden wash of heat through the night air. Porcelain Man was now a fiery shape rushing in a blur from the unfinished structure out into the night. Moments later, I heard what sounded like a splash, indicating he'd jumped into the water to douse the flames that had consumed him.

The way into the amphitheater had been utterly blocked by the flames feeding off the formaldehyde soaked into the wood. I lost my breath at the thought I was trapped, before swinging in the other direction through the shorter flames that had begun to sprout in that section of the structure as well.

I caught sight of a door, a dark chasm alight in the glow from the fire, and rushed toward it, doing my best to dodge the rising flames. I tumbled through a future emergency exit out of the structure to the ground, into a night that felt cool by comparison despite the fetid humidity. I back-crawled from there, aware now that the wall timbers were catching fast, the entire structure an inferno coughing fluttering embers into the night. As I watched the embers lighting the darkness and chasing away the fog, arms fastened tight around me and dragged me farther away from the heat of the flames.

I looked up and recognized Deputy Andy and one of his fellow deputies, as Mort rounded a corner between a front loader and a backhoe and dropped his hands to his knees to catch his breath. Before he could, though, headlights blazed through the night, seeming to stop when they hit the flaming shell of the building.

Men spilled from what looked like a dozen vehicles, big dark SUVs mostly, all wearing tactical vests and wielding automatic weapons.

"Dejong!" I heard one of them near the front bellow in Mort's direction. "Dejong! Where is he?"

Mort had his hands in the air, didn't respond, the speaker and the rest of the armed-to-the-teeth SWAT-like squad holding their positions, lit by the shroud of flames increasing their hold on the night.

"The water!" I cried out, realizing who Dejong must be, though not who these men were or what they were doing there. "He jumped into the water!"

The men surged past me, their heavy boots thumping over even the volume of the crackling flames and the crumbling wood frame of what would've been the Westhausen Garden. I could feel the whoosh of air as they charged past me, a single black wave silhouetted by an orange tint from the glow of the flames, rushing in the general direction of where Porcelain Man had disappeared into the night and the water.

"Well, you've really gone and done it this time, Jessica," Mort Metzger said, crouching over me, still trying to catch his breath. "Wait until the mayor and selectmen hear about this."

I watched the flames consuming what remained of the building's shell, wondering what was transpiring in the waters beyond them.

"They can bill me," I told Mort.

Chapter Thirty-eight

The battle-garbed commandos, it turned out, were FBI, CIA, or something similar—I never found out for sure. They'd been drawn to Cabot Cove after Chad had hacked databases in search of Porcelain Man's true identity. The ping he'd detected had been the product of someone recognizing his clearly serious interest in a much-wanted fugitive. Armand Dejong, it turned out, was a private contractor who'd left a trail of bodies both during his special ops military career, which had ended dishonorably, and after, when his deadly services became available to the highest bidder.

The special ops team had followed the trail to Chad's computer at the Wirth home, where Harry Mc-Graw had put up a fuss for all of three seconds before telling Chad he'd better come to the door right away. One of them, Harry probably, had told the team where they could find me and, thus, hopefully Dejong. Harry had guessed he must have been hiding out on that cabin cruiser with the registration ME2006Y.

Two mornings later, a fully recovered Mort took me and Seth Hazlitt to breakfast at Mara's Luncheonette, toasting me with his coffee mug.

"To Jessica, who cracked yet another case and brought yet another murderer to justice."

I didn't raise my tea. "The body of that murderer still hasn't been recovered, and I haven't cracked anything."

"Uh-oh," I heard Seth mutter.

"Whoever hired Dejong to do their bidding is still out there."

Mort looked toward Seth. "What do you think the chances are of her giving up the ghost?"

"Not very good, ayuh."

"Oh, man," Mort followed, turning his gaze on me. "I'm guessing you've got an idea of where to go next."

"As a matter of fact," I told him, "I do."

The wheelchair-bound man I'd known as Richard Fass when we'd dined in New York lived in a fancy Chelsea apartment that featured a wonderful view of the iconic Flatiron Building on Fifth Avenue. His real name was Mark Falco and he answered the knock on his door from a pair of NYPD detectives who'd accompanied Mort and me there. Only this time, Mark Falco was standing on two feet instead of sitting in a wheelchair.

Falco's gaze drifted past the detectives and settled upon me. "I thought I recognized you."

"I'd like to say I get that a lot, but I really don't."

He shook his head in bemused fashion, the detectives holding their ground on either side of him, stopping just short of drawing their guns. "Done in by a paperback pulp writer who makes shit up for a living."

"Actually, Mark, my books are published in hardcover as well. E-book, too."

"How'd you figure it out?"

"It started with your sneakers," I said, looking down to see he was wearing the very same ones. "I looked them up online. Turns out they cost almost three hundred dollars per pair. You want to tell me what kind of man bound to a wheelchair spends three hundred dollars on sneakers?"

He shrugged, waiting for me to continue.

"Then there was the wheelchair. Once I drew my conclusions from the sneakers, I asked myself, why bother with such a ruse? I'm guessing because it was the perfect way to hide the machines that lifted all the data from my cell phone. Tell me, were they built into the chair's arms?"

"How'd you know?"

"Just a guess, actually. Sometimes it pays to be lucky instead of smart."

"I thought the phrase was 'lucky instead of good,'" Falco said, watching the detectives draw closer on either side of him.

"That, too. You can still help yourself out here, Mark."

"Do I have to go out on another date with you?"

"I was thinking more like telling us everything you know here and now. I count a whole bunch of

New York judges among my most ardent fans. Who knows? You might draw one of them and I'd be happy to put in a good word for you, even include the name of the judge's favorite grandkid in my next book."

"I can't help you, because I don't know anything. I do the deed, transfer the data, and get paid. Bing, bang, boom. Nothing else and nothing more."

"Why don't you tell me about the bing, the bang, and the boom and let me be the judge of that?"

I found Deacon Westhausen on the beautiful oceanfront property he'd purchased to build his lavish mansion and estate after the town had agreed to rezone a stretch of protected wetlands. That in return for his financial support of the marina expansion project, along with construction of the now incinerated Westhausen Garden.

In my mind, all thirty thousand square feet and four floors of the seaside mansion was an abomination from any perspective, a portrait in opulent decadence totally out of character in the rustic world of Cabot Cove. It was meant to be palatial, but its curves, angles, and notches, coupled with gilded doors and lavish marble accoutrements, made for a portrait in excess. It was more extravagant than exceptional, offering a window into the heart and soul of the man who'd built it. Had the mansion been located on a hill, instead of on the water, it might well be likened to Dracula's castle, the appropriateness of the comparison hardly lost on me, given the purpose of my visit.

"Jessica Fletcher!" Deacon Westhausen beamed when he saw me. "What brings Cabot Cove's second-most-famous resident to my soon-to-be humble abode? Maybe to give me a check for destroying my arena."

"You mean the former Westhausen Garden?"

"Almost as good as having my name on the top of a book jacket."

"Well, Deacon, you do have quite a story to tell."

He was dressed casually, mingling with the workmen toiling through the last of the construction on the sprawling home, which hadn't been ready in time for summer due to delays caused by lingering battles with the EPA and the state Department of Environmental Management. I guess Westhausen hadn't been able to buy off everyone.

"Starting with how you made a sizable portion of your fortune draining the assets of others," I continued. "Tell me, how many victims were there? How many people did you rob and send Armand Dejong, or men like him, to kill so there'd be no trail? How many fake heart attacks and accidents did you cause?"

Westhausen showed no reaction to my accusation at all, not even breaking a sweat. The only thing he broke into was a wide smile.

"Sounds like a great plot for a book, Jessica."

I shook my head. "Lacks credibility. Nobody would believe it."

"Really?"

"Really. We're probably talking about dozens of murders all over the country, maybe even the world. A high-tech crime spree I'm guessing has been going on for years with no signs of stopping. Until now."

Westhausen glanced over my shoulder in dramatic fashion, letting his gaze linger. "And yet you didn't bring the police or FBI with you. Not even your tag-along hick sheriff."

"Mort's on his way. To pick me up. I used Uber to get over here."

"I could have sent a car."

"I prefer to keep this all business."

"Your business is accusing me of these murders without a shred of proof?"

I just looked at him. "Who would believe a combination of Steve Jobs, Richard Branson, and Elon Musk was capable of murder?"

"Heady company for sure, Jessica."

"I doubt Branson and Musk would think so, especially once you're charged and the truth comes out. Then your assets get drained and, in a perfect world, returned to the victims you stole from."

Deacon Westhausen looked at me strangely, cocking his head to the side the way a dog might. "But this is far from a perfect world, isn't it? Tell me something. How is it someone who makes stuff up for a living thinks they can take someone like me down? Well, I suppose there's a first time for everything. Just not today."

"I figure we've got five minutes before Mort arrives," I told him. "Just enough time."

"For what?"

"For me to tell you about my visit in New York with one Mark Falco. Falco was one of your stooges who stole data off the cell phones of marks like Hal Wirth after being matched with them on a dating service. He claimed he knew nothing, and he was telling the truth. He didn't know a thing, but something he gave us—well, that helped a lot."

Westhausen remained silent, his expression remaining flat and fixed.

"Nothing about the information he collected going out, but from the money coming in. The money that magically appeared in Falco's account thanks to an offshore, off-the-books bank in the Caymans. Impossible to trace with one exception: the most obtuse of links to that same shell company that owned the boat Armand Dejong was living on in Cabot Cove Marina. Probe a bit deeper and I'm sure we'll find that account is yours."

"No one's going to believe it, Jessica. You're smart enough to know that."

"I guess I have more faith in people's ability to believe the truth than you do, Deacon. See, you thought this all out so well, covered your tracks at every juncture, except one."

I watched him stew, enjoying the upper hand I was holding even as I stalled just a bit for Mort and his deputies to arrive.

"Hal Wirth trusted you, considered you a friend. But you saw him as nothing but a mark, a dollar sign followed by a whole bunch of zeros to add to your coffers."

"I barely even knew the man."

"You came to his Labor Day party."

"Everyone in town came to his Labor Day party," Westhausen sneered, recovering a measure of his bravado. "You can't prove any of this and you know it."

"You're right. I can't. But Hal can."

Westhausen's expression seemed to crack as he tried for a laugh and then a smirk, failing both times. "Hal's dead, Jessica. Do I need to remind you about that? And he was little more than a total stranger to me."

I nodded at him, taking the bait. "The thing about books, Deacon, is that they live on, published or not. And Hal Wirth dedicated his memoir to you."

The moment froze between us; even the air stilled, until I resumed.

"That dedication reads, 'For my friend Deacon, who understands that life is about more than money.'" I stopped to let those words sink in. "Strange for a man you didn't know to dedicate his book to you, instead of to his wife and daughter. Then again, you were someone he trusted, someone he considered a friend, someone who recommended a matching service called LOVEISYOURS to him," I told him, recalling the words from the manuscript of Hal's memoir:

A good friend, a man whose judgment I trusted, recommended I give them a try, swearing by his own experience. I won't mention his name because you probably wouldn't believe he'd ever need to use an Internet dating service. And if it was good enough for a man like him, what did I have to lose?

Only his life, I thought sadly, returning my attention to Westhausen.

"You owned LOVEISYOURS, didn't you? The whole site was a setup. You hired Larry Dax, aka Sean Booker, to be your stooge. He might not have known exactly who he was looking for, or maybe he was afraid to tell me in so many words because he knew the FBI was listening in on our conversation. So he slipped me that boat registration he knew would lead me to you."

Westhausen stood before me motionless, not seeming to even breathe.

"So, Deacon, how many of these victims did you know personally, like you knew Hal?"

He smirked at me, the gesture lacking all measure of confidence.

"Let's try another question, then," I resumed. "How long have you been doing this?"

"I honestly can't say."

"But it's how you made your initial fortune, isn't it? The nest egg from which you built an empire. So here's what I really can't figure out: Why keep doing it once you became rich beyond comprehension? Why take the risk, especially of personally selecting a victim?"

Westhausen's eyes flashed as he processed his options. I knew those eyes all too well from my experiences over the years: the eyes of a predator sizing up its prey, assessing its size and strength and whether it was vulnerable to attack.

His smirk stretched into a thin smile. "With all your money and success, why do you keep writing?"

"Because I enjoy it."

Deacon Westhausen didn't speak, only nodded and let a tight grin claim his expression as Mort's cruiser headed up the drive, trailed by a pair of his deputies. Lights flashing but no sirens.

"Tell me one thing, Jessica," Westhausen said to me. "Have you ever encountered anyone like me before, in fiction or fact?"

"No," I said as I heard tires grind to a halt behind me. "But you're right, Deacon. There really is a first time for everything."

Ready to find
your next great read?

Let us help.

Visit prh.com/nextread